ENTER THE SEDUCTIVE WORLD OF LUST, GREED, AND REVENGE . . . WHERE MURDER AWAITS

Did my grandpa kill your grandpa or did yours kill mine? Asking too many questions about the past, the present, and eternity can be dangerous.

He had enough rage to annihilate the world. But he never guessed who his final victim would be.

She knew who the murderer was. Why would she take a killer's identity to her grave?

He went to incredible lengths to get what he wanted . . . until someone went even farther to stop him.

Thirteen outstanding mystery writers explore the unlucky fates of those who indulge their most murderous fantasies.

Sharyn McCrumb

PRESENTS

MALICE DOMESTIC 7

AVON
TWILIGHT

AVON BOOKS, INC.
1350 Avenue of the Americas
New York, New York 10019

Copyright © 1998 by Malice Domestic Ltd.
Published by arrangement with Malice Domestic Ltd.
Visit our website at **http://www.AvonBooks.com/Twilight**
Library of Congress Catalog Card Number: 98-92459
ISBN: 0-380-79406-3

First Avon Twilight Printing: September 1998

AVON TWILIGHT TRADEMARK REG. U.S. PAT. OFF. AND IN OTHER COUNTRIES, MARCA REGISTRADA, HECHO EN U.S.A.

Printed in the U.S.A.

WCD 10 9 8 7 6 5 4 3 2 1

Contents

Sharyn McCrumb
**Introduction:
The Cosy Nostra**
ix

Stephanie Barron
Jane and the Spoils of Stoneleigh
1

Eleanor Taylor Bland
Getting Robert
33

Michael Bond
Monsieur Pamplemousse Tells the Tale
44

Harlan Coben
A Simple Philosophy
66

Carola Dunn
Unhappy Medium
77

CONTENTS

Hazel Holt
After All . . .
95

Dean James
The Village Vampire and the Oboe of Death
112

Gillian Linscott
Rock of Ages
133

Amy Myers
Murder at the Soirée
154

Jennifer Rowe
Mystery Man
175

Barbara Burnett Smith
Writer's Revenge
196

Daniel Stashower
A Deliberate Form of Frenzy
215

Margaret Yorke
The Error of His Ways
228

Introduction:
The Cosy Nostra

Sharyn McCrumb

If Jane Austen were writing novels today, she might well be penning "traditional mysteries" of the sort that are celebrated in a *Malice Domestic* anthology because her gentle love stories like *Pride and Prejudice* would be marketed in the romance genre, featuring bare-chested gentlemen and swooning ladies on the cover. Miss Austen might well want to spare Darcy and Elizabeth such a fate by including a little mayhem in the plot. Since Jane Austen's novels were intended to be social commentaries on the middle-class society of her day, she might be pleased to discover that she has much in common with this century's writer of traditional mysteries, whose interests are much the same.

The form of crime fiction designated the "traditional" mystery is more about sociology than it is about forensic science. Today's practitioners of the

soft-boiled crime story (as opposed to police proce-
durals or private eye novels) are interested in character and psychological development, in motivation
and the social pressure to conform.

Middle-class society is full of conventions and little
hypocrisies that are often more rigidly observed than
laws. (Lots of people ignore the speed limit; but hardly anyone makes eye contact with a stranger in an
elevator.) To make "respectable" people break the social conventions, you have to do something pretty
drastic—put the cat among the pigeons. Murder is a
useful way of shaking up suburbia, because it is the
one irrevocable crime. One can pay back stolen
money or repair damaged property, but when one
has killed another human being, the error is past res-
titution. When first-degree murder was always a cap-
ital crime, the stakes were even higher, because the
suspects were protecting their very lives, but even in
the modern world of plea bargains and Twinkie de-
fenses, a murder charge is enough to cost you your
social standing in the neighborhood. Middle-class
people are usually very concerned with appear-
ances—more so than with actual morality, which is
why so many large crimes are committed to cover
smaller gaffes: *"I can't divorce my wife. Think of the
scandal! I'll kill her . . ."*

Generally speaking, it is the living who interest
crime writers, not the dead, which is why the victim
often dies in the early chapters of the book. The author sets up a little social order, and gets it ticking
away for a couple of chapters, with everyone's fa-
cades in place, and then murder is introduced to upset the balance. It's like throwing a rock into a
stagnant pool, and then watching the ripples change
the surface. Agatha Christie often compared this observation of the social order to watching pond life
through a microscope. It takes considerable psycho-

logical insight to plausibly predict what motivation will be required to drive a respectable middle-class person past the bounds of civilized behavior.

Those who write soft-boiled mysteries are interested in people who have some reputation to lose. If a gangster is killed, and the suspects are the pimp, the hit man, and the pusher, I don't much care who did it, because they'll all be dead or jailed soon anyhow; if not for this, then for something else. But when the Unitarian minister kills the Girl Scout leader, then there is respectability at stake, and the killer's struggle to escape detection and still maintain his position in the world can be harrowing to watch—and fascinating.

The authors featured in this volume of *Malice Domestic* are all skillful writers and perceptive observers of the human animal. The one thing that they have in common is that none of them has appeared in a previous edition of a *Malice Domestic* anthology. You will notice a wide spectrum among these writers: Overseas and American, male and female, funny and serious, rural and urban. The genre has come a long way since the old days of *Murder at the Vicarage*, and it is no longer possible to generalize the "cosy" as a tale about well-to-do people in an English village. Now these crime novels may be psychological studies of abnormal personalities, or sharp-edged satires of a particular subculture, or any of dozens of other permutations. The stories take place anywhere that people have private lives—that is to say: everywhere.

I think traditional mysteries have grown so much in substance and style in the past few decades that the best of them can be considered direct descendants of the nineteenth-century narrative fiction of Charles Dickens and George Eliot: they entertain with a satisfying story, but they also impart wisdom to the reader about some aspect of the human condition.

Writers tend to be quiet types, not known for being the life of the party. Like that reticent spinster Miss Jane Austen, writers at a social gathering will be sitting somewhere on the edge of the action, while the rest of you mingle, and chatter, and tell social white lies. Be warned, though; the writers are watching you very carefully. Here's what they've observed . . .

Sharyn McCrumb is a New York Times *best-selling author whose critically acclaimed success in Southern fiction has been both scholarly and popular. Her novels are studied in universities throughout the world, translated into German, Dutch, Japanese, French, Greek, Czech, Russian, Danish, Spanish, and Italian, in addition to being national bestsellers in the United States.*

Sharyn McCrumb has won more awards in crime fiction than any other author, including all of the major U.S. awards in the field, although critics and scholars are now recognizing her as an author of serious, nonmystery fiction. She has been awarded the Edgar, two Anthony Awards, two Macavity Awards, three Agatha Awards, and the Nero. She has also won the Sherwood Anderson Short Story contest, and twice been awarded the Best Appalachian Novel Award. Sharyn McCrumb is the author of fourteen novels, including the "Ballad Books," consisting of If Ever I Return, Pretty Peggy-O, *and* The Hangman's Beautiful Daughter, *and the* New York Times *bestsellers* She Walks These Hills *and* The Rosewood Casket, *all of which were named* New York Times *or* Los Angeles Times *"Notable Books." Her most recent novel is* The Ballad of Frankie Silver *(Dutton, 1998).*

Jane and the Spoils
of Stoneleigh

Stephanie Barron

6 August 1806
at Stoneleigh Abbey,
Warwickshire

*Emily shuddered as she held the lamp over it, and
looked within the dark curtains, where she almost
expected to have seen a human face; and, suddenly
remembering the horror she had suffered upon discovering the dying Madam Montoni in the turret
chamber of Udolpho, her spirits fainted . . .*

"Jane! My dear Jane! Where can you have got to?"
my mother's voice called from the dimness of the
gallery.

"I am in the library, with Mr. Hill," I replied; and
at her present appearance in the doorway, held aloft
my book with a satiric eye. "Only think, dear ma'am!

1

2 JANE AND THE SPOILS OF STONELEIGH

The late lamented Mary Leigh betrays a taste for horrid novels! I have been perusing the first volume of a quarto edition of Mrs. Radcliffe's *Mysteries of Udolpho*, and reflecting upon the similarities to be found in the relative situations of Emily St. Aubert and Miss Jane Austen."

"You would cast yourself in the guise of heroine, then?" enquired the solicitor, Mr. Hill, as he turned in some amusement from the letter he was writing. "You indulge the current fashion for the Gothic?"

"What else would you have me to read in an abbey, sir—Fordyce's Sermons?" I retorted mockingly. "I will have you know that I slumbered the better part of last night enveloped in just such a canopy of green silk as Mrs. Radcliffe here describes; and the wonder of it is that I did not dream of sepulchres!"[1]

"I am sure I did not sleep a wink," my mother reflected, and reached a hand to her cap. "The sheets, though dry and well-aired, were excessively chill, and it being August, one cannot very well solicit the housekeeper for hot bricks."

"Then pray take *Udolpho* as your guide, Miss Austen," Mr. Hill continued imperturbably, "and pay no attention to me. For with green damask curtains a man of the law may do nothing. They are quite beyond the reach of his reason."

"*Udolpho* may serve, up to a point," I said judiciously, "but I cannot think, Mr. Hill, that even its turreted keep, with all its splendid terrors, may equal Stoneleigh Abbey's portentious gloom; and I confess myself amazed that we have survived so much as four-and-twenty hours within these dreadful walls!"

---

[1] Austen's perusal while at Stoneleigh of Ann Radcliffe's *Mysteries of Udolpho*, a work of romantic suspense with which she was well acquainted, calls to mind the themes of her own *Northanger Abbey*. In that novel, the impressionable young Catherine Morland—also a devotee of *Udolpho*—confuses fact and fiction while visiting a venerable abbey.—*Editor's note*

My mother let slip an involuntary shriek, but the solicitor was not so easily moved. He fixed his bright blue eyes upon my face with good-humored shrewdness. "I perceive that you would sport, Miss Austen, with a poor fellow so benighted as to know nothing of *novels*. Are such horrors as you describe the stuff with which all young ladies fill up their heads?"

"Decidedly not. Only the most intelligent and charming of the ladies among my acquaintance admit to reading them—and the gentlemen, never. They are all for great folios of Plutarch and Aristotle, I believe—preferably in Latin and done up in the most indecipherable of typefaces."

"From the appearance of these shelves," my mother observed thoughtfully, "the Honourable Mary was entirely to our taste. Do you observe, Jane—here is *The Midnight Bell*, and Mrs. Sleath's *Orphan of the Rhine*. I have not yet looked into *The Black Forest*; perhaps I shall attempt it by and by—but she has also *The Castle of Wolfenbach*, and I should like to read it again."[2]

"There are volumes and volumes of such penetrating stuff, Mamma, and not a one is known to the unfortunate Mr. Hill! Do admit, sir, that you have never in your life looked within Mrs. Radcliffe's *Udolpho*, and I shall be confirmed in my opinion of human folly."

"I cannot disappoint you, even in this," he returned obligingly, "and I see that you shall be content with nothing less than the most malevolent of

---

[2] *The Midnight Bell* was written by Francis Latham, and published in 1798. Jane's father borrowed it from a circulating library, and it was read by the entire family. *The Necromancer: or the Tale of the Black Forest*, was translated from the German of Lawrence Flammenbergy by Peter Teuthold, and published by the Minerva Press in 1794. *The Castle of Wolfenbach*, by Mrs. Parsons, appeared from Minerva in 1793, while *Udolpho* and the *Orphan of the Rhine* appeared in 1794 and 1798 respectively.—*Editor's note*

plots and sinister of signs while resident in Stoneleigh Abbey. May you enjoy the swiftest revelation of both, Miss Austen. I may admire the application of such wit, as may turn an affair of tedium into a prospect of delight."

I laughed aloud, for indeed our journey yesterday to Stoneleigh Abbey—undertaken at the behest of another, and in all the discomfort of sudden flight—had threatened to be excessively tedious. It is not that the place is devoid of charm—rather the contrary, being a grand house of warm sandstone, founded on the ruins of a Cistercian monastery that dates to the twelfth century. It sits in a slight declivity, well back from the River Avon, with some very fine woods rising behind; the interior is vast and furnished in the style of a vanished age, all velvet hangings and hideous wood, exactly suited to a desperate heroine; and full five-and-forty windows grace the front facade alone! My mother is all amazement at the cost of the glazing and the window-tax.

But our delights in the abbey are a good deal mitigated by the nature of our visit. We are come into Warwickshire as the baldest of usurpers, and feel ourselves to move under the concerted suspicion of every domestic in the place. For not least among Stoneleigh Abbey's curiosities is the nature of its disposition: the fifth baron, Mad Sir Edward, left it in life tenancy to his sister, the Honourable Mary Leigh; and upon that lady's demise, ". . . *unto the first and nearest of his kindred, being male and of his blood and name, that should be alive at the time.*"

The Honourable Mary Leigh had recently fulfilled Sir Edward's clauses by dying at her London residence, and my mother's first cousin, the Reverend Thomas Leigh, was the foremost of the abbey's claimants. In the normal course of things, his nephew Mr. James-Henry Leigh, the head of the Adlestrop branch of the family, should have inherited before his uncle; but the curious wording of Mad Sir Edward's Last Will and Testament had given rise to a different construction. To the *first* and nearest male relation the abbey would go; and Reverend Thomas was certain these terms could signify only the eldest Leigh extant—himself.

There remained, however, some little uneasiness in the Reverend's breast. Of his nephew he had nothing to fear—the point had long been settled between *them*—but the Leighs are a distressingly numerous breed, running to variegated branches in far too many counties, and it was not unthinkable that some rival sexagenarian might dispute the Reverend's claim. Relative degrees of consanguinity and maleness would be debated, at great embarrassment and expense; the sordid expediency of lawyers should be required—and so, in the belief that possession was decidedly nine-tenths of the law, to Warwickshire the Reverend descended, in company with his entire family party.

There was the nephew, Mr. James-Henry; the nephew's wife, Julia; and her mother, Lady Saye and Sele, of the relentless tongue and careless morals. Lady Saye and Sele possessed the distinction of having raised one child to adultery and another to divorce; and in her wits I placed not the slightest confidence.[3] The three Austen ladies had been taken up with the rest, through the singular misfortune of

---

[3] Mary-Cassandra Twistleton, the younger of Lady Saye and Sele's daughters, eloped in 1790 with the eventual Viscount St. Vincent; was detected in adultery 1797 with Charles-William Taylor, a member of Parliament; was divorced 1799; and remarried in 1806 Richard-Charles Head-Greaves. Having seen her once in Bath, Jane Austen thought her to look "quietly and contentedly silly, rather than anything else." Her brother, Thomas, took to the stage in his youth and eloped with an actress, by whom he was cuckolded and divorced in 1798. Surprisingly, he remarried a year later and subsequently became a prominent clergyman.—*Editor's note*

having been resident in the Reverend Thomas's home at the moment of his fateful decision. And as he had been urged to it on the advice of his solicitor, Mr. Joseph Hill—who was undoubtedly the agent of any tedium Stoneleigh might afford the Austens—I had no inclination to spare that gentleman my reproaches. He was gazing at me now with such frank goodwill, however, that I forebore to be cross.

"I positively exult at our prospects in this noble old pile, Mr. Hill," I told him with a generous air, "and should not give up my place to the most shocking of Mrs. Radcliffe's heroines. Only observe—we shall have thunder this evening, I am sure of it; for the day is grown excessively close, and there is nothing like an abbey, you know, for storm and tumult of an evening."

"I had not understood how gravely we were circumstanced," he replied, folding up his letter, "and shall expect to be presented at every turn with a singular black veil, or a mouldering pile of bones, or at the very least a long-forgotten priest's hole, marked with the last struggles of a dying man."

"Indeed," my mother broke in, "and only consider what I have found myself in the cushions of the settee! I do not speak of the drawing-room piece, for I cannot abide such a quantity of crimson and wood, it puts me quite out of countenance—but of the striped one in the little breakfast parlour. As I settled myself with the intention of taking up my letter, the cushion positively *moved* beneath me! I was never more startled in my life! And what do you think it was?"

We were both of us devoid of speech.

"A nest of field mice!"

"Poor Mamma!" I exclaimed. "Were they very *large* mice?"

"Not *very* large," the good lady replied in a doubtful accent. "I should not be obliged to call them *rats*, Jane. But it cannot signify what their relative size may have been. Mr. Stanley has been at them with a poker and a few of the dogs, called up from the stables for the purpose, and great slavering brutes they were—the dogs, I would mean, not the mice, which are all run off or et up entirely, I suppose. But the impression of dirt *will* linger most uncomfortably. I cannot think that the Honourable Mary was excessively nice in her domestic arrangements, for all that Mr. Stanley is so superior; and I have not adventured the breakfast parlour since."

Mr. Stanley is the steward of Stoneleigh Abbey, and stands firm as a heart of oak before a legion of domestics. There are upper housemaids and lower housemaids, rank upon rank of liveried footmen, three butlers, a head gardener and his under-labourers charged with caring for the broad avenues and terraces of the grounds, a pastry cook, and a bread baker. Two French cooks divide the field of the kitchen between them, and the issue of the contest— to judge by the previous day's dinner and this morning's breakfast—is as yet undecided. We are all of us a little in awe of Mr. Stanley. I did not wonder that my mother had failed to request a hot brick; and determined for my part to do so this very evening.

"Then do oblige us by accepting a chair near the fire, ma'am," Mr. Hill suggested, and rose to secure her comfort. "I may attest that this particular seat can offer no unpleasant sensation, from having occupied it myself this quarter-hour."

"You are very good, sir," my mother rejoined, "but dinner cannot be very far off, and I must attend to my dress. I am bound to lose my way in searching for my bedchamber, you know, and must allow for the interval. I have beseeched the Reverend Thomas to place direction posts at the angles of the hallways, but he will not do it!"

"Then I shall wish you a successful journey, ma'am," he gravely concluded, "and hope to find you presently restored without incident."

The lack of direction posts notwithstanding, we found our way through the abbey's vast hall, and from thence (with only a trifling error that led us first to the billiards room, and subsequently into the apartments of the Reverend Thomas himself), to our own chambers. Along the way we were happy in encountering others of our party, similarly bewildered by the multitude of doors and galleries; but it was not much above an hour before we were all once more assembled around the long dining-table.

Fully twenty dishes lay upon its gleaming surface, comprising the first course; and I little doubted that a second, equally grand and equally impossible to consume, should follow at a respectable interval. A glance revealed every chair to have a footman ranged at its back, while the Clerk of the Kitchen, one Blackwell, stood behind the most elevated of the guests—Lady Saye and Sele. She was arrayed this evening in all the awful grandeur of puce satin with jet beads, and a feathered turban.

It was rather, I reflected, as though we dined under armed guard. Any attempt at easy conversation must be impossible. Even my sister Cassandra, who had the delights of Mr. Hill for enjoyment at her left hand, appeared utterly subdued.

But I had reckoned without Lady Saye and Sele.

"Good God, Blackwell, what in heaven's name is *that*?" she ejaculated, and pushed back her chair from the table with every evidence of horror.

"A little boiled chicken, my lady," the Clerk of the Kitchen informed her with a bow. "It is very wholesome, I assure you, and tender to the bone."

"I thought as much." She peered up at the fellow with an expression of contempt. "Since my unfortunate husband destroyed himself, I have been incapable of stomaching the dish. I shall take a little macaroni, if you please. It is made, I suppose, with Parmesan?"

"It is, my lady," Mr. Blackwell imperturbably replied.

"Very well."

"La, Mamma!" her daughter Julia declared, with a roguish twinkle, "have you not got over your dislike of chicken yet? And Papa is dead these eighteen years at least! You must know, Uncle Thomas," she confided to the Reverend Leigh, "that when my father cut his throat in Harley Street all that while ago—I was but a child, in fact, not even out of the schoolroom!—Mamma shut herself up for a fortnight, and would take only boiled chicken. Nothing so disgusts her in consequence as a well-poached fowl. But I continue to relish it, I assure you."[4]

"That is very well, my dear," Reverend Thomas said in answer to this foolish speech, "for there is a quantity of it in the kitchens, and I will not have it thrown to the dogs."

"On no account," my mother agreed, "for it cannot be good for their throats, you know, Cousin. Such little bones as a chicken possesses must choke the stoutest dog. I wonder whether a mouse might do the same? Only now that I consider of it, Mr. Stanley

---

[4] Thomas Twisleton, thirteenth baron Saye and Sele, attempted first to drown himself in Kensington gravel-pits, and eventually committed suicide in 1788 by both slitting his throat with a razor and stabbing himself with a sword. According to family history, he did so to end the pain of an incurable disease, although his choice of wife may have proved an added inducement.—*Editor's note*

did not seem anxious upon the point, when he loosed them in the breakfast parlour."

Before the Reverend could summon a reply to this interesting conjecture, my sister had marshalled her resources, and enquired whether he was satisfied with his impressions of the abbey.

"Quite satisfied," he replied, with an air of gloom; "for it is a very great estate indeed, and remarkably well-tended. Happy I should be to lay claim to it without encumbrance! But that is not to be, I fear!"

"Not to be?" Mr. James-Henry cried, with an air of astonishment, and set down his knife and fork. "Dear sir, what *can* you intend to intimate? Are we then come too late to prevail in our claim?"

"Our claim is immaterial, my dear boy, until we may lay our hands upon the necessary deeds of the estate."

"Deeds?"

"There are several. I would speak of the document of Elizabeth's time, conferring the abbey grounds to her Lord Mayor of London, Sir Thomas Leigh, in the midst of the Dissolution;[5] and of the confirmation of the Leigh family's ownership in the time of the Civil Wars, by Charles I, who was received at Stoneleigh when he had been turned away from Nottingham. These documents, along with the emblems of peerage conferred upon the first Baron Leigh in 1643, are priceless. By convention they are known as the Spoils of Stoneleigh, and have passed from father to son for nearly two centuries; but the Leigh line being now extinguished, they should rightly proceed to me, and to yourself in time."

---

[5] The Dissolution is the period roughly from 1539 to 1547 when Henry VIII confiscated property belonging to Roman Catholic families, monastic orders, and churches and sold or presented the bulk of it to supporters of himself and the newly formed Church of England. His successors, including the early Stuarts, completed the process.—*Editor's note*

"Naturally," Mr. James-Henry rejoined with asperity. "They are lodged with the Honourable Mary's solicitors, I must suppose?"

"So had we all. But I have been closeted with that firm's representative, a Mr. Smallgood, the better part of the morning; and most distressing have I found the business. Smallgood is only now returned to London, an unhappier man than when he journeyed hither."

Reverend Thomas seemed little disposed to say much more; and it was left to Mr. Hill to enlighten us.

"Mr. Smallgood thought to have found the deeds in an ancient strongbox stored in the late baron's study," the solicitor said, "but when he unlocked the box before the Reverend and myself, he found only a letter composed in the Honourable Mary's hand. She removed the documents at her discretion, it seems, and placed them elsewhere."

"Elsewhere?" Mr. James-Henry ejaculated. "*Elsewhere*? Are we to conclude from this, Hill, that you have not a notion of their present location?"

Mr. Hill seemed about to smile, but saved himself. "A notion, indeed, is all that the Honourable Mary left—a few lines of verse, that must indicate the deeds' hiding place. But for the life of me I cannot understand her meaning, any more than the Reverend Thomas."

I looked up from my chicken with a sinking heart. Melancholy was the fate of the Austen ladies, indeed! For until the Reverend Thomas should be happy in the disposition of Stoneleigh, our own plans should be utterly waylaid. And tho' this little visit to Stoneleigh is not entirely without interest, I should not wish it unduly prolonged. The society is too incongenial, Mr. Hill excepted. I cannot *like* my cousin, any more than I may admire his nephew (and on the subject of Lady Saye and Sele it is better to be silent). The Reverend Thomas is possessed of an unfortunate character in one united to the Church—too concerned with his own consequence to consider the feelings of others; too attentive to the *form* of his actions and address, to give thought to the nature of their ends. He is illiberal in his opinions, mean in his understanding, and complaisant in his admiration for himself; and at the last, so unlike my own dear departed father—from whose loss we must continue to derive the greatest misery—that I cannot but sigh over the irksome nature of his company.[6] The sooner we might assist him to the possession of Stoneleigh, therefore, the sooner we might be on our way to Staffordshire—and happy in the exchange.[7]

"Might we not endeavor to help, Mr. Hill?" I enquired. "Surely the application of the entire party may succeed where merely one or two, working alone, should fail!"

"An excellent notion, Miss Austen. If the Reverend Leigh will permit, I shall read the burden of the Honourable Mary's letter."

"Read it, for all love," Reverend Thomas said hastily. "It cannot possibly harm our cause, and may substantially aid it."

The solicitor bowed, and then reached within his coat for a single sheet of paper. " 'My dear Reverend Leigh,' " he began, " 'if you are reading this letter, I am undoubtedly gone on to my reward. I shall not

---

[6] Jane's father, the Reverend George Austen, had died 21 January 1805, leaving his wife and daughters largely dependent upon his five sons.—*Editor's note*

[7] The Austen ladies spent much of the summer of 1806 in visiting various relations before taking up residence that fall in Southampton with Jane's brother Frank and his bride. From Stoneleigh they went to another clergyman cousin, Edward Cooper, with whom they remained five weeks.—*Editor's note*

bother to conjecture as to its nature—I am too well acquainted with the blessings and errors of my life, to feel much apprehension regarding its conclusion. But if my days were hardly blameless, they may at least have been considered most interesting. Your own, I fear, will never suffer either the distinction of notoriety nor the satisfaction of pleasure. And so, as my parting gift, I am offering you a quest. If you see fit to abandon the torpor in which you have lived— the dull rectitude of piety and convention—you may win the Spoils of Stoneleigh, and a bit of amusement besides. You may even succeed in clearing my dear brother Edward's name of the gross injustice under which it fell in 1774. If, however, your habits are incapable of change at so advanced a period in life, you shall win nothing but my most heartfelt regret. A poor substitute for Stoneleigh, I must believe. I remain,' etcetra etcetra." Mr. Hill glanced up from the paper. "There is only the verse, appended at the letter's end. To wit:

> *Ah! paint her form, her soul-illumined eyes,*
> *The sweet expression of her pensive face,*
> *The light'ning smile, the animated grace—*
> *The portrait well the lover's voice supplies;*

Hardly a distinguished poet, I should think, and one with whom I am happily unacquainted."

"The merest doggerel!" cried Mr. James-Henry. "The woman was as mad as her unfortunate brother. It is all an outrage! I must implore you, Uncle, to throw yourself upon the mercy of the courts!"

"What would the Honourable Mary indicate, Mr. Hill," I enquired, "in speaking of her brother?"

"I cannot undertake to say. She mentions 1774, as

you will have noticed; and all I can learn is that Sir Edward was declared lunatic in that year. He was then but two-and-thirty years of age."

"So young!" Cassandra cried. "Pitiable soul!"

"It was a dreadful business, even without the suspicion of murder," Mr. Hill agreed.

"Murder!" Lady Saye and Sele set down her spoon with a clatter.

"Yes. So dreadful an enormity was never proved, of course, but the rumours persisted. Sir Edward was believed to"—Mr. Hill paused, and glanced feelingly at the footmen ranged imperviously behind our chairs, before dropping his voice to a whisper—"to have *strangled* a young lady while in the throes of one of his fits."

"How dreadful!" Her ladyship's looks were avid.

"And it is *this* that motivates the Honourable Mary's quest," I mused. "She would have us to learn the truth."

"Then she has chosen an odd way of going about it," the Reverend Thomas broke in bitterly. "Hill and I have been poking among the abbey's portraits for the better part of the morning. There are women enough in the long gallery—sweet, smiling and pensive alike—but what does that signify? We have pressed the frames and beat upon the wainscoting, to no avail; and I believe I shall have Mr. Stanley and a few of the footmen tomorrow, about the dismantling of the pictures."

"Does not the verse seem familiar, Jane?" my sister Cassandra whispered across the table. "I am sure we are acquainted with the poet. But I cannot call to mind the work in question."

Mr. Hill's bright blue eyes fixed upon my sister's face. "Pray continue, Miss Austen. You interest me extremely."

She blushed, and studied her plate. "If you might read the verse aloud once more, sir—"

He patiently did so, while the chicken was forgot and the macaroni cooled.

"*The portrait well the lover's voice supplies* . . . Of course," I cried, throwing down my napkin. "*Udolpho!*"

"Not the ubiquitous Mrs. Radcliffe?" Mr. Hill enquired, astonished.

"The same. Do not you remember, Cassandra? The sonnet pencilled by an unknown hand in Volume the First?"

"On the wall of the cunning fishing cottage, near the picturesque of the river!"

"Exactly!"

We both pushed back from the table, intent upon the book, but Mr. Hill arrested us with a single word.

"Ladies," he said, "some explanation, if you please."

"It is not a portrait that the Honourable Mary's verse would indicate," I told him, "but a particular building. The lines you found secreted in the strongbox are taken from the initial chapters of *Udolpho*, a work our cousin Mary appears to have prized. In the relevant passage, Emily St. Aubert discovers these verses scrawled upon the walls of her family's fishing cottage by an unknown hand. Has Stoneleigh anything to resemble such a building, Mr. Hill? Near the banks of the Avon, perhaps?"

"Let us find if it does," he said immediately, and rang for Mr. Stanley.

We assembled the following morning in the ramshackle boathouse, grey with disuse, that declined gently toward the thread of the River Avon. The weather was fine, although a trifle hot; my cheeks glowed, and a perceptible dew stood out on Mr. Stanley's brow. He had readily acceded to our request for a tour of the estate's outbuildings, and stood armed with a quantity of keys.

"These doors have rarely been opened in Miss Mary's day," he assured us, as he fumbled with the lock. " 'Twas the late baron, Sir Edward, as once had the use of the place. He thought to have gone to sea, the late baron, while a boy—until the duties of his position made it impossible."

"You astonish me, sir," I told him, with an eye for the door's hinges. "Is not that a glint of oil I perceive about the hasps? Surely someone has attended to the place since Sir Edward's day?"

The lock sprang open, and with a noiseless motion the door swung inward. "One of the gardeners, I'll be bound," Stanley said with a frown, "interfering where he had no right." He stood aside to admit the ladies' passage, and we hastened within, our sight somewhat impoverished by the dimness of the interior. The Reverend Thomas and Mr. Hill followed hard upon our heels.

A quantity of dust, lying thick as a pall on every surface; several wooden boats depending from the rafters, their sweeps long since shipped; and a small table near a shuttered window, with two chairs arranged as though for tea.

On the table, leaning slightly against one cobwebbed shutter, stood a heavily framed object—draped with a sinister black veil.

"Cassandra!" I whispered, with a hand to her arm. "Do you observe?"

She paled, and was momentarily at a loss for speech. "It cannot be Laurentini's skeleton!"

"Nor yet a waxen image, eaten by worms," I agreed. "But I doubt we find it here by chance. We are treated to the Honourable Mary's hand. Let us summon our courage and throw back the veil!"[8]

To our relief, no relic of the sepulchre appeared to our wondering eyes—only the portrait of a young lady, attired in the fashion of a vanished age.

"The sweet expression of her pensive face," Cassandra murmured. "It is as Miss Leigh described." It was a sweet face, assuredly, and young—not above seventeen, perhaps, with all the unblighted beauty of youth; her hair and dress were such as my mother might have worn in girlhood, and a band of black ribbon was tied about her throat. *Lucinda* was painted with a flourish along the canvas's lower edge, and a date—1774.

"How beseechingly she gazes from the frame," my mother observed. "Great liquid eyes, all supplication and love."

"Yes. Did she beseech him thus as she died, I wonder?"

Cassandra's look met mine. "Sir Edward, you would mean?"

"Do not you perceive his signature in the corner?"

"Then you believe this to be the lady he *murdered*?" Cassandra shivered. "No man—no matter how mad—could have ended that creature's life."

At her words there was a cry to our rear—and we turned to find our party arranged in attitudes of consternation, and Mr. Stanley insensible upon the floor.

"Lucinda Carmichael was her name," Mr. Stanley said, and mopped at his brow with the kerchief so kindly extended to him by the excellent Mr. Hill. The steward was propped against the boathouse's outer door, and although once more delivered into sunshine, his eyes seemed fixed upon a darker past. "I

---

[8] The heroine of *Udolpho* discovers a similarly veiled frame, and when she peers beneath the drape, perceives a horror that is revealed at the book's close as having been a waxen image rather than a corpse.—*Editor's note*

hadn't thought to look upon her face again in this world—forgive me, Reverend Leigh, for losing hold of my senses as I did. I'm that ashamed."

"No matter," the Reverend said dismissively. "But pray enlighten us, Stanley. Who is the lady?"

"No one of importance," the steward said, "but she was everything to Sir Edward. And in that she found her death, I suppose."

"You mean—that is to say, you would accuse— you are suggesting that Sir Edward ended this girl's life?" the Reverend Thomas said slowly.

"So the world would have it. The baron was found with his hands about her throat—and she was certainly dead. We all saw the mark of his fingers on her poor white skin."

Mr. Hill's bright blue eyes met mine. "And when did this dreadful business occur, Stanley?"

"At the turning of the year, it must have been— 1774, or thereabouts. I was just a boy at the time, and understood only a little of what happened, but it was enough to strike the heart dumb. My revered father was steward then, a position to which I acceded; and for years I prayed God to forget the lady's face," he said with a gesture to the portrait. "And God was good enough to grant me that peace."

"You observed her in death?"

He nodded. "A bitter night in January, it was, with the wind howling and the snow in great drifts about the abbey's walls. Mr. Simkins, the baron's valet, found the master gone from his bed; and fearing for his mind, he roused the whole household. It was then we saw the young miss was absent as well—and thought first of an elopement. A flight to Gretna Green, perhaps. But when the torches were fired and the dogs sent out, we saw the trail clear enough. Two sets of footprints, leading down to the river—and there we found them, the master and his love: half-drowned in icy water, with one of them howling like the devil's own, and the other quite fled from this world."

We were all of us silent with apprehension and dread, as though the cold of that winter might yet freeze our bones. "Miss Carmichael was a guest, then, in the abbey?" I enquired.

Mr. Stanley looked up sharply. "Of course," he said. "She was Sir Edward's ward, and thought to have married him before the year was out. But the physicians from London meddled in the business, and put it about that the baron was mad. Not fit to marry, they said, and would have prevented it—for the lady was an heiress, and her funds at the baron's disposition. They worried Sir Edward to death between them, the physicians and the solicitors, begging your pardon, sir," he said with a nod to Mr. Hill, "and drove Miss Carmichael to tears. Just a slip of a girl she was, and innocent of the world and its cruelties; but she learned too much in her last days."

"A melancholy tale," I said. "And the baron could offer no explanation for her death?"

"Neither explanation nor sense," Mr. Stanley replied. "It was days before he was calm again, and then only in a manner no one could like—as though his body was present, but his mind was gone. He never spoke from that night forward—not even at his death, so they say."

"And yet he was never charged?"

"Neither the coroner's jury nor the local magistrate could bear to try a man so plainly driven out of his wits. And there remained a point of confusion— whether two sets of footprints led through the snow to the banks of the river, or perhaps a greater number still, arguing for the baron's discovery of the deed, rather than its commission. None of the search party could agree upon the point; and the fall of snow that night continuing heavy, the marks were quite invisible by morning."

"And so he was declared insane," the Reverend Thomas said, a curious light in his eye, "and kept under the guard of physicians until his death. Do you recall the year of his passing, Mr. Hill?"

"1786, I believe, sir," the solicitor said immediately.

"Twelve years," the Reverend mused. "Twelve long years of grief and remorse. Good God! A swift hanging should have been the kinder."

"If indeed he was guilty," I objected.

The Reverend's countenance—so usually peevish with injury—was all alive with interest. "You would credit the Honourable Mary, Miss Jane? You believe our Sir Edward to be innocent?"

"I am so well acquainted with the vagaries of justice, sir, as to suppose that very few who land in the dock are deserving of the injury," I replied. "I am ready enough to acquit Sir Edward of killing his lady-love, on the mere evidence of all the world's believing it!"

"Very well," the Reverend replied. "We shall go forward, you and I, and pursue the hare our cousin Mary has loosed. What next, Mr. Hill?"

Like a conjurer, the solicitor turned the portrait on its face, and probed the frame with a careful finger. A slip of paper was his reward; and he held it up for all to see.

"Another note from the great beyond, I think," he said.

Those who really possess sensibility ought early to be taught that it is a dangerous quality, which is continually extracting the excess of misery or delight from every surrounding circumstance . . . and since our sense of evil is, I fear, more acute than our sense

*of good, we become the victims of our feelings, unless
we can in some degree command them.*

The Reverend Leigh looked up from Mary Leigh's
note, a puzzlement at war with curiosity in his countenance. We had repaired within doors to seek re-
freshment and counsel, and had found our way from
breakfast parlor to library with remarkably little difficulty.

"I confess the sense of this eludes me," the Reverend said, "and I cannot believe it to point to a particular place where the Spoils might be held. Nor
may it be thought to derive from a horrid novel, as
the previous direction—for in tenor and object it
might rather be taken for one of my own sermons."

"The sermon of a dying parent to a child," I observed dryly. "I know that I will astonish you, cousin
Thomas—and to contradict your words must always
bring me pain—but the passage is from *Udolpho*, of
that you may be certain."

"The plaintive scene in the woods, Jane!" my
mother said excitedly, "among the dancing peasants.
When St. Aubert is at the point of death."

"The very one."

The Reverend Thomas seemed about to dispute the
notion, but thrust himself toward the bookshelves instead. "Where is the wretched work?" he cried. "I
cannot remain in ignorance of it any longer."

I helped him to the pertinent volume, and was
even so good as to leaf through several chapters until
the particular passage was found; and we remained
in some suspense while the Reverend examined the
text.

After the first transports at his discovery, Mr. Hill
had fallen unwontedly silent. I observed him now at
a little remove from our party, brows knit and gaze
abstracted, and moved to his side.

"I may venture to guess the subject of your thoughts," I said lightly. "You are lost in lamentation of the wasted years of your youth, spent all in the study of philosophy, when a wiser man might have looked into the Gothic."

He could not suppress a smile. "I wish that my mind were so pleasurably engaged—but I fear it is otherwise."

"You are gravely troubled," I said slowly. "Do not deny it, I beg."

"I am merely all wonder that so mature a gentleman as Mr. Stanley should faint dead away at the sight of a portrait of a mere acquaintance—however disastrous her end. Do not you find it singular, Miss Austen?"

"I do," I replied, "and have been at a loss to explain it. So extreme an anxiety—so decided a disruption of his usual serenity—must suggest a severe shock."

"Of guilt, perhaps?"

"The same notion has seized both our minds. He describes himself as a child—but perhaps *youth* was a more appropriate term. Might it not be likely that he was of an age with Miss Carmichael? And jealous of her love for Sir Edward?"

"Jane!" my sister cried from her position at Reverend Thomas's elbow. "Was it not upon his deathbed that St. Aubert extracted from Emily her final promise?"

I frowned in thought. "To burn his private papers?"

"Papers secreted in a hidden chamber among the floorboards of a closet adjoining his apartments!"

"But of course! We must enquire of Mr. Stanley," I said, with an eye for Mr. Hill.

The steward was summoned, and appeared with a

greater expression of composure upon his countenance than heretofore.

"Ah—very good, Stanley," the Reverend said
briskly. "Pray be so good as to show us to the late
baron's rooms."

"The Blue Rooms, sir," he offered, "at the head of
the staircase. They have been shut up these thirty
years at least."

Mrs. Radcliffe had placed *her* heroine's papers beneath a certain floorboard, that might be known by
a distinctive knot in the wood, and opened by concerted pressure along the joints; and so, on hands and
knees, my sister and I crept the length of the baron's
dusty dressing-room, pushing and prying at every
plank. But we were not to prevail. No squeak or complaint from broken wood did we hear, and if the
Spoils of Stoneleigh reposed beneath Sir Edward's
abandoned slippers, they were destined to slumber
undetected.

At length I sat back on my heels—tired, cross, and
smudged with dirt. "Mr. Stanley," I enquired, "was
the Honourable Mary resident in the abbey at the
time of Miss Carmichael's murder?"

"She was, ma'am."

"And of an age to comprehend events?"

"Oh, decidedly, ma'am—she was only two years
younger than Sir Edward, you know."

I glanced sidelong at Mr. Hill. "Quite a bit older
than yourself, obviously."

"Some twelve or thirteen years, I should think. She
was always the young lady to me, even when I was
little child—but very kind and attentive, just the
same."

Twelve or thirteen years' difference would make
Mr. Stanley decidedly of an age with the dead girl—
and I was certain that Mr. Hill at least had compre-
hended the fact. Would any boy of seventeen remain

unmoved by Lucinda Carmichael's golden loveliness, however plighted to his master?

"Miss Leigh was well out of the schoolroom, then, and tarrying in the single state," I mused. "Did she mean to live with her brother after his marriage, I wonder, or form a separate establishment in London? And what were her opinions of the fair Lucinda?"

"The two ladies were hardly of an age," Mr. Hill observed.

"No. And yet the younger—with both charm and fortune to recommend her—bid fair to displace the elder in situation and consequence." I accepted the solicitor's hand and rose to my feet. "It is a prospect to counsel the most desperate of deeds to a lady reared on the pap of horrid novels. Flight by night in a stolen carriage—embarkation for the coast of France—or an application for the protection of an elderly aunt, I should think. Very well, Mr. Stanley— if the Reverend Thomas will indulge me yet a moment more, I should like to be shown Miss Leigh's own apartments."

"They are just opposite, ma'am—the Yellow Room, which Lady Saye and Sele occupies."

We were thankfully bereft of Lady Saye and Sele's company this morning, Mr. James-Henry having driven his wife and her mother to Kenilworth Castle. "I am certain she would not object any disturbance of ours, in pursuit of her daughter's eventual inheritance," I declared, with a hard look for Mr. Stanley.

"Naturally not," he said immediately, and turned for the Yellow Room.

The objections of her ladyship's private maid were overborne, entry gained to the dressing-room itself, and a few minutes' work upon the floorboards rewarded our presumption. With a sharp creak, one plank slid beneath another—and a cunning little chamber was revealed to our sight.

Mr. Hill crowed aloud and the Reverend dropped to his knees, his fingers scrabbling—but no Spoils did we find. Only a calf-bound book of stiff buff paper, such as a lady might employ for her private jottings.

"Should we burn it, Jane?" Cassandra said with amusement.

"Even Emily St. Aubert permitted her eyes to stray." I opened the little book's cover, and read a single inscription upon the flyleaf: *Mary Elizabeth Cassandra Leigh, Her Book, July 1773 to August 1774.*

"I think, sir, that you should have the reading of this," I said, and placed the volume in the Reverend's hands.

It was then that a small pendant slid from the pages of the book—a miniature portrait of a dark-eyed, handsome man not much above thirty. I picked it up, and espied a few words engraved on the ob verse. *To Lucinda, my everlasting love.*

"Is this Sir Edward, Mr. Stanley?" I enquired.

And the faithful steward nodded.

It was a tousled Reverend Thomas who appeared in the breakfast parlour the next morning—a gentleman robbed of sleep and quelled in spirit, with barely a word to spare for our entreaties. He had failed to assist at the household's morning prayers, conducted daily by Mr. Stanley in the abbey's chapel—a singular remission in one so apparently correct.

"Come, come, my dear Reverend," cried Lady Saye and Sele, who had learned the better part of our adventures over tea and toast, "we are positively with child to know it all!"

"I am in no position, madam, to act as midwife," he replied in a fit of temper, and tossed the offending volume on the table linen. "I am done with frivolity and dissipation. *All night* I have been turning these wretched pages—aye, and Mrs. Radcliffe's too—and not a hint of the Spoils do I find!"

"But Cousin," my mother objected, "surely you have learned *something* to the purpose. The Honourable Mary cannot have failed to relate the events of January 1774."

"I know not whether she wrote of them or no. The revelant pages have been excised from the book with a razor. Whatever Mary Leigh may have felt or done, it is as a blank to us now. I cannot think why she directed us to the volume, if only to snatch the truth from our fingertips."

"But sir—surely she must give some picture of her relations with her brother," I protested, "or of her opinion of the charges against him! She retained his miniature for decades after his death. Does not that speak eloquently of undiminished affection?"

"You may judge for yourself, my dear Jane," the Reverend wearily replied. "I cannot find anything in these pages but an overweaning love for Stoneleigh itself. It might almost be a guide to the building's history, or the transformation of its landscape, than a record of her year. The Honourable Mary was a singular woman; and if she felt a strong affection, it was for stone and mortar rather than living things."

I frowned, quite put out by impenetrability of the lady's character, and reached for the discarded journal. "And there was nothing else?"

"Only a scrap of verse. There, tucked into the back cover. I cannot say whether it is intended for us or no."

I extracted the slip of paper and read the few lines.

Him the vindictive rod of angry Justice
Sent quick and howling to the centre headlong;
I, fed with judgment, in a fleshly tomb, am
Buried above ground.

"How dreadful," said Lady Saye and Sele. "It quite works upon my nerves."

The Reverend Thomas commenced to pace before the breakfast-room hearth. "I have been tearing through Mrs. Radcliffe the better part of the wee hours, searching for that verse."

"My dear sir," I said in some amusement, "tho' I must commend the energy that takes so worthy an object as *Udolpho* for its study, I fear your researches have been in vain. These words are not from Mrs. Radcliffe's pen, of that I am certain."

"Surely it is Mr. Cowper's work?" Cassandra suggested.

"From 'Lines Written During a Period of Insanity,'" Mr. Hill said softly. "I have the words by heart."

"You are an enthusiast of Mr. Cowper, sir?" I enquired.

For the first time in my acquaintance with the solicitor, I observed him to flush with embarrassment. "I had the honour to correspond with Mr. Cowper, right up to the year of his death. He possessed a formidable intellect."

"However beset by periods of madness," Cassandra observed thoughtfully. "We must wonder why Mary Leigh took the verses so to heart."

I studied the few lines in private once more. "I wonder, Mr. Stanley, whether there is a crypt at Stoneleigh?"

The steward stood wordlessly in the parlour doorway, neither removed from the party nor yet quite of it; but at my words he started. "There is a family vault in the abbey chapel. It is presently draped with black in respect of Miss Leigh, as you will have observed during morning prayers."

I had noted the lengths of crape; but the presence of a vault had escaped my notice. "It has been re-

cently opened for the interment of the Honourable
Mary, I collect?"

"Yes—and well before the date of her death, for
the erection of her sarcophagus. It seems she had a
presentiment of her end, and ordered stonecutters to
the business only last June."

"Did she, indeed." I looked to the Reverend Leigh.
"Perhaps this presentiment instructed her to remove
the Spoils at about the same time. I believe, sir, that
we should pay our respects to the Honourable Mary.
I cannot think how we should have neglected the
duty so long."

We repaired as one to the abbey chapel—a dim,
cool height beneath soaring arches of stone, where
one might almost glimpse, from the corner of an eye,
cowled figures ranged in stalls—silenced in their
chants, but eternally watching. To the iron grill in the
wall, fastened with a ponderous lock that opened
easily enough to Mr. Stanley's ministrations; and at
last, hesitating upon the chill threshold, into the vault
itself. If I confess I thought of Emily St. Aubert, and
countless other horrid heroines, before I plunged
with my wavering candle into the mortal dark, I may
perhaps be forgiven a foolish shudder.

"Where does the lady lie?" Reverend Thomas
whispered.

"Just there—against the nearer wall."

"You must help me, Hill, to lift the sarcophagus."

"But sir," the solicitor protested, "she cannot have
taken the Spoils to her grave—for she was buried
from London; and who should have placed the deeds
within her coffin?"

In the hope of forestalling some gruesome revelation of the Honourable Mary's present condition, I
said quickly, "Search first about the tomb's surface,
or perhaps the adjacent wall. It will be there, in a

hidden chamber created by the stonecutters for the purpose, that the Spoils are hidden.''

We held aloft our candles, and commenced severally to examine the granite walls. Here, an inscription to a long-dead Lady Audrey; there, yet another of the numerous Thomases in which the Leigh family abounds. And then to my wondering eyes, the flame revealed a quite fresh inscription carved upon a single stone—

> *The lady that hath no music in herself,*
> *Nor is not mov'd with concord of sweet sounds,*
> *Is fit for treasons, stratagems, and spoils;*
> *The motions of her spirit are dull as night,*
> *And her affections dark as Erebus:*
> *Let no such lady be trusted.*

"Cousin Thomas!" I cried. "Here they lie, I am certain of it!"

My fellow searchers hastened to my side, and held aloft their candles, a hushed silence falling over the entire party as they read.

"Shakespeare," my mother said with satisfaction. "*Julius Caesar*. Only she has put *lady* where it ought to read *man*."

"So she has," Mr. Hill said briskly, "and thus we may consider her to have achieved a final balance— having placed a *man* where a *lady* should have stood, many years ago."

I looked at him swiftly, but said nothing.

"A chisel, Stanley, I think," said the Reverend Thomas.

The steward called for just such a tool, and at its being quickly provided, commenced to hammer diligently at the newly laid stone.

*   *   *

"I cannot quite accept it, Jane," my sister Cassandra said the following evening, as she raised her head from Mary Leigh's journal. "I can only assume that the lady was even more lunatic than her brother."

"Find solace in that reflection if you must, my dear," I said from my place by the fire. "It can do very little to comfort *me*." For I, too, had read the pages excised from the Honourable Mary's journal, and found her possessed of a formidable courage and coolness.

Madness was nothing to it.

Stoneleigh Abbey,
January 9, 1774

Tonight I crept into Lucinda's bedchamber, and gazed at her in the light of my candle. Such a frail little thing as she is—a gossamer faery, too lovely for life. Delicate bones under a translucent skin; hair that might have been spun from gold. I cannot fault poor Edward for loving her. She is everything a man might prize.

And utterly unlike myself.

His miniature, hanging slack on its rose-colored ribbon, rose and fell with every indrawn breath. I bent down quietly, gently, as though to embrace her, and took the ribbon between my fingers.

It was a small thing only to strangle her.

And when it was done—when she had ceased to flail and choke, her eyes wide open with awakened horror—I lifted her gently in my arms and carried her out into the snow.

I laid her on the riverbank and returned to the house, careful to muddle my own footprints. And the house once regained, I hastened to my dear Edward's bedchamber, and called out in whispered alarm: "Brother! Come quickly! Our Lucinda is gone!"

He rose immediately, and dashed to her room—
saw the bedcovers flung wide—and turned to the
staircase.

"Go quietly," I said in some little urgency. "We
cannot have the servants know as yet. It would not
do to incite a scandal."

One wild look—and he was out of doors.

In a little while I heard the sounds of his lamentation; and it was then I roused Simpkins, and bade
him to go in search of his master.

March 15, 1774

The ides of March, an auspicious day for gross be-
trayal. The solicitors have come for Edward.

His madness is no more than they expected. The
signs of it—reported dutifully by myself for months
before Lucinda's death—could not hope to encourage
the London physicians in sanctioning his marriage;
and now that his ravings are full-blown, his grief
inconsolable, and his guilt in her death beyond question, there is nothing for it but to declare him lunatic.

And so Stoneleigh at last is mine.

I am safe from that terrible exile, granted lovingly
at the whim of a mere child. She presumed to my
place at her peril.

Thrones, dominions, principalities, realms—they
are as nothing to me now, who am come into my
little kingdom. I have taken lives for it—wreaked
havoc among those I love; stolen the very breath of
meaning from a sensitive soul, and consigned myself
to eternal damnation.

They have given Lucinda's miniature into my
keeping, in remembrance of Edward. I shall treasure
it always.

These journal entries were secured along with the Spoils of Stoneleigh—slumbering perhaps forever, had my cousin, the Reverend Thomas, not consented to look within a *novel*. But for his dissipation he has won this bit of earth—so contested and marked by malice through the ages.

Shocking as the admission of Mary Leigh's guilt may be, there is nothing more to be learned from her pen. Neither words of remorse nor plea for absolution—unless they might be found in the few lines graven upon her tomb's wall. Had she felt, at the last, what it was to be a soul unmoved by music? To know her spirit was as dull as night? That she lived a life fed on judgment, enclosed within a fleshly tomb?

Pitiable woman.

Even Mrs. Radcliffe can give us nothing like her.

Miss Austen closes the book on old secrets in a Gothic mansion in Stephanie Barron's latest case for the shrewd and observant novelist. The immortal Jane also appears in Jane and the Unpleasantness at Scargrave Manor, Jane and the Man of the Cloth, *and* Jane and the Wandering Eye.

Getting Robert

Eleanor Taylor Bland

Catherine Matthews hooked her cane over the shelf above the fireplace and eased onto the sofa. The swelling in her joints made every movement painful. She didn't bother to turn on a lamp. A clock ticked on the mantel but she couldn't see the face. She guessed it was close to midnight. The house sat back from the street, and a row of tall yews stood sentry near the porch, blocking out street lights and moonlight as well. The room took on texture and shades of darkness. The curtains lighter than the walls, Aunt Hattie's ginger jar lamp squatting on the table, Aunt Winnie's blue parakeet, stuffed now, with wings spread as if in mid-flight as it perched, still caged, in the curio cabinet. Small noises, comforting and reassuring, made her feel less alone. Glass rattling as the wind blew against the windows, the settling and resettling on the wood frame. The knocking of the pipes as they cooled.

She hadn't wanted to buy this old house when she

and Robert got married fifteen years ago. They would have been able to afford better if it wasn't for Julie, Robert's first wife. Julie and her three daughters got the vacation home in Lake Geneva and the estate in Lake Forest that had belonged to Robert's parents. Something in their will, he said. They had liked Julie. Pain jolted her and she felt her nails cutting into her palms and flexed her fingers. Julie had always had so much and appreciated so little.

Catherine rubbed the back of one hand with her fingertips, then the other. The swelling in her joints had increased. She could smell the BenGay, but the heat was little more than a distraction. Nothing could touch the ache. She had done too much driving today, driven farther than she had in years, all the way to Wisconsin. She had sat in that cold car for over two hours, her legs cramped beneath the steering column. Not even wool slacks and a heavy coat, Robert's socks, a blanket, and a thermos of coffee could keep out the cold. She parked just beyond the bend in the road that led to the house, the small white Escort camouflaged by white snow and out of sight beneath the tall pines. She was paying for it now, but it had been worth it. That was one trip that neither she nor Robert would ever have to make again.

When Robert retired right after they were married, they settled here, homebodies, both of them, her with her gardening and needlework, Robert with his birding at nearby nature preserves and golf at the army base and fishing along the shores of Lake Michigan. Everything would have been perfect if it wasn't for Julie. She just couldn't let go. Robert had been forced to travel to get away from her. They must have seen half the world while he tried to stay away from Julie. Robert would have given anything to stay here in Highwood and live a quiet, settled life, but there was always Julie, just thirty minutes farther north and a moment away by phone. The calls would begin, Robert's voice furtive as he whispered into the phone, trying to keep her from becoming upset as he pleaded with Julie to leave them alone. When he couldn't take it anymore, he would make reservations. Poor Robert, he was always so eager to leave. He would begin packing three days ahead of time, get to the airport two hours early. Then he would stare out the window the entire trip, and fidget from the time the landing gear went down until they disembarked.

Once there; in London, or Barcelona, or Venice, Robert would put her into a cab, send her off to a small bed sitter, and hasten away, just in case Julie had discovered where they were staying. He would return after dark and go out early each morning, careful to leave unobserved. Robert loved the confusion of a marketplace and the cool quiet of a museum. She didn't want to go sightseeing. She had no curiosity about strange places and didn't like the food. She didn't speak the languages that Robert and Julie were fluent in and had no interest in the local customs. While Robert revisited places he had seen as a child with his parents, she settled in with her books. How she hated all of that chatter that she couldn't understand and cars careening along the roads. And the animals. They always seemed to be running loose somewhere.

Despite all his efforts to get away from her, Julie followed them wherever they went. Malicious and spiteful, Julie would call her with lies about Robert. As if she would believe anything that woman said. Besides, Robert slept in her bed every night and there wasn't even a hint of Julie's White Diamond perfume on his clothes.

It was such a relief to come home. Robert seemed to age on the ride to the airport. He was always ex-

hausted during the flight back and, face drawn,
looked ten years older. He would have heart palpi-
tations by the time they landed, then his ulcer would
act up on the drive home. For days he would be almost a ghost of himself, saying little, taking walks in
the morning and long naps in the afternoon. In a few
months the calls would begin again, and he would
begin planning another trip.

Her arthritis had put a stop to all the travel. Three
years ago, her doctor agreed, no more. Fifty seemed
too young to be getting so crippled, but now they
had to stay home. At sixty-five, Robert was getting
too old for it anyway. He still subscribed to all those
travel magazines and brought home brochures as fast
as she could throw them away, but there was no trav-
eling now. Dear Robert. Such a good man. And now
he was hers, hers alone.

Catherine reached for the shawl she kept handy,
eased it around her shoulders, and folded her arms
beneath the soft warm wool. She smiled, thinking
back to that night sixteen years ago when she knew
Robert would be hers. He had been such a ladies'
man then. She had gone to work for him right out of
secretarial school. As his secretary, she had made so
many hotel reservations for two that didn't include
Julie. Until Yvette, Robert's interest in a woman
didn't last for more than two business trips. He dated
Yvette for almost a year.

Good thing she was there the night Yvette died.
Good thing she knew where the two of them were
staying and booked a room for herself. Yvette, with
her phony French accent—so young, so dangerous.
Robert was ready to divorce Julie to be with her. He
had an appointment with his attorney. If she hadn't
gone to Yvette's room . . . if she hadn't succeeded in
getting the barbiturates into Yvette's drink, if she
hadn't helped Yvette to bed and then put that plastic

bag over her head until she stopped breathing...
Poor Robert. Yvette would have ruined his life.

Robert was like a little child when she found him
in Yvette's room, standing over her body. He held
her hand and kept nodding as she explained what
they would tell the police. Yes. Yes. They were together all evening, attending to the business that
brought him to the convention. If it wasn't for her,
Robert would have been found in that room and arrested. Not that she thought for one minute that
those detectives believed them. Robert was so terri-
fied of being arrested, of going to jail, so relieved
when the police could not break their alibi, so grateful to remain safe and free.

Of course there was still Julie to contend with. To
Julie she was invisible then, just the secretary. There
was never so much as a hello when Julie came to the
bank. Until they were ready to marry, Catherine
doubted that Julie even knew her name. Julie came
into Robert's office as if she owned it, and never ever
paused long enough to read the name plate on her
desk. After the headlines in the newspaper about
Yvette, Robert practically hid in his office. He
dreaded going home, and waited until hours after the
bank closed. He wanted so desperately to be free of
Julie that Catherine suggested they might let everyone think they were reconciled, and take a short trip
abroad. Something was always happening to tourists.
Or, there was his parents' yacht. The waters off shore
in Lake Michigan could be quite treacherous. There
was nothing unusual about someone falling over-
board and drowning. After Yvette, it seemed so easy.
Too bad Julie relented and agreed to the divorce, just
when Catherine had everything planned. And, finally, after all of these years, everything that Julie
couldn't let go of then was hers, especially Robert.

Last year, when Julie finally realized there would

be no more trips abroad, and understood just how much Robert loved *her*, how considerate he was and how much he loved being with her, Julie began to have heart trouble. One of Robert's daughters would call. Mother has been taken to the hospital, Mother has chest pains, Mother has fainted. And, because he had never gotten past the guilt of Yvette's death, off he would go. This time he'd been at Julie's place in Lake Geneva for over three weeks. This was the first time he'd stayed away for more than a day. When she called, he sounded frantic to come home, but always there was this whining, adult daughter, standing nearby. Daddy, we need you. Daddy, mother is sick.

Robert had been gone so long that she sent him the copies of the newspaper articles about Yvette's death so he could signal her on the phone if he wanted something to happen to Julie. And, last night, he had. When she called and asked if he'd received her letter, he said that he never wanted to see her again. Of course, with Julie and his daughters right there, he couldn't say who he meant, but she knew who it was and she had gone there before daybreak this morning.

The furnace kicked on. The fan began to whirl and cool air, then heat swirled from the vents. A hot soak would feel good. She had overexerted herself today. It was her first trip to the summer house, but not her last. The place wasn't anything like what she'd expected. A sprawling single-level home, with no stairs to climb, and so much land. It was so isolated, a perfect hideaway for her and Robert. Everything was so quiet. No traffic sounds, no people sounds, just an occasional bird.

She sat there, without any plan other than to wait until Robert went for his morning walk and bring him home. She could not hear Julie as she jogged down the path. She didn't see her until she rounded the bend. Julie, with the bad heart, jogging. Julie, lying again. For a moment there all she could see was a hazy kind of orange. When her vision cleared, she just wanted to run, but Julie was in the way. The engine didn't turn over on the first try, when it did, the car seemed to leap forward. There was a thud as metal hit flesh and bone. For a moment she glimpsed a red parka as it bounced on the hood, then was flung to the side of the road.

She had been waiting for Robert to come home ever since she got back. The car, with the broken headlamp and dented fender and what she hoped looked like rust, was in the garage. She couldn't call him, couldn't tell him what to say this time, but, there was no need to. He wouldn't have had any idea of what had happened. She wanted him to know, just as she had wanted him to know about Yvette, but perhaps she would wait until after the funeral to tell him. He would have to go to Julie's funeral, because of his daughters. Three of them. What were they like? If they were anything like their mother . . .

The phone rang. Robert! She ignored the cane and rushed to the hall without stopping to turn on the light. Robert! She reached for the phone and knocked the receiver off the cradle.

She grabbed the receiver. "Robert!" She almost shouted his name. She couldn't have broken the connection. "Robert!"

"Yes, Catherine. It's me."

He sounded so tired.

"You must have had a terrible day."

He didn't answer.

"Robert, you can come home now. You've been gone so long, but now you can come home."

"No," he said. "I'm never coming back again."

"But of course you are, Robert. Oh dear, it's the

girls, isn't? Those daughters of yours. I knew they were just like their mother. Never you mind, darling, I'll take care of that. I'll take care of everything." She didn't know how, but she would. "Things always work out for us in the end now, don't they? Don't be upset, and don't you worry."

She waited. He was breathing as if he'd been running.

"Robert? Are you having another panic attack?" He hadn't had one since that night in the hotel. "Don't worry, darling. If you have to stay there a few days to help make arrangements, I'll understand. This time when you come home there won't be any more trips, not ever. It will just be me and you. Isn't that wonderful, darling?"

He still did not answer.

"Robert, I've missed you so much. If it weren't for my arthritis I'd drive up there again right now. You are coming back soon, darling, aren't you?"

"Yes."

It was almost a sigh. A sigh of longing. He had missed her almost as much as she had missed him.

"I'm at a filling station, Catherine. I'll be there soon."

"Goodbye, darling. It's been so lonely here without you."

She went upstairs without leaving any lights on. Robert would think it was wasteful, and she wanted his homecoming to be perfect. She straightened the coverlet on his side of the bed, then adjusted the blinds so that moonlight filtered into the room. Robert, always modest, still came here like a newlywed, hesitant and shy, waiting until he thought she was asleep, worried about her arthritis. Their room, no more strange beds. Her wedding pictures, several dozen, hung above the bed, and she had put the fifteen-by-eighteen wedding portrait on the opposite wall where they could see it as they lay back on the pillows. She looked almost regal in that white gown and veil, and Robert was so handsome, so solemn in his tuxedo, even though his hair was receding. How he hated losing his hair. She thought it made him look distinguished.

Aunt Hattie and Aunt Winnie had raised her, then died, old maids in a nursing home. "Died without a man between 'em," an elderly neighbor said when she went home to arrange their funerals. But not her. Not only had that spinster Catherine Fonk managed to get herself a man, but she had gotten herself a wealthy, attractive bank vice president. All those who thought her too dull, or too plain or not well enough educated had watched in amazement. And she hadn't had to make do with someone nobody else wanted either. Julie wanted Robert very much, so had Yvette, but he was hers. And she had been happy all these years. She had been. She was. Happy. With Robert.

She went over to the bed and sat down on her side. Tonight he would sleep beside her. His age and her infirmities would hinder much else, but he would be with her in this bed. Dear Robert. He sounded so happy when he called from the filling station, so eager to be coming home. It was Julie's fault that he had asked her for a divorce when she called him last night. How they must have been pressuring him. He must have felt awful afterward. A divorce, not her and Robert, they were too much in love. That's why it was so difficult for him to come back to her. She had known as soon as he said it that nothing could ever change as long as Julie was alive. There had been moments where, sitting in that car, she had been afraid that Julie really did have a bad heart, that she only went jogging in the morning when she was at the estate in Lake Forest. There was so much property surrounding the house that she wasn't sure she had chosen the right place to wait. It looked like the main road, but what if Julie took a different path? What a relief it had been to see Julie come around that curve. Now Robert was rid of that woman forever.

She heard a whap as the screen door closed. Robert! There was an abrupt silence as he turned down the thermostat and the fan went off. She would have to get out the extra blankets and wake up to a cold house in the morning, but she would never wake up alone again. Robert had come home to her forever. She wanted to run to the door, rush down the stairs, give him a big hug, but Robert disapproved of displays of affection. Instead she stood there, savoring the sound of his footsteps coming toward her. When he reached the first landing where the stairs turned, she tiptoed over to the window, stood there with her back to the door, hugging herself as she listened to Robert coming closer.

She could hear her heart beating, feel it pounding in her chest. It was so hard to just stand there, to let him come to her. The stairs creaked just a little. He was still a big man, a little stoop-shouldered now so he didn't appear as tall, and thanks to Julie, he had probably put on a few more pounds. The floorboards in the hallway gave beneath his weight. Then the door squeaked. Creaky old house, not like that mansion in Lake Forest that was hers now.

She shivered as he came into the room and hugged herself tighter to keep from turning and throwing her arms around him. Unable to remain silent, she whispered his name.

"Robert, oh Robert, you've come home."

Instead of sitting on the edge of the bed and taking off his shoes, he came over to where she was standing. She could hear him breathing. Was he going to kiss her? Eyes closed, she waited for his touch. She smiled as he fumbled in his pocket. He had brought her a gift! That strand of pearls that Julie wouldn't give her when they were married! Yes! He was slipping something around her neck. Yes.

"Oh, Robert. You—"

No! It was a cord! Dear God. No. Before she could say his name again, the cord tightened.

This story centers on a marriage of a murderous kind. Bland, who lives in the Chicago area, writes a regular series featuring black Illinois cop Marti MacAlister and includes Done Wrong.

Monsieur Pamplemousse
Tells the Tale

Michael Bond

"**Sadly,**" **said Monsieur** Pamplemousse, "I never did get to eat *chez* Picot. It was on account of a dead Chinaman in the cold store. That, and Pommes Frites's nose being mistaken for a truffle when he rested it on a lady's knee . . ."

His pause did not go unrewarded. The mere mention in the same breath of two such legendary figures—Pommes Frites, bloodhound *extraordinaire*, late of the Paris *Sûreté*, sometime holder of the "Sniffer Dog of the Year" award, and Picot—until recently chef-patron of France's premier restaurant—was sufficient to bring all other conversation in the room to a halt.

Pommes Frites, on the other hand, gave a deep sigh. He'd been toying with the idea of taking a midnight stroll in the shrubbery, but from past experience he knew that once his master got going with a story there was no knowing when he would get back into the house. Concealing his disappointment in as pointed a manner as possible, he closed his eyes and went to sleep.

The occasion was the annual staff party given by Monsieur Henri Leclercq, Director of *Le Guide*, France's oldest and most respected gastronomic bible.

The venue was, as usual, Monsieur and Madame Leclercq's summer residence in Normandy. It was past midnight and the host and hostess had long since made their excuses and retired to their rooms, pleading urgent business the following morning, although everyone else knew that July 15 marked the start of the flat racing season in nearby Deauville.

One by one the office staff drifted away. The food had been beyond reproach and the wine had flowed freely; a little too freely as far as some were concerned, for Monsieur Leclercq was not one to stint his guests. Even Madame Grante from Accounts, not usually given to lowering her guard without good reason, had joined in the singing of the "Marsellaise" as the last coach headed up the driveway to begin the long drive back to Paris.

It was left to the inspectors, accustomed as they were to serious eating and drinking, to wind up the evening with a glass or two of the Director's Roullet Très Rare Hors d'Age cognac. It was one of the few times in the year when they were able to meet and exchange notes and they always made the most of it.

The tail lights of the coach had hardly disappeared from view when someone told a story about a Frenchman, an Englishman, a German, and an American who were shipwrecked on a desert island. The Frenchman was the only one who lived to tell the tale, but he did say the sauce had been particularly good.

After the laughter had died down, that led to a discussion on the essential differences between nations.

Bernard made the point that had France been populated by the English, restaurants would have been staffed by foreign waiters, for the English do not like serving others. They consider it beneath their dignity and resort to making funny voices or trying to appear infinitely superior to their guests, sometimes to the extent of ignoring them altogether.

Allard was of the opinion that had France been run by Americans, Paris *restaurateurs* would no longer get away with removing the ashtray from one small table near the toilet and designating it the "No Smoking" area.

Glandier had a theory that with the Germans in charge it would have been dumplings with everything.

However, it was generally agreed that these same differences made life more interesting. As Duval rightly said, it is the people who mold a nation, which gave France a head start, *naturellement*.

As the night wore on conversation turned to the problems of running a restaurant, particularly the few—some eighteen in number—which enjoyed the supreme accolade of three Stock Pots in *Le Guide*. The annual wages bill for staff alone in such establishments could run into millions of francs; the price of ingredients went up all the time and during the season truffles alone could cost a small fortune.

That triggered off a discussion about the current trend of certain well-known chefs to embrace the cuisine of the Far East: Vonglerechon in New York was one of the first. Paul Bocuse was forever flitting to and fro between Collonges-au-Mont d'Or and Tokyo. The name Picot came up because in recent years he had acquired a reputation for flirting with that most dangerous of Eastern fish, the fugu; one bite of which, wrongly prepared, was capable of causing death from tetrodotoxin poisoning within moments, for there was no known antidote.

That, of course, led on to the subject of crime, which was when Monsieur Pamplemousse dropped his bombshell, and in so doing managed to encapsulate each and every one of the subjects they had been discussing.

"You may remember," he began, "that unfortunate business last year when there was talk of awarding Picot a golden lid to his Stock Pot."

A murmur of assent went round the room. The top awards in *Le Guide* had remained unchanged for many years. Recently there had been talk of introducing an extra accolade for the very best in the top echelon—a kind of holy grail to which others might aspire, but for one reason or another it never materialized. Picot had been nominated, but at the very last moment not only did it not make the grade, but it failed to gather even so much as a Bar Stool—symbol for a venue where it was possible to obtain a good snack. At the time it had caused something of a sensation in culinary circles. To lose one Stock Pot was bad enough; to lose all three in one go was unheard of.

It had also caused a major upheaval in the offices of *Le Guide* itself. If the name Picot was to be expunged from its pages not only did they have to move quickly, they also had to be absolutely sure of their facts.

"So what really happened?" asked Glandier. "Give us the dirt." Glancing up at the ceiling to make sure there were no discreetly placed cameras or microphones—the Director was very security-minded and in these high-tech days one couldn't be sure of anything—Monsieur Pamplemousse began his story. "It started with the chief," he said.

"Early one morning, on the very eve of publication, I received an urgent message requesting me to join him for *petit déjeuner*, not at Headquarters, but at a small café some distance away from the office. I was to bring Pommes Frites with me.

"The chief was already there when we arrived and he looked as though he hadn't slept a wink all night. There were dark shadows under his eyes and he had a plaster on his chin where he had cut himself shaving. His coffee was cold and his croissant lay untouched.

"I tell you, he was in such a state he hardly knew where to begin and for a moment or two we just sat there. I remember some pictures of monks on the wall. They were chopping firewood and I spent the time counting their halos and wondering what they did with them at night."

Having set the scene, Monsieur Pamplemousse closed his eyes in order to transport both himself and his audience back in time . . .

Monsieur Leclercq spoke first. "Tell me, Aristide, how would you describe Picot?" (Monsieur Pamplemousse captured the Director's booming voice to perfection. It was so realistic Pommes Frites twitched nervously in his sleep.)

"I see the equivalent of a piece of exquisitely delicate machinery, monsieur. A musical box perhaps, or a rare example of the watchmaker's art—each separate piece perfect in itself, yet when the many parts are joined in unison they become something else again. I see subdued lighting and waiters seemingly endowed with extrasensory perception as they materialize out of the shadows, anticipating each and every customer's slightest whim.

"I see Ministers dining together, immersed in affairs of state; others perhaps discussing affairs of the heart. Here and there a captain of industry, possibly celebrating the successful conclusion of some mammoth deal or other. I see a scattering of gnomes from Zurich. Film producers accompanied by their starlets . . ."

"Pamplemousse . . ." the Director raised his hand. "That, I agree, is how one would normally picture Picot. Unfortunately, it is far removed from what actually took place yesterday evening when I took my wife there to celebrate her birthday.

"As we entered, Chantal automatically turned her back on a minion so that she might be relieved of her coat; a coat which I might add cost a small fortune when she had it designed—over one hundred wild Russian mink went into its making. Then, as she walked away, all eyes turned in her direction." The Director shuddered at the memory. "You will never guess what had happened!"

Seeing that something was clearly expected of him, Monsieur Pamplemousse made a hasty stab at a possible answer.

"Madame Leclercq had forgotten to put on a dress?"

The Director clucked impatiently. "Something even more unthinkable. Without so much as a second glance, the waiter let go of her coat. It fell to the floor where it lay unregarded while he emptied an ashtray."

Monsieur Pamplemousse gave a start. "He retrieved it for her, of course?"

"No, Pamplemousse, he did not," snorted the Director. "By the time she realized what had happened the man was nowhere to be seen."

"Perhaps he was a member of Animal Rights, monsieur. A lover of mink in their natural habitat."

"I think not, Pamplemousse," said the Director grimly. "There was worse to come."

"Worse, monsieur?"

"Can you guess what the maître d's words were as he approached our table?"

Conscious that his success rating could do with a boost, Monsieur Pamplemousse decided to play it safe. *"Bon appetit?"*

"Far from it," said the Director. "They were, and I quote them verbatim for they are indelibly imprinted on my mind: 'Ah, monsieur, the third time this week!' "

"There are those who would say you are very fortunate, monsieur. To dine *chez* Picot once is beyond most people's wildest dreams, but three times in one week . . ."

"There are others, Pamplemousse," said the Director grimly, "who would say that, given the circumstances, I was extremely unfortunate. I had spent the earlier part of the evening telling Chantal how much I was looking forward to the occasion since it was many moons since my last visit. To say that conversation became minimal from that point on is to put it mildly.

"It being near the end of the truffle season I tried to make amends by ordering the *Menu aux truffes*. It was a disaster. The scallops were overdone. The *poulet* when it eventually arrived tasted like tinned chicken of the very worst kind—which it may well have been. And throughout it all the accompanying truffles tasted of nothing, absolutely nothing.

"As for the wine service . . . at one point the *sommelier* offered a bottle of Latour '85 for tasting, but before I had a chance to comment the wretched man grew impatient and began pouring it. His hand was shaking so much he allowed some of the wine to go down the outside of the glass. That would have been

bad enough, but he caught the drip with his finger
and redirected it into the glass. Then he covered the
stain on the cloth with a butter dish.

"The final indignity came at the end of the meal
with the arrival of a cake which I had ordered spe-
cially for the occasion. The candles turned out to be
those dreadful ones which are impossible to blow
out. Chantal was not only rendered breathless, she
was mortified, for it gave those at neighboring tables
ample opportunity to count them. She blamed me, of
course, for getting the number wrong.

"I tell you, Aristide, it was not a happy evening. It
was no wonder Picot spent his time skulking in the
kitchen rather than brave the dining room.

"To compound the injury, as we were leaving the
maître d' inquired after the health of my wife, adding
that he hadn't seen her lately.

"I am paying dearly for his crass behavior. Chantal
informs me she is visiting Dior with a shopping list
this morning." Monsieur Pamplemousse stared
across the table. He couldn't help feeling that all
things considered the Director was getting off com-
paratively lightly.

"My previous visits were merely to seek a variety
of opinions, Pamplemousse," said Monsieur Leclercq, reading his thoughts. "The fairer sex are often
able to spot little imperfections that we mere males
tend to miss. That being so, I suggest when you go
there tonight you do not go alone."

"Tonight, monsieur?"

"Tonight," repeated the Director firmly. "I want
you to note down all that transpires and report back
to me as quickly as possible. Something untoward is
going on and we must take immediate action. I cannot hold the presses for long."

Monsieur Pamplemousse considered the matter.
The Director was right to be worried. The disastrous

meal apart, discretion had always been one of the restaurant's hallmarks. In his time Monsieur Picot must have been privy to more state secrets than the whole of the French cabinet put together. It was one of the main reasons that he'd been awarded the *Legion d'Honneur*.

"But, monsieur, will I get a table without saying where I am from? The waiting list is normally many months for those who are not regulars."

"Rest assured, Pamplemousse, there will have been cancellations. Word travels swiftly in the higher gastronomic circles of Paris. Bad news spreads like wildfire.

"However, you are absolutely right. You must remain incognito. An *homme* dining alone will be an object of suspicion. I suggest you take Madame Pamplemousse. And Pommes Frites. I would value his opinion on the *foie gras*. It seemed to me more than a trifle overcooked."

Monsieur Pamplemousse looked dubious. "Doucette will not be happy, monsieur. She hates going to places where the guest menu is unpriced. Besides, it is very short notice. She will undoubtedly say she has nothing to wear."

"Buy her a new dress then," said the Director. "If necessary," he added recklessly, "buy her two."

"Suspicions will be aroused, monsieur. It will be outside the norm."

"In that case," said the Director, "you must arrange for someone else to partner you. There must be people who deal in such matters."

"They call them escort agencies," said Monsieur Pamplemousse dryly.

"Don't be difficult, Pamplemousse," said the Director testily. "You know very well what I mean."

He fell silent for a moment or two, then the merest

hint of a smile spread over his face. "Leave it to me, Aristide," he said, "I think I know the very person."

Monsieur Pamplemousse chose that point to break off, allowing the others time to recharge their glasses before continuing.

"Our arrival at the restaurant that evening went smoothly enough," he said, when order had been restored. "We received a gracious welcome from Madame Picot; although I thought I detected signs that she had recently been crying. Despite skilfully applied makeup there was a slight puffiness below the eyes, and the right one looked distinctly bloodshot, possibly as a result of mascara running into it.

"The Director was correct in his forecast. There were a number of empty tables, so I was able to decline the first we were offered in favor of one nearer the kitchen. As I'm sure you all know, Picot is one of those restaurants where the *brigade* can be seen at work behind a picture window and I wanted to be as near to the action as possible.

"A place was laid for Pommes Frites beneath the table and while a waiter went to fetch him a bowl of water he made himself comfortable on a cushion, doubtless with the intention of keeping an eye on things from his own vantage point.

"I sometimes wonder," he mused, "what I would do without him."

Their eyes closed, Monsieur Pamplemousse's audience maintained a respectful silence while they contemplated the unthinkable, at the same time allowing themselves to be transported back once again to the realms of *chez* Picot . . .

Left to his own devices, Pommes Frites focused his attention on some domes being lifted at the next table. Pommes Frites liked domes. If pressed he wouldn't have minded having one on his bowl at home; used with discretion, of course. The element of surprise sharpened the taste buds. He licked his lips as he saw meat rather than fish being revealed. In his humble opinion fish was strictly for cats.

He sniffed as a cheese trolley the size of a small market stall went slowly past and stopped a few tables away. Using the blade of a knife, the elderly wine waiter pointed with pride as he went through the names, summing up the clients with a practiced air as he made the choice for them.

Meanwhile, Monsieur Pamplemousse began his routine testing of the system by helping himself to an olive. He deposited the stone in the center of a large Bernardaud plate discreetly initialed with the letter "P" in gold leaf. It was promptly whisked away, only to be replaced seconds later by an identical one. It was the kind of attention to detail that might be construed by some as the ultimate in perfectionism and by the less charitable as an attempt to unnerve the diner.

Two could play at that game. Monsieur Pamplemousse helped himself to a second olive and resorted to the *eau mineral* ploy by requesting a bottle of Chateauneuf.

"I will ask the *sommelier* to bring you the *carte du vin*, monsieur," said the waiter.

"That will not be necessary," said Monsieur Pamplemousse patiently. "Chateauneuf is also the name of a mineral water . . . from the *Massif Central*."

Deuce, but with bonus points to Picot if they turned up trumps.

Glancing through the window to his left he saw the *patron* moving about among the staff. Not for the first time he was struck by the parallel that could be drawn with the world of ballet; a choreography that was performed night after night, day in day out, each and every player carrying out the moves with ease and precision.

And yet . . . he eyed the scene reflectively . . . was it simply his imagination, or was there something odd about the ballet master himself? Monsieur Picot had a reputation for being a "hands on" chef, yet not once did he so much as dip his finger into a sauce or pick up a spoon to taste one of his creations. If anything he seemed to be acting like a fish out of water. Plates offered for inspection on their way to the dining room received only a cursory glance; not a single one was commented on or sent back. Nor was their any sign of him coming out front to circulate among the guests; rather the reverse; it almost looked as though he was in hiding from someone.

His behavior was echoed on at least one occasion by others; and even as Monsieur Pamplemousse watched he detected a definite *frisson* of alarm as heads turned to watch something happening outside his own line of vision.

Although, given his own weakness for truffles, Monsieur Pamplemousse had more or less decided to follow the Director's lead and indulge himself, he ordered an *aperitif* and turned his attention to the *carte* while waiting for his unknown guest to arrive. He glanced at his watch. Clearly, whoever she was, punctuality was not her strong suit.

A ripple of laughter came from a party of Japanese ladies occupying a large table on the far side of the room. They looked as though they had been on a shopping spree, probably paid for by their company as a reward for good work during the year. Hermes scarves abounded.

And everywhere there were fresh flowers. Madame Picot was noted for her good taste and no expense was spared in expressing it.

A waiter went past bearing a silver platter. He

crossed to a bureau near the reception area and placed a platinum Amex card discreetly inside a drawer along with the validating machine, pushing it shut lest the sound of the tiny printer disturb the other diners. Monsieur Pamplemousse reached for the notepad he always carried in a hidden compartment of his trousers. Another bonus point.

So far, so good.

Seeing a waiter approaching with his *aperitif*, he was about to remove the menu to make room for the glass when the man stumbled and almost dropped it in his lap.

"Forgive me, monsieur . . . I . . ."

"*Sacré bleu!*" Following the direction of the man's gaze, Monsieur Pamplemousse felt his heart skip a beat as he saw a familiar figure emerging from a room at the back of the kitchen. She had a clipboard in one hand and as she caught sight of him she waved, then blew him a kiss.

"Elsie!" he exclaimed. "I do not believe it!"

"I do not believe it either, monsieur," said the waiter miserably.

Elsie was the very last person Monsieur Pamplemousse had expected to see, and at first he wasn't sure whether to be pleased or sorry. One thing was certain, for all her funny ways he couldn't have wished for a better ally, or one he would have trusted more.

He paused . . .

As ever, the mere mention of Elsie's name caused a stir among his audience. Glandier's cognac went flying in the excitement. Elsie was like a comet or a shooting star; once seen, never forgotten. For a short while she had worked as an *au pair* for Monsieur and Madame Leclercq. Her cooking had been out of this world, but from the word *go* the writing had been on the wall. Nature had been more than generous in its manifold gifts; a fact which hadn't escaped Madame Leclercq's notice, and she'd lost no time in putting her foot down. Elsie had to go.

She surfaced again briefly when the Director offered her a post as the first, and to date the only, female Inspector ever to work for *Le Guide*. Monsieur Pamplemousse had been charged with looking after her, but his moment of glory had been short-lived. Once again, she had returned home to London.

Monsieur Pamplemousse waited patiently until the wolf whistles and obscene grunts had died down before returning to *chez* Picot . . .

"What on earth are you doing here?"

Elsie gave Monsieur Pamplemousse a dig in the ribs. "Couldn't keep away, could I? I'm only 'uman.

"Besides . . ." She brandished the clipboard. "I'm here on official business. Public health."

"You? A Health Inspector?"

Elsie looked hurt. "What's the matter with that? Are you saying I'm un'ealthy or summock?"

"No, of course not. But . . . you are not French . . ."

"We're all in the Common Market, aren't we. It's a matter of flashing the right papers and Ron saw to that. Work of art. Can't tell them from the real thing. 'Ere, 'ave a decko." Fishing inside her handbag she took out a pass.

"Soon as he 'eard from the Director what was going on he said, 'Better get in there quick, love.' "

Monsieur Pamplemousse examined Elsie's papers. She was right. They were, indeed, a work of art. "And how is your husband?"

"All right," said Elsie. "Sends 'is regards. Only got another three months to do. The trouble is he keeps getting 'is sentence reduced for good behavior. Like I say, that'll teach him."

"He does not want to get out of prison?"

"Why should he? 'E's got it made where he is—all

mod. cons—television, fax machine, e-mail on 'is computer, most of 'is friends around him. No aggro. Apart from that we see each other every weekend to catch up on you know what."

"They allow such things?"

"I wouldn't like to be the warder what tried to stop 'im," said Elsie. "Accidents can 'appen. A lump of concrete falling off the roof can give you a nasty 'eadache."

Monsieur Pamplemousse decided to change the subject. "So, having carried out your inspections, what are your conclusions?"

"Well," said Elsie mysteriously, "if I was you I'd stick to the fish."

"Why do you say that?"

"Because," said Elsie, lowering her voice, "there's a dead body in the cold meat room . . ."

Monsieur Pamplemousse stared at her. "A dead body? A stiff?"

"They don't come any stiffer," said Elsie. "Looks like a Chinaman. All wrapped up in butter muslin, 'e is. They tried to pretend it was a side of beef."

"Are you sure it wasn't?"

"Sides of beef don't come wearing white trousers," said Elsie. "Also," she continued, "if you ask me, somebody else dressed him in a hurry; shoes on the wrong feet, trousers back to front. Little things, you know . . ."

"I was thinking of ordering the truffle menu," said Monsieur Pamplemousse inconsequentially, his mind racing with other things. It was possible, of course, that a member of the staff had died on the job. Death in a restaurant during opening hours was always a problem. The arrival of morticians to dispose of the body tended to cast a gloom over the proceedings.

"Talking of truffles," broke in Elsie. "That reminds me." She was about to feel in her lap when she gave a squeak. "Ooh! You don't change, do you?"

"*Comment!*" Conscious of other diners looking their way, Monsieur Pamplemousse held up his hands. "What are you suggesting?"

Momentarily thrown, Elsie looked under the tablecloth. "Beg yours. I should 'ave known. Your nose doesn't get any drier, Pommes Frites, I must say—or any warmer. You want to watch it. Any more of that and I shall tell Ron."

She held up a round black object about the size of a golf ball. "I brought this for you."

Pommes Frites emerged from under the table, gave the object a passing sniff, then dismissed it in favor of resting his head on Elsie's knee again.

"Now there's a funny thing," said Elsie thoughtfully. "Saying no to a truffle, that's not like you."

"He may have a point," mused Monsieur Pamplemousse. "I wonder . . . perhaps we should dine elsewhere, this evening. One way and another there is a lot to talk about."

"Somehow," said Elsie, "I 'ad a feeling you might say that."

"We went back to Picot later that night," said Monsieur Pamplemousse. "There is nothing like catching people at the end of a long day when they are tired and all they want to do is get to bed.

"At first they tried to bluff their way out, denying all knowledge of a body. They even took us into the cold room to prove their point. They must have used the time to put it elsewhere. But Elsie stuck to her guns and it didn't take long before it all came pouring out, helped on its way by a few choice warnings about them all being accessories after the fact.

"The story, as told by Madame Picot, is that the previous afternoon, between lunch and dinner, Monsieur Picot returned to his restaurant and found a gang waiting for him. Having read somewhere of the daily turnover—a figure that doubtless had been trebled or even quadrupled by the media—they had come to stake a claim. They reckoned without the fact that in such establishments very little actual money changes hands. It is all done on account or by credit card.

"Despite all Picot's protests, they refused to believe him—even when he showed them the contents of the safe—so they resorted to a particularly fiendish form of torture. They sat him on one of his stoves and threatened to keep turning up the heat until he talked.

"As Elsie so succinctly put it: 'I've 'eard of people putting things on the back burner, but that's ridiculous!'

"Fortunately, before they could carry out their plan other members of the staff began to arrive back and came to his rescue. A fight broke out, during the course of which one of the gang drew a knife but was himself stabbed by a member of staff wielding a kitchen blade. The man was fatally wounded. Everyone denies seeing who was responsible, of course, and it could have been one of a dozen. It may even have been Picot himself. In any event the rest of the gang fled and *chez* Picot suddenly found itself with blood everywhere and a dead body on its hands.

"Imagine the panic. Three visits in one week from the Director of *Le Guide*, and so close to publication day; it didn't need a mathematician to put two and two together to know why. They were desperate. One breath of scandal and their chance would be gone for another year."

"The chief wouldn't be pleased if he knew he'd been recognized," broke in Glandier. "Imagine the fuss he would have made if it had been one of us."

"Monsieur Leclercq is like a great many people in a position of power," said Monsieur Pamplemousse.

"They go to great lengths to avoid being recognized, then get upset when nobody does. At such moments he has an endearing habit of turning his profile to the audience.

"Anyway, by the time they had cleaned up and got rid of all the blood, the first of the evening guests were starting to arrive. They did what seemed to be the best thing at the time—they put the body in the cold room."

"So it was there while the chief was dining," said Bernard. "It explains why Picot kept out of the way."

"He not only kept out of the way," said Monsieur Pamplemousse. "He wasn't even there. He'd gone to see a doctor to have his burns treated."

"Then who was it?" asked Glandier. "Don't tell us they found a look-alike at five minutes' notice."

"It wasn't necessary," said Monsieur Pamplemousse. "There was one all ready to hand. Picot had a twin brother.

"I tackled Madame Picot on that very point and in the end she showed me a family photograph. Picot's brother is an accountant with no interest whatsoever in food—he cannot even boil an *oeuf* without burning the saucepan. He was brought in until things could be sorted out and they were safe for another year."

"They planned to carry on like that until after publication day?" exclaimed Allard. "I don't believe it. No wonder the staff didn't know whether they were coming or going."

"At that point it was still panic stations," said Monsieur Pamplemousse.

"Besides it wouldn't have been for very long. Once *Le Guide* goes to press there is no turning back. I doubt if anyone had thought it through. Picot, to coin a phrase, was 'going for gold' and nothing was to be allowed to stand in his way."

"What did Monsieur Leclercq have to say about it when you told him?" asked Duval.

Monsieur Pamplemousse assumed his Director's voice. "We are none of us perfect, Pamplemousse, and chefs are only human. The heat and the steam play havoc with their metabolism. I think we should err on the side of leniency and let artistry receive its just reward. Strings can be pulled. That is what they are there for. It just so happens that in a few days time I shall be dining with the appropriate Minister . . ."

"If that was the case," broke in Glandier, "why didn't Picot himself send for the police. Surely, with all his contacts it wouldn't have been too late."

"I asked myself the same question," said Monsieur Pamplemousse, "and there was only one possible answer. He had something to hide.

"The clue was in the way Madame Picot told the story. Not once did she mention the nationality of the gang, and yet Elsie swore the body she saw had been that of a Chinaman.

"Which was where Pommes Frites came in. He didn't win the title of 'Sniffer Dog of the Year' for nothing."

Reaching into his pocket, Monsieur Pamplemousse removed a ball of silver foil, carefully unwrapped it, then held up the contents between thumb and forefinger for the others to see. "I would like to show you Exhibit A—the Black Diamond of French cuisine. Only in this case it happens to be gray in color. Elsie gave it to me as a souvenir. I carry it with me as an occasional reminder of the standards we are all honor-bound to uphold.

"It is not, as one might think, a *tuber melanosporum* from Perigord, smelling and tasting of the very earth of France from which it sprung. It is a Chinese truffle from the province of Szechwan, and on the wholesale market costs a third the price.

"For some time Picot had been passing them off as the real thing. If it hadn't been for Pommes Frites turning up his nose and revealing it for what it is, he might have carried on doing so. My guess is that the gang who attacked him were not after money in the safe, but had a more long-term interest—blackmail. They were threatening to reveal all. That, on the eve of *Le Guide*'s publication, would have been a total disaster."

"But why?" asked Allard. "Why would he do that? A man in his position who stood to lose everything."

Monsieur Pamplemousse shrugged as he slowly rewrapped his exhibit. "Greed, perhaps? We shall never know. All that glistens is not gold. Running a great restaurant these days is not all champagne and caviar; more and more it is a matter of balancing the books. Unfortunately, though, there can be no short-cuts to perfection."

"So that's why the chief dropped Picot," said Glandier.

"For Monsieur Leclercq," said Monsieur Pamplemousse simply, "publisher of the most prestigious food guide in the land, there was no other choice. There is no greater crime in the world of *haute cuisine* than that of 'passing off.' The perpetrator received his just punishment, but it was an ignominious end to a glittering career."

"It could only happen in France," mused Bernard. "Going back to our previous argument, if it had been the Germans they would have closed the restaurant down on the grounds that keeping a dead body in the cold store was contravening their laws on hygiene."

"The English press would have had a field day," said Bernard. "They like nothing better than a good scandal, and if it involves us French so much the better. They are also jealous of other people's success. It strikes them as unfair."

"The Americans would have moved in because Picot hadn't got an import license for the Chinaman," added Glandier. "After that lawyers would have grown fat with everyone suing each other, left, right, and center."

"True," said Monsieur Pamplemousse, "very true. But sadly, it was the reason why I never did get to eat *chez* Picot. And now I never shall. Although come to think of it, I did have an olive or two on the house, so I shouldn't really grumble."

"How about 'you know who'?" Someone broke the silence. "What do you think he thought of it all?"

"Perhaps," said Monsieur Pamplemousse, "you should ask him." All eyes turned automatically in Pommes Frites's direction. For a moment or two he gave no answer, then he gave vent to a long drawn-out sigh as he stretched himself luxuriously on Monsieur Leclercq's favorite Caucasian rug.

To the uninitiated it might have sounded suspiciously like a snore, but those in the party who knew him better recognized it immediately as the canine equivalent of *c'est la vie*—and somehow that said it all.

Witty Britisher Bond, creator of the beloved Paddington Bear and a recent recipient of the OBE from Queen Elizabeth II, continues his mystery series featuring the hapless Guide Michelin *critic Pamplemousse and his discerning* chien Pommes Frites. *This story finds Pommes Frites sniffing out suspects amid some mysterious truffles. Dog and master's adventures in* haute cuisine *and crime include*

M. Pamplemousse and the Secret Mission, M. Pamplemousse Rests His Case, M. Pamplemousse Stands Firm, M. Pamplemousse on Location, *and* M. Pamplemousse Takes the Train.

A Simple Philosophy

Harlan Coben

Killing someone is so easy. Even your own sister.

My name is Christina Matthews. My sister is Edna Wentworth. Or at least, she *was* Edna Wentworth. Right now her corpse is entering an early stage of rigor mortis, hardening in front of me like drying plaster. Her eyes seem to be staring at something just out of sight. I am crying very hard. But do not fret. I am not sad. You see, the police are here. I need to put on a good show.

"No marks on her," the tall police officer says.

The coroner shakes his head. "Nope. Not a thing."

"Think it's natural causes?"

"Could be. She seems kinda young though."

The tall cop looks at me. "How old was your sister?"

I hitch my chest. I pretend that speaking takes great effort. "Tw . . . twenty-six."

"Was she ill or anything?"

"Edna has always had physical problems," I tell

them. It's true, of course. It has nothing to do with her death, but she was a sickly woman. "Her heart, you know."

The cop turns to the coroner. The coroner nods knowingly.

Our momentary silence is shattered by a voice behind us. "What the . . . ? Let me pass! Please!"

The voice belongs to Henry. My Henry now. He runs into the room and looks down at the floor in shock. His face collapses in horror. I am amazed by his acting ability. He is not shocked. He knows very well what is going on. He must.

"My God . . ." he utters. Quite convincingly, I might add. Henry falls to the ground as though someone has ripped the bones out of his legs. He looks up, wounded and confused. "What's going on here? Is she . . . ?"

"Are you Henry Wentworth?"

"Yes."

"I'm sorry to tell you this, sir. Your wife is dead."

He gasps. "What? But that's not possible!"

Henry looks at me for a moment. To the others in the room, it appears as though he's a shocked man seeking confirmation. But I know better. You see, Henry loves me. He married my sister for her massive trust fund. Daddy always did love Edna best, gave her all the money. But now it's mine. Henry's look is telling me that all is well, that he loves me dearly, that now, at long last, we can be together.

I play my part. "It's true," I say.

He lets out a guttural scream, a horrible sound, and again I am impressed with his acting. I did not tell him what I was going to do, of course. I kept it to myself. Henry and I share a spiritual love, you see. It is a chaste love, love expressed with the eyes. Henry is a beautiful man with Superman blue-black hair and green emerald eyes to die for—and in this case, I mean that literally. We have never so much as kissed. But I know. His eyes say it every time they gaze into mine.

I love you, his eyes whisper. Your sister is in our way. We can be so happy if only . . .

So I killed her.

Oh, wait. You are probably wondering how I did it. Simple, you see. Poison. The technical name is Arbetamocine. It is fairly undetectable because the symptoms so closely resemble a heart attack. Arbetamocine takes a few hours to take effect and then whammo, Heart Attack City.

Just so you know, I did not put it in Edna's drink. That would have been way too obvious. But Edna always had chapped lips, poor dear. She kept a cherry lip balm with her at all times. It was so easy. I work for a pharmaceutical company. I stole the poison and, well, like the old commercial said, a little dab'll do ya. The cherry flavoring disguised the subtle smell. And best of all, though Arbetamocine works through the skin—or in this case, the lips— the fact that Edna would undoubtedly touch it with her tongue—swallow some, if you will—just made it hit the bloodstream that much faster.

The tall police officer escorts us out of the room. I take Henry's hand. The morons. I can see by their faces that they think that I am merely comforting my brother-in-law. How noble it all must appear. We are a grieving twosome, gathering strength from each other—or so the fools believe. But I can feel Henry's heat. Passion is there, just under the skin, waiting to explode. I can hardly wait for this part to be over, for us to be alone and rich and oh-so-happy.

I have handled this all beautifully. Henry will be so impressed when I tell him. No one will ever suspect. I loathe clichés, but there is no denying that I have indeed committed the perfect crime.

Well, almost perfect. I confess that I made one teensy mistake:

I called the police too fast.

You see, as soon as I saw my sister lying on the floor, I faked a scream. That was part of my plan. Come home, find her dead, scream so the neighbors would hear me, then call 911. So I did all that. But I forgot something.

The cherry lip balm.

That was the only clue that Edna's death was anything other than natural causes. My plan was to get rid of it, you see. But I got a bit carried away. I screamed first. After that, I had to call 911 right away. Still I had time before anyone showed up. All I had to do was fetch the lip balm from Edna's purse. That's where she always kept it.

But when I checked the purse, I found no cherry lip balm. Then I checked Edna's night table and her bathroom. Nothing. I searched frantically for the ten minutes it took the police and paramedics to arrive. But I could not locate the cherry lip balm. Panic seized me. A mistake. A mistake could cost me everything.

But I quickly calmed down. If I could not locate the lip balm, neither would the police. Soon Edna would be wheeled out of here. The police might casually glance about, but they would never find nor confiscate something as innocuous as a container of cherry lip balm.

There was, I realized, nothing to worry about.

Henry and I are sitting on the couch now. We are both crying. The tall officer is very understanding. Henry, I must say, is a much better actor than I. Tears stream down his face. His nose becomes stuffed. His face is ashen. Perhaps I should have warned him ahead of time. Perhaps Henry is the squeamish type, and seeing a dead body—even one belonging to a woman he loathed—is causing this strong reaction.

The tall officer prattles on, but my mind is already whirring with thoughts of the future. Of course, Henry and I couldn't just rush into marriage. There would have to be a suitable mourning period—at least, in public. In private, well, that was another matter. Henry and I love each other. We have been denied for too long already. Trust me on this, friends: you can only hold back such burning passion for so long. Then, ka-boom.

Time passes. We answer questions. Then Edna is zipped up and carted away like the trash she is. Henry feigns as though he can't look when she passes him. I suppress both a smile and the desire to wave bye-bye. The tall policeman offers us one more condolence before leaving.

Henry and I are alone now. We sit on the couch in silence. I wait for him to say something, to profess his love, to thank me. But his eyes stare straight ahead, not unlike poor Edna's.

"I need to make some calls," he says.

"Do you want some help?"

"No, Christina, thank you."

I smile at him. He does not smile back. I wait for him to take me in his arms. But he doesn't.

"Henry?" I say.

"Yes, Edna."

"We're alone now."

He looks confused. "I realize that."

"We don't have to pretend anymore."

"Pretend what?"

I open my mouth to explain, but his confusion looks so genuine, I stop myself. The shock, I thought again. The shock of seeing her body. Maybe I should have done more than hint. Maybe I should have told him after all.

"I'll be upstairs," he says.

Henry begins to cry again. He ascends the staircase, and then I hear him making phone calls. "Edna is dead," he tells people. Then he cries some more. "What am I going to do without her?"

I smile and nod to myself. Henry is laying more groundwork—in case someone gets suspicious. I understand that. He loves me. And oh, I love him. With all my heart. I think I always have. Four years ago, Edna, the witch—the *engaged* witch at the time—stole him from me without a thought for her own fiancé, her college sweetheart who never even lasted long enough for us to meet. But my sister was like that. She saw something bright and shiny and new— something *I* had—and so she simply discarded the poor boy.

You see, I met Henry first. A friend set us up on a blind date. But Edna, the engaged tramp, the "pretty one," fluttered by and sunk her teeth into him. Or so I thought. Only later did I understand Henry's genius. Edna had the money. He was marrying her for it. Then, once enough time had passed, we could do away with Edna and be together forever.

And now, well, here we are.

I hear Henry put down the phone. Footsteps. More sniffles. My goodness, he is taking this far, isn't he? I decide to check up on him. I creep up the stairs. More sniffling. He is in the bedroom. The bedroom he used to share with my sister. While I slept on the third floor. Alone. Hearing the two of them coo and laugh and, well, you know.

The bedroom door is closed. I hear more sniffling. I knock softly. There is no answer. I put my hand on the knob and turn it. The door swings open and then I see a sight that makes my heart slam into my throat.

"NO!" I scream.

In Henry's right hand—clutched between forefinger and thumb, being raised slowly toward his mouth—is the cherry lip balm.

He freezes as though I've fired a pistol. "What is it? What's wrong?"

"Put that down," I tell him.

He looks confused again. "What are you talking about? It's only lip balm."

"Please, Henry, put it down."

He studies me for a moment. "You're distraught about Edna," he says. "I understand that. But it's only her lip balm, Christina. Calm down."

He starts to raise it back to his mouth.

"No!"

I dive across the room, but I see that I am going to be too late. The balm touches his lips as I collide into him. I hear a whooshing sound; I've knocked the wind out of him. But I've also made a terrible mistake. The balm falls into his mouth. Not for long. For just a few seconds. But it is long enough.

"Nooooo." But this time, my voice is little more than a whisper.

Henry sits up. "What's the matter with you, Christina?"

I grab his arm. "Quickly, come with me. We have to wash your mouth out."

"What? What are you talking about?"

"The lip balm! It's poisoned. That's how I did it!"

Henry stops, his face a mask of confusion and horror. "Did what?"

"There's no time, Henry. Please."

"DID WHAT?"

I look at him. Time is of the essence, doesn't he see that? "Killed Edna, of course. Just as we always planned."

His face falls. "Like we planned? Are you out of your mind?"

"You love me, Henry. I know that. So I did it for

us. I didn't tell you before now because I didn't want you to worry. But now she's gone. We can be together. But only if you live, my love. Only if you . . ."

A sound stops me. The door behind us opens. The tall police officer steps into the bedroom. Henry steps back, his eyes wide with repulsion and loss.

The tall police officer smiles. "And we have it all on tape." I look above the armoire. A video camera is pointing at me.

Henry shakes his head. "I still don't understand." He looks at me. "Why, Christina?"

Now I am the one who is surprised. "Because we love each other, Henry," I say. "We have always loved each other."

His stricken face softens a bit now, turns from abject horror into something approaching pity. The tall police officer grabs me. He pull my hands behind my back hard. A pain rips down my shoulders. Handcuffs are snapped on me.

"Please don't hurt her," Henry tells him. "She"— he stops, swallows hard—"she's not well."

See? He does love me.

A few hours later, Henry sat with the tall police officer. "She's confessed?"

The officer nodded. "I just took her statement."

"But what made you suspicious of Christina in the first place?"

"An anonymous tip," the tall officer explained. "A chemist at the pharmaceutical company she works for saw her steal from the lab. But by the time we got here—about five hours ago—your wife was already dead. The lip balm was still clutched in her hand. That's what made me wonder. So our lab ran a quick check and found Arbetamocine on it."

Henry looked surprised. "The poison was on the lip balm?"

"Not on the one I gave you, of course. The poison one is back at the station. Alone it wouldn't have been enough to convict her. That's why I called you with my plan. Of course, running a sting operation like this is not exactly standard police procedure—that's why I asked you to keep it to yourself—but, well, with what happened today, it all worked out. Christina Matthews had no choice. She had to confess."

"She's a sick woman."

The tall officer rolled his eyes. "Wasn't hugged enough as a child, is that it?"

"No. But she needs professional help."

He shrugged. "Not my place to decide. My opinion? Murderers should pay, no matter what. An eye for an eye and all that." He stood and spread his hands. "A simple philosophy, no? I'll show myself out. I'm sorry about all this, Mr. Wentworth, but thank you for your help."

Henry said nothing.

When the tall officer left, Henry leaned back and opened the humidor. He picked out a cigar—a Cuban, mind you—and then a smile slowly came to his lips. Well, it'd taken longer than expected, but in the end, his plan had worked to perfection.

Edna's old man had set up a hell of a trust before he died. In the event of Edna's death or divorce, all of the money would revert to Christina, not Edna's husband. But now, of course, Christina had murdered her own sister. How did the saying go? You can't profit from the fruits of a crime. No—the fruits of a *poisoned* tree. Something like that. He chuckled to himself. No matter.

The money was his now, clear and easy.

God, he'd been brilliant. All it had taken was some well-placed whispers, some hints of love, quick asides on how wonderful it would be if Edna were dead. It had taken a tad longer than expected, but eventually Christina got with the program. He'd kept his eyes on her the whole time. And he'd learned of her plan.

Henry was the one who'd found Edna dead early that morning. The cherry lip balm had been in her purse. Not obvious enough, he decided. So he placed it in her dead hand. Even a complete dolt like that tall cop would not be able to miss that clue. Then he called in the anonymous tip from a phone booth on his way to work and posed as a chemist. So perfect. Everything wrapped up neat and careful. Oh, Edna's lawyer might have tried to argue that Henry was behind it all—that he had been in cahoots with Christina and had in fact urged her to act—but after today, he'd have no chance of floating that particular trial balloon. She had confessed. And the videotape proved that he had nothing to do with Christina's demented little scheme.

Henry inhaled deeply on the cigar. The taste was heavenly until he felt a tightness in his chest. The cigar fell to the floor. Pain now. Like a fist squeezing his heart.

The front door opened and the tall officer stepped inside.

"Putting the lip balm in her hand," he said. "That was overkill, Henry. Calling in that anonymous tip so close to the time of death—not to mention making the call from one of only three pay phones on the route between this house and your office. That was another boo-boo. But they were circumstantial things. Nothing that would stand up in court. So what would I have? The testimony of the actual killer who, to put it kindly, is a few french fries short of a Happy Meal? No jury would buy it."

Henry fell to the floor. Death tightened its grip on his insides, making it impossible to breathe.

"I gave you the poisoned lip balm, of course. But no one will ever be able to prove that. You have to remember that nobody but you and I knew about our little sting—and nobody else ever will. With Christina's confession, I can get rid of the videotape now. The poisoned lip balm is back safe and sound in the evidence room. And when someone finds you dead in a day or two, I'll be put in charge of the investigation. My conclusion? The pressure of losing your beloved wife was too much for your heart—or, if the poison gets detected in your system, maybe I'll conclude that Christina Matthews poisoned you too. After all, she only knows I burst in on you two and overheard her confession. She doesn't know that we set this whole thing up. She'll probably just blame herself." He grinned. "Ironic, no?"

The tall officer bent down and looked into Henry's eyes.

"It's like I said before, Henry. Murderers should pay, no matter what. And so should men who steal fiancées from other men."

The tall police officer smiled as Henry's eyes rolled back in death.

"An eye for an eye and all that," he whispered at the corpse, spreading his hands again. "A simple philosophy, no?"

Native New Jerseyan Harlan Coben reveals murder is more than simple in this crime of dubious passions. Coben's series featuring smart-aleck sports agent Myron Bolitar has won Edgar and Anthony awards and includes Deal Breaker, Dropshot, Fade Away, *and* Backspin.

Unhappy Medium

Carola Dunn

"A séance?" **Daisy** exclaimed. "I didn't think you believed in all that tommyrot."

"I don't," Lucy said languidly, locking the door of her mews studio behind her. "Absolute eyewash, and too, too tedious, darling! But this one should be rather a lark. Actually, Binkie asked me to trot along to keep an eye on his aunt, Lady Ormerod."

"It doesn't sound like much of a lark." Daisy led the way across the tiny courtyard garden to the back door of the *bijou* residence she shared with her photographer friend. "Lady Ormerod's the most fearfully depressing female."

"That's just the point. She'd been that way ever since Binkie's cousin Jerome was killed in the trenches."

"Her only son, wasn't he?"

"Yes, and in her eyes daughters definitely play second fiddle," Lucy said tartly.

"She pulled herself together enough to do a couple

of seasons in town and marry them off," Daisy
pointed out.

"Only *just* enough. Now she hasn't even got that
to take her mind off Jerome. Of course one is sorry
and all that, but after all other people have it worse.
You lost your fiancé and your only brother in the
War and your father soon after, and you haven't
gone around for the last five years looking like the
middle of a wet week."

"Keep a stiff upper lip," Daisy said ironically, trying not to remember the first few days, months, even
years.

"Well, Lady O not only doesn't want to hear about
stiff upper lips, she spends simply pots of money trying to communicate with Jerome through those
frightful mediums."

"Lord Ormerod must be a bit peeved."

"More than a bit. He called in one of those Psychical Research johnnies to investigate the last psychic Lady Ormerod patronized. She was arrested for
fraud, but it doesn't seem to have put Lady O off in
the slightest. I think there are a couple of digestives
in the tin." They were in the kitchen by now, and
Lucy was at the sink, filling the kettle for tea. Their
daily, Mrs. Potter, went home at four.

Daisy set down the Royal Worcester cups and sau-
cers on the well-scrubbed kitchen table and reached
for the biscuit tin. "Aren't there any choccy biccies
left?"

"No, and it was you who ate them. *Some* of us
watch our figures, darling."

With an envious glance at Lucy's boyish shape,
sleekly elegant in her low-waisted, mid-calf-length
voile frock, Daisy sighed. It was no use feeling guilty.
However hard she dieted, she would never be
straight up and down. All she could do was wait for
hips and bosoms to come back into fashion.

"These have gone soft." She took a digestive biscuit anyway, nibbling as she sat down. "So Lady O has found a new medium to put her in touch with Jerome?"

"Madame Vasilieva. The second consultation is tomorrow evening, and Binkie says his uncle has arranged for the scientific chappie to attend. He hopes seeing the woman exposed as a charlatan right before her eyes will disillusion Lady O. Binkie's afraid she may be a bit upset, though."

"I should jolly well think so," Daisy said, her opinion of the strong, silent Lord Gerald Bincombe's sensitivity soaring, "if she's convinced she's been talking to her dead son."

"She is. She's obsessed with it. Binkie has a feeling she may be heading for a nervous breakdown. He's rather fond of her, and he thinks she ought to have a woman's support when the new psychic is unmasked, but Lord Ormerod has forbidden the family to go, so he asked me to. Be a sport, darling, and come with me."

"Oh, right-o." It sounded less and less like a lark, but Lady Ormerod might need more sympathy than she was likely to get from Lucy. "Where is it?"

"Maida Vale." Lucy grimaced. "Too frightfully dreary, but Binkie will stand us a taxi. I'm going to take the new camera I bought at the Kodak place in Regent Street. It's small enough to hide in my handbag, and I'd hate to miss a chance to photograph an apparition. Maybe you'll get an article out of the unmasking."

"Now that's a spiffing notion!" Daisy said with enthusiasm. "The whole beastly business is in the news at the moment, with Houdini's exposés of just how the mediums create their effects. I shan't mind adding my mite to bring down the rotters who exploit other people's sorrows."

* * *

The setting sun painted the smoky sky an angry crimson as the motor-taxi dropped Daisy and Lucy in a drab suburban street lined with semidetached villas.

"The Laurels," Daisy read on the gate, as Lucy paid the taxi driver. "Trite, but at least appropriate."

She regarded the high evergreen hedge with a jaundiced eye. Already the shiny new leaves of early summer had gathered a dingy film of city soot. It looked a fitting place for all sorts of horrid mysteries.

Not that anything a medium could produce, from ectoplasm to levitation, was a mystery to Daisy any longer. A visit to the Chelsea Free Library had produced Harry Houdini's recent book, *Miracle-Mongers and Their Methods*. In the *Times* and *Manchester Guardian* files, she found newspaper reports of discredited and confessed frauds. The only thing still capable of astonishing her was how otherwise intelligent people allowed themselves to be taken in.

Sir Arthur Conan Doyle, creator of the supremely rational Sherlock Holmes, was not merely a firm believer but a proselytiser. He remained convinced his friend, Houdini, performed his feats by psychic means, even after the magician explained his methods!

What struck Daisy most was the meaningless triviality of most phenomena. Why should the dead bother to return from beyond the veil simply to make knocking noises, move a table, or play a few notes on an accordion? The voices and automatic writing tended to produce pure drivel, or garbled, rambling messages at best, as open to interpretation as the Oracle at Delphi.

If the spirits really wanted to communicate, surely they'd do better than that?

Adding to Daisy's disillusionment was the fact that

almost every aspect of the subject had been written about extensively. The only opening she found for a fresh point of view was to portray the grief of those forced to acknowledge that the manifestations of their dead loved ones were nothing but trickery.

And that, she felt, would exploit their grief as surely as did the crooked mediums. In particular, she could not do it to Lady Ormerod, whom she had come to comfort.

"Here's Lady Ormerod," Lucy said as a gleaming silver-grey Isotta Fraschini, chauffeur-driven, drew up at the curb.

"Does she know we're coming?"

"Yes, Binkie asked her to take us in with her, in case they wouldn't let us attend a private sitting otherwise. Not without paying through the nose, anyway. Remember we're just interested observers."

"Right-o." Daisy wanted to ask if Lucy knew how the Psychical Research man intended to sneak in, but Lady Ormerod stepped down from the motor and greeted them.

In their alter egos as, respectively, daughter of a viscount and granddaughter of an earl, Daisy and Lucy were distantly acquainted with Lady Ormerod. A tall, gaunt woman, clad in unrelieved black draperies with a black veil over her face, she drooped. That was the only word for it, Daisy decided. She drooped along the short garden path and stood drooping as they waited for the doorbell to be answered, whereupon she drooped into the house.

"I have brought friends," Lady Ormerod told the tall, fleshy man in evening dress who admitted them. "I hope their presence will not discommode Madame Vasilieva?"

He bowed. "My wife is always happy to accommodate believers, milady," he said suavely, in a deep, sonorous, accented voice. The accent sounded

Russian to Daisy—unless she was just influenced by the medium's name, for somehow it did not quite ring true.

"Miss Fotheringay and Miss Dalrymple."

He bowed again as Daisy followed Lucy into a commonplace entrance hall such as might be found in any of thousands of small, middle-class suburban houses.

At least, it would have been had not the wall opposite the hall table been hung with far from commonplace photographs. Each showed a woman with masses of black hair, her eyes closed, and hovering above her one or two misty faces. Daisy recognized the late czar of Russia and the Czarina Alexandra in one. Another had Disraeli, Earl of Beaconsfield, and a third Queen Elizabeth, dead centuries before the invention of photography.

Lucy looked at them and gave a quiet snort. "I could fake those," she muttered to Daisy.

"Hush!"

At the last moment, a small, nondescript man in a bowler hat and a baggy suit slipped in behind them. Removal of the bowler revealed thinning grey hair and steel-rimmed spectacles with thick lenses which effectively hid his eyes. The investigator from the Society for Psychical Research, Daisy guessed, glancing sidelong to avoid drawing attention to him.

She had read about the society. For the most part, the members were not, as she had assumed, sceptics out to show up Spiritualism as sheer hocus-pocus. On the contrary, they were would-be believers. Their merciless denunciations of fraudulent mediums sprang from their eagerness to discover true psychics.

The little man made no attempt to introduce himself, and no one took any notice of him. Presumably Vasiliev assumed he was one of Lady Ormerod's friends, and her ladyship thought he belonged to the medium's entourage.

Vasiliev ushered them toward the back of the house. He moved with a lightness which belied his bulk and reminded Daisy of her mountainous friend, Detective Sergeant Tring. As with the sergeant, the result was a feeling of leashed energy, of power held in check, an uncomfortable feeling when the man responsible was not on the side of the angels.

He showed them into a smallish parlour. The furniture consisted solely of a number of straight chairs set against the walls, which were hung with midnight-blue plush curtains. A thick carpet of the same shade covered the floor, and the ceiling was painted to match. A central electric light fixture was turned off. The only light came from the twilight sky outside french windows leading to a narrow, straggly lawn surrounded by more high laurel hedges.

Despite herself, Daisy shivered. The sinister gloom was impressive—and no doubt intended to impress.

The curtains could conceal any amount of skulduggery, she realized. Against the dark blue, black threads used to suspend objects in midair and telescoping rods for moving them about would be invisible. The carpet would deaden the sound of footsteps, allowing spirits to glide silently about the room in their white gauze draperies dyed with luminous paint.

The will to believe would do the rest. That was really the only frightening thing.

A woman was already present in the room, sitting on one of the chairs. A pudding-faced, mousy, middle-aged creature in dark grey, with wispy hair escaping from beneath a black cloche hat, she gave an uncertain smile as the other entered.

Vasiliev gestured toward her. "Mrs. Baine also has

a loved one on the other side. She will join us, if your ladyship has no objection."

"None, as long as Madame concentrates on trying to contact my son first," said Lady Ormerod with a sort of desperate belligerence.

"Naturally, milady. Will you be seated? My wife is in her cabinet preparing herself for the trance. Excuse me while I go to see if she is ready."

He slipped out between the curtains opposite the french windows. Daisy guessed that they partitioned the room from another at the front of the house. Most convenient for ghoulies and ghosties and things that go bump in the night. She was glad spiritualists didn't go in for long-leggity beasties.

"Isn't it simply too ghastly?" Lucy whispered to her.

"A bit different from an evening of table-turning at a weekend house party."

"I need a breath of fresh air." She went to the french windows, opened one leaf, and stood gazing out. The set of her shoulders indicated to Daisy a sort of uneasy boredom.

The bespectacled man hovered indecisively by the door, wearing a convincingly vacant air, though Daisy was sure he was studying every detail. Lady Ormerod wilted onto a chair, as far away as possible from Mrs. Baines, and turned back her veil.

Daisy politely joined her. "This is jolly interesting," she said.

"Have you never attended a séance before? You lost a brother, didn't you? But I expect Lady Dalrymple has spoken to him since he passed over."

"I don't think Mother has even tried to talk to Gervaise, actually."

"Oh but she must!" said Lady Ormerod with fervour, her pale, hollow-cheeked face unexpectedly animated. "Tell her I can't recommend it too strongly.

It's such a comfort to hear the voice of the dear departed himself, to know he is happy and still remembers and loves his family, though translated to a higher sphere."

"I'm sure it must be."

"Jerome has spoken to me several times. The darling boy has been trying to pass on a warning to me, but a mischievous spirit, a medieval Hungarian called Istvan, constantly interrupts."

"What a nuisance," Daisy murmured. And what a way to keep the anxious believer returning time after time! And how convenient that the meddler was Hungarian, a language as unlikely as the commonly claimed Ancient Egyptian to be recognized, let alone understood, by anyone present.

"I'm sure Jerome was about to get through with a clear message. Akhenaten, Mrs. Blackburn's spirit guide, had almost managed to subdue Istvan when those horrible, interfering research people had her arrested on trumped-up charges," Lady Ormerod said angrily.

"Oh dear."

"Goodness knows how long it will take to get to the same point with Madame Vasilieva. Her reputation is marvellous, but of course she has a different control, so it means starting all over again."

Certain that the medium or her husband was listening behind the curtains, Daisy decided it was time to feign ignorance. "Control?" she asked.

"Another word for the spirit guide. Every medium has a friendly spirit who acts as a go-between on the other side, much as the medium does on this plane. Madame's control, Devaki, is a rather childish Indian girl."

"Devaki can't stop Istvan interrupting?"

"Oh, my dear, Istvan hasn't turned up yet. I have only had one consultation with Madame Vasilieva.

At first Devaki could not grasp who was wanted. She brought several young officers killed in Flanders, each of them expecting and eager to speak to his mother, and terribly upset to be disappointed. It was quite shattering!"

"It sounds simply frightful," Daisy said sincerely.

Lady Ormerod turned an earnest gaze upon her. "So you see why I say Lady Dalrymple really must make an effort to communicate."

"Perhaps Gervaise will speak to me today, and give me a message for Mother," Daisy said, rather less sincerely. "Did Devaki find your son in the end?"

"Yes, but by then she was tired and wanted to go and play. I had no more than a word or two from Jerome, just to reassure me he was anxious to speak to me. It should be easier this time, since she knows him. And with luck, Istvan won't have followed him to the new guide."

Daisy suspected the best way to dispose of Istvan would have been not to discuss him within hearing of the Vasilievs. They were hardly likely to pass up such a chance of keeping Lady Ormerod on the hook.

They would not be pleased to lose so rich a prize when the man from Psychical Research exposed their tricks.

He had gone over to Lucy now. As he spoke to her, his spectacles glinted enigmatically in the sombre light from the darkening sky. He'd be no match for Vasiliev if the brawny Russian was angry enough at his wife's exposure to resort to fisticuffs. Daisy studied the chairs, wondering whether a biff with one of them would be enough to knock the big man out if it seemed advisable.

They were flimsy objects of faux bamboo with cane seats, quite useless for bonking anyone over the head. The investigator would just have to take his chances.

What was he saying to Lucy?

"No." Lucy's usually penetrating soprano was deadened by the draperies. "*I* haven't come to consult the medium. Not this time," she added hastily, no doubt recalling that she and Daisy were supposed to be interested onlookers.

The man spoke again, too low for Daisy to make out his words.

"Really, I can't see that it's any of your business." Lucy had small patience with presumption in the lower orders. She turned a cold shoulder.

"What on earth is Madame doing?" said Lady Ormerod fretfully. "She could have started preparing herself earlier. I want to speak to Jerome."

"I don't suppose the spirits have much idea of time," Daisy soothed her, as Lucy came to join them. "I'm sure she doesn't mean to keep you waiting."

Vasiliev's prompt reappearance confirmed her opinion that he had been eavesdropping. He popped through the dividing curtains and drew them back to reveal a sort of Punch-and-Judy booth without a stage. Instead of gaily striped canvas, it was entirely enclosed with dark blue plush to match the draperies of both rooms.

"The spirit cabinet," explained Lady Ormerod.

In front of this, in the centre of the double room, Vasiliev placed a small round table. As flimsy as the chairs, it would be easy to tilt with a toe or fingertip, Daisy noted.

Lady Ormerod surged eagerly to her feet. "Madame is ready?"

"She has prepared herself to enter the trance, milady." He started to set chairs around the table, and after a moment the other man went to help.

The front curtains of the booth were parted from inside. A slight, pale woman stood there, a faraway expression on her face. She was dressed in black—

Daisy's pale blue and Lucy's amber flowered summer frocks began to seem positively garish. The bird's nest of black hair piled on the psychic's head gave her an Edwardian look. Daisy immediately suspected a wig. She probably had bobbed fair hair underneath, to help make her unrecognizable when she exposed it to appear as a spirit.

"Lady Ormerod," she said in a soft, contralto voice, "be so good as to sit on my right. I must have my husband on my left to lend me his strength."

Like her husband, she had a vaguely Russian accent, with rolling r's and guttural h's, but Daisy caught the flat tones of Birmingham beneath. Neither used the speech patterns of Russian, she realized. Since meeting a couple of Russians recently, she was familiar with the distinctive rhythm, the tendency to skip pronouns and articles.

For the first time, Daisy was rather sorry for the medium. To escape Birmingham, practically any expedient was reasonable. Exposed as a fraud, she would lose her livelihood and maybe even go to prison.

After all, from her point of view she was going to a lot of trouble to provide a valued service for which many people were happy to pay well. Perhaps she even saw herself as easing the pain of the bereaved. They might be gullible fools, but she gave them what they sought: comfort in their affliction.

The only harm was to their pocketbooks, and they shelled out willingly.

On the other hand, as with gambling the obvious victims were not the only victims. Even in these days of female emancipation, Lord Ormerod had a right to put a stop to his wife's bleeding of the family coffers. Also, Lady Ormerod might have emerged by now from her pitiable state if not for her belief in the possibility of communicating with the dead.

Daisy sighed. How much easier life was for those who didn't see both sides to every question!

Lucy sighed. "I suppose Binkie expects me to sit next to Lady O," she murmured. "I hope that research bounder gets a move on with doing his stuff, so we can get it over with and go home."

She sat down beside Lady Ormerod, and Daisy took the next chair. Mrs. Baines moved to sit next to Vasiliev, but the nameless research chappie, still surprisingly unquestioned, got there first. Mrs. Baines's mouth tightened with annoyance, though she did not protest aloud. She took the place between the man and Daisy.

Seated in the spirit cabinet, Madame Vasilieva requested, "Gloves off, please, and everyone hold hands. Do not break the circle, or the power will depart."

Mrs. Baines took Daisy's hand with a deprecating smile. "Most mediums prefer physical contact," she said in an undertone.

To give the illusion that their hands are restrained, Daisy recalled from her reading. In this case, Madame and her husband obviously each had a hand free to produce phenomena.

For some reason, Daisy had assumed Mrs. Baines was new to the séance business. She must have attended several, though, to make such an observation. Daisy regarded her with more interest than hitherto, but the room was too dark by now to pick out more than a pale patch of disembodied face.

"I'm getting the creeps," Lucy whispered on her other side.

Daisy turned to smile at her. She too was nothing but a pale blur, so Daisy squeezed her hand instead.

"Hush!" hissed Lady Ormerod. "Madame needs quiet to enter the trance."

After a few minutes of silence, during which the

last hint of light vanished, strange mutters and moans came from the direction of the cabinet. It was jolly eerie, Daisy admitted to herself as Lucy's grip on her hand tightened.

Suddenly a high, shrill voice cried out in an exotic tongue—an Indian language? More likely nonsense syllables.

"Is that you, Devaki?" came Madame Vasilieva's lower tones.

More shrill nonsense.

"Please speak English. We need your help. Will you help us?"

"No, I don't want to. It's no fun."

"Just for a little while," Madame coaxed. "Only you can bring comfort to a sorrowful mother."

"I don't—" The petulant voice broke off. "Oh, here is someone who wants to speak."

"Who is it?"

"A soldier."

"Devaki, we don't want just any soldier again."

A high giggle: "A soldier . . ."

Her words were drowned by the blare of a trumpet playing the Reveille. The sound came from the far side of the room. A ghostly, phosphorescent trumpet floated there, suspended in mid-air.

Lucy gasped.

The brassy notes died away. "Who is there?" the medium queried sharply.

"Je . . . Je . . ."

Gervaise? thought Daisy, her heart somersaulting.

"Jerome!" cried Lady Ormerod.

"Jemmy Heatherwood." The slow, country voice came from behind Daisy. She twisted her head to look back. A luminous sword hovered there.

"What do you want?" asked Madame.

"Kilt on Bosworth Field, I were, wi' nary a chance to bid me mam farewell. Mother, are ye there?"

"Your mother is not here, Jemmy."

The sword slashed the air and a horrid, keening lament rent the darkness, fading into a silence shattered by the clang of the sword landing on the table. It lay there, glimmering. Daisy shuddered.

"Devaki, please find Captain Jerome Ormerod for us."

"There are no ranks on this side," scolded the childish spirit guide. "No ranks, no titles, no . . ."

"Mater?" A clear, light tenor, very public school. A muted trumpet sounded the Last Post, the mournful notes bringing tears to Daisy's eyes.

"Who is it?" the medium asked.

"Jerome? Is it you?" cried Lady Ormerod. "Oh, my dearest boy."

"Hullo, Mater. Can you hear me? This is Jeremy."

"Not Jerome?"

"Not Jerome," the voice confirmed sadly. "Hold on half a tick. There's this frightful little Hungarian blighter . . . Hullo? Are you there?" It was like a bad telephone connection. "Jerome is here. He wants to speak to you, but . . ."

"Mater?" This voice was very similar, perhaps a shade deeper, coming from the opposite direction, to Daisy's left, well behind Lady Ormerod. A filmy white figure stood there, hovering above the floor. Its indistinct, moustached face suggested a handsome young man—any fair, handsome young man.

"Jerome!"

"Don't break the circle," snapped Madame Vasilieva, "or the spirit will vanish."

Daisy imagined Lady Ormerod frantically trying to see her son without losing hold of the medium's and Lucy's hands. She'd not be able to get a clear view, but even if she did, in the frenzied state she was in she would be convinced it was Jerome.

"Jerome, speak to me! Are you happy?"

"It's absolutely ripping over here, Mater. But I have to tell you . . ."

A burst of rapid gibberish interrupted him.

"Go away, you perishing bounder!"

At that moment the beam of a powerful electric torch shot out. From somewhere to Daisy's right, the dazzling light crossed the medium's pallid, shocked face, probed the empty space where Vasiliev ought to be, and swung back. It struck the spirit figure in the face, pitilessly illuminating a crude mask, then sank past the billowing gauze to focus on a pair of black trouser turn-ups and black-socked feet.

Toes twitched. Their owner bolted for refuge behind the cabinet.

Caught in the scattered light on the edge of the beam, Lady Ormerod opened her mouth in a sobbing wail of desolation and fury. Springing to her feet, she leaned forward, hands outstretched. The table went flying. The torch fell with a thud on the carpet and lay there, still shining, its reflection from the plush curtains providing a dim, ghostly light in which unrecognizable figures moved.

A ghastly shriek rang out.

Daisy made for the nearest door. Feeling for an electric light switch, she snapped it on.

The glare blinded her momentarily but, expecting it, she was the first to recover. The tableau which met her eyes made her wish she hadn't.

The shabby little investigator lay flat on his back on the carpet, glassy gaze fixed on the ceiling. A crimson stain crept across his white shirtfront, spreading out from the spot where Jemmy Heatherwood's sword protruded from his chest.

His mouth twitched once and then fell open, still and slack.

Lady Ormerod was on her knees at this head, her face hidden in her hands, rocking back and forth. A low, steady moan issued from her blanched lips. Beyond him the medium clung to her husband's arm. They both stared down with appalled fascination at the inert clay whose spirit was passing "to the other side" even as they watched.

Lucy stood by her chair, transfixed, camera forgotten, too utterly astonished to be horrified yet. Mrs. Baines knelt and reached for the man's wrist.

"He's gone," she said tersely.

Lady Ormerod threw back her head and laughed. The hysterical cackle rose to a screech, fell in a whimper to an incoherent mumble. Hurrying to her, Daisy snapped, "Lucy, you'd better go and telephone the police."

"But . . ." She turned an aghast gaze on the Vasilievs. "Daisy, I can't leave you here with them. It's not safe."

"It wasn't them." Gently Daisy raised Lady Ormerod to her feet and supported her tottering steps to the nearest upright chair. "It was her."

"Lady Ormerod? Impossible!" As if the scene had suddenly sunk in, Lucy paled, the rouge on her high cheekbones standing out starkly, horribly like the crimson smears on Lady Ormerod's gaunt cheeks.

"Look at her hands, her face. Don't you understand? He parted her from her son, drove Jerome away. He's the investigator from the Society for Psychical Research."

"No, no, my dear," said Mrs. Baines in a shaky voice.

As she rose awkwardly from the floor, she drew from the man's sleeve a black rod with a hook on one end. She pulled on the hook and the rod lengthened telescopically. Comprehending, Daisy drew in a sudden breath.

Mrs. Baines continued, "This man is Agnes Potts's—Madame Vasilieva's—uncle, who was once

a stage ventriloquist. My information suggests that
his was the brain behind this swindle. No, her ladyship made the same mistake as you did. I am the
psychical researcher. I very much fear the sword was
meant for me."

*In this spirited tale, the Honourable Daisy Dalrymple un-
settles the living and the dead at a 1920s séance. Dunn's
aristocratic photographer sleuth appears in* Death at
Wentwater Court, The Winter Garden Murders,
Death of a Mezzo, Murder on the Flying Scotsman,
and Damsel in Distress.

After All . . .

Hazel Holt

The whole village was talking of nothing else. Not surprising, really, considering we haven't had a murder in Yenworthy since some time in the 1890s when a farm labourer ran amok with an axe in what is now the Honeysuckle Cottage Tea Room.

"It's a complete mystery," Richard Blackburn said. "The facts are beyond dispute." Richard is a retired naval commander who runs the village shop (most village shops nowadays seem to be run by retired service personnel) and is very keen on facts. "There was no sign of a forced entry and the burglar alarm was on."

"The classic body in the library situation," Alastair Milburn said. He is a retired headmaster and our self-appointed authority on all things literary. "Though the weapon should have been an oriental dagger of curious design rather than a blunt instrument, as I believe was the case here."

"Not the library," Richard corrected him, "he

doesn't have a library. He was in his study and he was hit over the head with *something*, though they don't know yet what it was."

The fact that we were all able to take a purely academic interest, as it were, in this unpleasant crime was due to the fact that the victim, Norman Dixon, was a thoroughly unpleasant man and deservedly disliked by the whole village. We were shocked, of course, as one is by any sort of violence, but no one, I believe, felt any actual sorrow. I myself had a particular dislike of the man, together with a slight feeling of guilt, since I was, in a way, instrumental in his coming to Yenworthy. When my husband, Philip, died five years ago, I faced up to the fact that I could no longer afford to live in the Old Rectory. It had been too big for just the two of us for years, ever since the children had grown up and gone away, but we loved it so much that we'd somehow managed to hang on, even though it was a bit of a struggle to make ends meet. So I sold it to Norman Dixon.

I wasn't terribly happy about it, since I hadn't taken to him, though he was perfectly civil and said all the right things about how beautiful the house and grounds were. He was a heavily built man, in his early fifties, with that sort of sleeked-back dark hair that always reminds me of 1930s Hollywood gangsters. He had a self-satisfied air, which was unappealing, and an unpleasant brusqueness toward those he considered unworthy of his attention.

But there hadn't been any other offers—at least, none that would give me enough money to buy a small house in the village with sufficient left over to eke out my widow's pension. Money seemed to be no object to Norman Dixon, who, I heard, had "made a killing" in some sort of commodity market, or was it futures? I don't understand these things. Anyway, he certainly spent a great deal of money on the house, even though he was usually down here only at weekends. Then there were noisy parties, with cars driving too fast through the village in the early hours of the morning. There was no Mrs. Dixon (I believe he was divorced) but a succession of young female companions certainly gave the village something to gossip about.

We didn't care for his lifestyle and the fact that he appeared to hold the village and all who lived there in contempt, but when he began to buy up more land, put up fences where fences had never been before, and close footpaths, he became even more deeply unpopular.

"He never set foot in this shop," Richard said, "not even to buy a stamp!"

"I called to ask him to sign a petition about the new bypass," Alastair said, "and he was extremely rude."

"What do the police think, then?" I asked. "Have you spoken to George?" George Bishop is our local police constable.

"Oh George isn't in charge," Richard said. "There's this Detective Sergeant down from Taunton. He's doing the investigating."

"Oh?"

"George isn't too happy about that," Richard went on, "and I don't think he likes this new chap much—a bit of a know-all. Anyway I did have a word with George last night, in The Royal Oak, and he said that the latest theory was that Norman Dixon knew the murderer and let him in—this chap hit him on the head and then went out, putting the alarm back on again as he went. Marjorie Kemp said it was definitely on when she arrived the next morning." Marjorie went in daily to do the cleaning and some cooking.

"Well if it was someone he knew," Alastair said,

picking up his *Times Educational Supplement* from the counter, and preparing to leave, "it can't have been anyone from down here. It must have been one of those people from London."

Richard and I gave little nods of agreement. It did seem most likely that, unpopular as Norman Dixon may have been in Yenworthy, he almost certainly had even more enemies in London.

That afternoon I received a call from the police. When I answered the bell I found George Bishop standing on the doorstep with another, younger man.

"Oh, Mrs. Forsyth, I wonder if you can help us . . ." George began, when the other man interrupted.

"It's about the murder of Norman Dixon, can we come in?"

I led them into the sitting room and asked them to sit down.

"This is Detective Sergeant Brady," George said "from Taunton CID."

"How can I help you?" I asked.

Sergeant Brady, who was unexpectedly dressed in jeans and a leather jacket, took charge briskly.

"How well did you know Norman Dixon?" he asked.

"How well? Not at all, really."

"But he bought the Old Rectory from you?"

"Yes, but I had very little to do with him afterward."

"You never visited him there?"

"I went once—he invited me to see what alterations he had made."

"You didn't approve of what he'd done?"

"It was all very elegant—he had some sort of interior designer, I believe, but I was sad to see things so changed."

"I see."

There was a pause and Mitzi, my cat, pushed open the door and came into the room. She went toward Sergeant Brady, making as if to jump on his knee, but he pushed her away. I stood and picked her up.

"I'll just put her outside," I said stiffly.

When I came back into the room, the sergeant continued.

"You didn't like him, then?"

"Mr. Dixon? As I say, I didn't know him."

I wondered if I was under suspicion—a snobbish old woman who resented the rich upstart who had driven her out of her house. The sergeant looked the sort of young man who might think along those lines.

Sergeant Brady got up and went to look out of the window.

"You have a good view of the village street from here. I don't suppose," he went on in a would-be jocular tone, "you miss much that goes on!"

A *nosy* snobbish old woman. I made no comment.

"Were there any strangers in the village the day Mr. Dixon died?" he asked.

I thought for a moment.

"There was a van driver delivering a parcel to Mr. Maybury at Pound Cottage, and two ladies who came to look round the church—we aren't on the tourist route as such, but, as you may know, St. Decumen's has a very fine rood screen which is mentioned in some of the guide books—that's all *I* saw, though other people may be more helpful. Oh yes! There was someone else—a young man, very scruffy and unshaven, with long hair, most unsavory, dressed in black jeans and a black leather jacket and those boots young people seem to wear these days. Quite suspicious—certainly not our usual kind of visitor in the village . . ."

"I don't think *he's* the sort of person we are looking for," Sergeant Brady said in a patronising tone, zip-

ping up *his* leather jacket. "Oh well, if you think of
anything else . . ."

He went to the door, followed by George Bishop,
who gave me a placatory smile and murmured
thanks as they left.

I went out into the kitchen to let out Mitzi, highly
indignant at her incarceration.

"Yes, I know," I said as I opened a tin of sardines
to placate her. "He was a disagreeable young man.
Very abrupt and rude—he obviously thought I was
just a silly old woman. Perhaps I am, but he might
have had the grace to disguise his opinion."

Mitzi, deeply engaged with the sardines, made no
reply.

I began to get my own lunch. I don't have very
much these days. When you are old you don't really
need a great deal, though I do try to eat sensibly and
always make an effort to have a proper meal in the
evening, as Philip and I always used to do, even if
these days I have it on a tray on my knee in front of
the television rather than in the panelled dining room
of the Old Rectory.

As I ate my ham sandwich and drank my coffee I
allowed myself a moment of nostalgia about my old
home. It was such a beautiful house. Although the
main building was Regency it was built onto a much
earlier farmhouse, dating back to Tudor times, so
that although the facade was of elegant simplicity
(square with a pediment and pillars on either side of
the front door with its elegant shell-shaped fanlight),
at the back there was a jumble of outbuildings—the
old kitchen and scullery, the bakehouse, the old
laundry and various storehouses. Inside, the rooms
led off the square hall—the dining room, the drawing room, the library and, down a stone-flagged passage, the kitchen with its great scrubbed wooden
table and the built-in dresser that covered a whole

wall. That was all gone now—the homely shabbiness replaced by shining new paint and paper, expensive antique furniture bought by the vanload, the kitchen a designer's dream of Cosiness and Old World Charm, with a large red Aga enthroned like some sort of household god where our old woodburning stove used to stand with its pile of logs heaped untidily beside it.

I don't know what he had done to the upstairs rooms. Norman Dixon had offered to show me that day I was there, but I'd seen enough. I made an excuse and left so that my memories of the house as it had been wouldn't be overlaid and spoiled by my impression of how it was now.

In our day the bedrooms had been papered in old-fashioned flowered wallpaper, mostly faded, and, over the years, the white paint had become a dingy cream, but it was comfortable and friendly and we had been happy there. There were five bedrooms—I hoped that Norman Dixon had not occupied the room that Philip and I had slept in at the back overlooking the garden, but I expect he would have preferred what he undoubtedly called the master bedroom, looking out over the drive. The bathroom was enormous, with a large bath, boxed in with mahogany, whose brass taps were stiff and awkward to turn. The rooms on this floor (there was, surprisingly no third floor or attics) were arranged in a higgledy-piggledy way along a series of corridors, interspersed with large cupboards. I think it was the cupboards I missed almost more than anything. My cottage is very pleasant, and quite big enough for my needs, but there are very few cupboards.

I've never been very good at throwing things away, and having to move the contents of the Old Rectory into a small cottage was dreadful! I could cope with the large things, like the furniture and so forth, but the smaller pictures and ornaments, to all of which I had a deep sentimental attachment, were so difficult. And my mother's linen. I *know* I shall never use it and I cannot imagine that the children will want it, but I simply couldn't get rid of the linen sheets, each embroidered with the intertwined HWS (Helen and William Swinburne), the formal damask tablecloths and napkins and the more delicate tea cloths with white drawn-thread work or lace edging. Finding somewhere to put it all in the cottage had been frightfully difficult. It was scattered in odd chests of drawers, the bottoms of wardrobes and the filled-to-overflowing ottoman, instead of all neatly together, as it used to be in my marvelous vast airing cupboard at the Old Rectory. This was a superb example of Victorian practicality, a sort of a walk-in cupboard, as large as a small room, with heavy slatted wooden shelves, a *dream* of an airing cupboard and I missed it very much.

Mitzi, wanting to be let out after her meal, gave a loud Siamese wail and suddenly I remembered another Siamese cat, thirty years ago—and the airing cupboard ...

Philip had gone to fetch the boys from school (they were at a boarding school in Surrey) and they were all going to stay overnight in London to see some exhibition or other at the Science Museum, so I was alone in the house when Tobit, my Siamese cat, went missing. It was not an unusual occurrence. He had been frequently rescued from trees, hauled out from the water butt, and once (a dreadful business) dug out from an old, disused rabbit warren, so I was accustomed to these disappearances. I searched the house, but there was no sign of him (not even under the eiderdown in Martin's room) and then went around the gardens calling and rattling his food plate (which sometimes worked), but still no Tobit. Agitated now, I went back into the house, calling and (foolishly) looking in places I had already searched, but to no avail. I told myself that he'd come back in his own good time, but, as always on these occasions, I couldn't rid myself of the thought that he might be trapped somewhere, unable to get out, trusting me to rescue him.

I went upstairs to get myself a warmer cardigan so that I could go out and look for him in the fields and woods around the house. As I went along the passage to my bedroom I noticed that the airing cupboard door was open and my heart leaped up. Cats have a natural affinity with airing cupboards, liking to curl up (preferably with muddy paws) on the piles of newly washed towels and sheets. Tobit, of course, loved it, and if the door had been inadvertently left open he was in there like a shot. I went in and switched the light on. There was no sign of him on the lower shelves and my heart sank again, but I called his name, just in case. There was no response, but I called again. This time, to my joy, I heard a muffled wail that was unmistakably Siamese.

"Tobit," I called. "Tobit, are you there?" Again the wail, from high up above my head. "Tobit, where *are* you, you bad cat!"

Now the wail became a muted bellow, demanding that something should be done. Now. At once.

I looked up. The shelves went right up to the ceiling, which, to promote the better circulation of air, was itself slatted. The wooden slats of the ceiling, though, had half broken away and it was obvious that Tobit had jumped up from the top shelf and was somehow stuck in the space above the ceiling. I was just wondering how on earth I was going to get up there when the doorbell rang. It was Patrick, the doctor's young son, who had called to see when Robert and Martin were due back from school.

"Oh Patrick," I said thankfully. "I wonder if you could possibly help me?"

Patrick surveyed the shelves of the airing cupboard with the practised eye of a habitual tree-climber.

"It's easy," he said. "The shelves make a sort of ladder. No problem."

As I watched nervously, he began to make his way up toward the ceiling, climbing from shelf to shelf.

"I'm going to have to pull out the broken bits of the ceiling," he called down. "Is that all right?"

"Yes, of course," I said. "Can you manage? Do you want any tools or anything?"

Patrick yanked at a piece of broken wood and a small shower of plaster fell down.

"No, it's okay. The wood's quite rotten, it comes away, no trouble. Right. Now then . . ."

I saw him reach up and swing his body into the hole. He seemed to go through quite easily, although he was big for his age, and disappeared from view.

"Are you all right?" I called anxiously. "Don't do anything dangerous."

"It's great!" a muffled voice came down. "There are sort of metal pegs in the sides of this small shaft, I can easily haul myself up—it leads right out onto the roof!"

"Do be *careful*!" I shouted, feeling guiltily that I shouldn't have encouraged a fourteen-year-old to go climbing about on roofs.

There was a short pause and then I heard a very loud and indignant miouw and Patrick appeared again in the hole, this time holding a squirming Siamese cat, covered in dust and cobwebs.

"I'll just put him down so," Patrick said, leaning down at a perilous angle to deposit Tobit on one of the top shelves. Then he wriggled round and got his legs through the hole and climbed back down the shelves. Tobit, meanwhile, had scuttled down from the shelf and bolted for the kitchen to make up for lost eating time.

"Are you all right?" I asked. "I really shouldn't have asked you to go up there!"

Patrick shook his head, his red hair now streaked with dirt.

"It's great!" he said with enthusiasm. "You can get right out onto the roof, easy as anything!"

"I don't know what your mother will say . . ."

"Oh she won't notice!" Patrick said. This was true, since she, as well as Patrick's father, worked at the local hospital and were hardly ever at home, which was why Patrick spent most of his time during the school holidays with us.

When Robert and Martin came home Patrick was full of the excitement of the Great Airing Cupboard Route, as they called it, onto the roof, which, being flat behind the pediment, made a splendid vantage point for a secret but minute examination of the surrounding countryside. They also, I regret to say, found a way down from the roof which involved climbing onto projecting window sills, then onto the roof of the old laundry and thence onto the ground. I didn't discover this for some time and promptly put the whole thing out of bounds as being too dangerous. Fortunately, Robert had a new rod for his birthday and, to my great relief, they all became mad about fishing. Philip had a loose cover put over the hole leading up onto the roof, and I forgot all about it.

Until now. It was unlikely that Norman Dixon knew about this way into the Old Rectory. The roof, which we had had (at great expense) repaired and renovated the year before Philip died, was about the only part of the house that had been left as it was.

So there was a way into the house that nobody knew about. Except me. And the boys, of course (though they are now in London and New York respectively)—and Patrick. A few years after the airing cupboard incident, Patrick's parents moved up to London to a larger teaching hospital there. It was taken for granted that he, too, would become a doctor, and he did complete three years of his course before he decided that medicine was not for him. For several years he travelled the world, as the young seem to do nowadays, and we had postcards from India, Japan, and South America. Then suddenly he was back in Yenworthy. Back to his roots, as he put it. He had taken a course in thatching at some rural crafts center and he went to work for Bill Prescott, our local thatcher, and when Bill retired, Patrick took over the business.

He seemed happy, though it is very hard work, balanced up there on roofs in all winds and weathers, packing down the bundles of straw; layer upon layer, so that, in the bitter cold of winter, his hands and arms were often red and raw. He settled back into the village as if he'd never been away, and, bless his heart, he always gave me a very special price for repairing my roof. I was grateful since thatch is a terrible drain on one's resources, needing constant attention, because, even if you cover it with netting, the wretched birds still pull out the straw in handfuls!

Patrick bought a small cottage just outside the village and, four years ago, he married Gemma. He'd met her at some craft fair, I believe, where she was selling handmade jewellery. She was really beautiful, with striking Pre-Raphaelite looks—tall and slender, with that short, curling upper lip, and masses of copper-coloured hair. They made a striking couple. "Well," Fred Munsey, my gardener, said, looking at them, "when them two have kids they'll be right little copper-nobs!" Though, actually, when little Jessica was born this year she had dark hair.

Gemma was an aloof sort of girl. It seemed to me that she didn't really like country life—she didn't join the Women's Institute or, indeed, take part in any village activities. She was hardly ever in the shop, that natural meeting place for the exchange of news and gossip, and, really, the only times we ever saw her in the village were when she drove through in her little red car on her way to Taunton or Exeter. I think Patrick was hurt by her attitude but he never said anything to me, so, of course, neither did I. I thought that when the baby was born we might see more of her, but she just put the child in its carry-cot in the back of the car and went off just the same.

About this time a change came over Patrick. He seemed morose and withdrawn, quite unlike his usual cheerful, outgoing self. Except when he was working, he hardly ever came into the village. I saw him at the garage one day, when he was filling up with petrol, and asked him if he was all right, if Gemma or Jessica was unwell. He muttered something about them all being a bit under the weather and I noticed, after that, he seemed to be avoiding me.

Although I still drive, these days I tend to avoid main roads, keeping to the back ways wherever possible. A little while ago I set out to drive into Taunton along a very unfrequented lane which I was especially fond of since it went past the back drive of the Old Rectory. The drive hasn't been used for years, being quite overgrown, and the gates have lost most of their white paint and sag badly, but, in our day, the boys used to like to slip in and out that way since it was a shortcut to the river.

On this particular day, as I was approaching the

driveway, I saw a small red car parked in the little
lay-by beside the gate. I slowed down and was
amazed to see the gates open and Gemma come out
followed by Norman Dixon. A slight bend in the road
hid me from their view, so I stopped the car and
switched off the engine. They seemed to be having
some sort of argument—a violent argument, because
I saw Gemma raise her arm as if to strike him and
he pushed her backward so hard that she nearly fell.
Then she flung herself away from him, got into her
car, and drove away, very fast, the tyres of her car
screeching on the road. Norman Dixon stood for a
moment looking after her, then turned and went in,
closing the gates behind him. Fortunately Gemma
had driven off in the other direction so that neither
of them realized they had been observed. I was very
shaken by what I had seen, so shaken, in fact, that I
turned round and went back home. I made myself a
cup of tea and put a little brandy in it, and while I
drank it I considered the scene I had just witnessed.
One thing was certain, whatever the argument had
been about, the way they had acted, their very ges-
tures, argued a degree of intimacy that implied only
one thing. Gemma was having, or had had, an affair
with Norman Dixon. I felt a great sadness for Patrick,
who loved her so deeply. But there was nothing I
could do, nothing I could say to either of them. When
Patrick became so moody, I wondered if he had
found out about the affair. Was it over? How long
had it been going on? I thought of Jessica's dark
hair . . .

When Norman Dixon was murdered, and under
such mysterious circumstances, I wondered about
Patrick. When I remembered the airing cupboard, I
was almost sure. But what should I do? Norman
Dixon was an unpleasant man, unloved, unmourned,

and Patrick—well, Patrick was almost like a son to me. What *could* I do?

I took the problem to bed with me and spent a restless night, rising early the next morning unrefreshed and with it all still churning over in my mind. I fed Mitzi and let her into the garden, following her out there in the hope that the fresh autumn air might clear my head. It had been a cold night; soon we would have the first frosts. I looked at the fine show of dahlias still in bloom and thought I would cut them all now before the frost blackened and destroyed them. Soon I had an armful. I took them indoors and shook them over the sink to dislodge the earwigs that always nestle within and then divided them into two bunches, one for the church and one for Philip's grave. I was going, as I always did, to put my problem to Philip, to talk it through with him, before I made up my mind.

As I walked along the village street on my way to the church I saw that there was a tarpaulin on the roof of Glebe Cottage and a scattering of straw on the road. I looked up and saw Patrick, balanced on the roof, his foot braced against the chimney stack. He was hammering wooden spars into the exposed roof timbers with a heavy wooden mallet. I called out "Good morning, Patrick. Nice day!" and he raised the mallet in salute and called "Good morning" in something resembling his old, cheerful manner. I walked carefully up the narrow path to the church, my walking stick clicking on the cobbles. I would have liked to arrange the dahlias in the church myself, since it was Maureen Blackburn's turn to do the flowers and her idea of flower arrangement was to stuff them any old how into whatever vase came to hand. But she was a touchy woman and would have been offended if I had, so I laid my offering in the church porch, filled a watering can from the tap by the crypt, and went on up the churchyard to Philip's grave.

It is at the top of the steep path from the church, and when you pause there and look around, you can see the sheep in the field on the other side of the low stone wall that circles the churchyard, and beyond that the hills and the open moorland, still rich with the muted colours of the heather and gorse—the hymn-writer's "purple-headed mountain." With some difficulty I got down on my knees and began to remove the dead roses from the stone vase on the grave.

"It *could* have been someone from London," I began my silent conversation with Philip, "goodness alone knows what sort of circles Norman Dixon moved in there or what sort of financial dealings he had, probably with all sorts of dubious people—criminal even. Yes, I know—you don't believe that either. The other—it all fits. The airing cupboard, Gemma and her affair, the fact that the murder was committed with a heavy wooden m—with a blunt instrument. But *Patrick*! How could I go to the police? And then there's little Jessica . . . You loved him, too . . . There's no evidence—it's all conjecture."

I filled the vase with water and began to arrange the dahlias.

"If I say nothing it will be on *my* conscience—yes, I know that. And, do you know, I think I am prepared to bear that, to take on the responsibility myself. There now, that's settled then."

I knelt for a moment, quietly thinking. Then I got stiffly to my feet and stood looking down at the grave. I brushed a little moss from the headstone that reads

PHILIP ARTHUR FORSYTH
1909–1991

with a space underneath for my name that would be there soon now

also HARRIET, his wife

"Yes," I said, "that's settled. And after all," I added, picking up the watering can and the plastic bag with the dead roses in it, "I'm just a silly old woman—who'd believe me?"

Hazel Holt, novelist Barbara Pym's literary executor, takes a break from her series with literary critic Sheila Mallory to investigate a corpse who may be connected to the past. Holt's latest book is The Only Good Lawyer.

The Village Vampire
and the Oboe of Death

Dean James

It's a good thing I'm dead already, or listening to
Cora Dembley's wretched oboe playing would be
enough to drive me to suicide. Geese in the climactic
stages of connubial bliss are probably less strident.
Who on earth ever persuaded the woman that she
could play the oboe?

My fellow members of the Snupperton Mumsley
Clarinet Ensemble were no less appalled than I, to
judge by the identical look of glazed horror on all
their faces. Our fearless leader, Alistair Dingleton,
however, seemed enraptured by the hideous screeching that Cora Dembley was wresting from her poor
instrument.

More likely, I thought, old Alistair had his eyes
fastened upon Cora's voluptuous bosom, which
heaved rhythmically to supply the wretched oboe
with air. How he could accompany Cora upon the

piano and still crane his neck around to stare at her breasts, I couldn't fathom. What straight men won't do for a glimpse of cleavage!

Cora had only just launched into this oboe concerto—composed especially for her by Alistair Dingleton—and I had no doubt we had several long minutes to endure until this travesty came to an end. There was always the possibility that Cora would collapse from attempting to play at least one note in tune. I brightened momentarily.

Not all vampires have perfect pitch, you see. Unfortunately for me, I do. You must realize, of course, that my fellow members of the Snupperton Mumsley Clarinet Ensemble don't know that I'm a vampire. They would all probably tell you that there's something more than a little "queer" about me, in more ways than one, but as yet they have no idea that a brash young American vampire has come to live in their anachronistic little Bedfordshire village.

So how *did* a nice American vampire like me wind up in Snupperton Mumsley? (God knows where that name comes from—it's probably a corruption of the Anglo-Saxon for "My, isn't this just too twee for words?")

Because of a man, naturally.

Isn't that always the story? Can't live with 'em, can't be undead without 'em.

In my case it was one Tristan Lovelace, he of the impeccable Oxbridge accent, who was spending two years as a visiting scholar at that august southern institution of higher learning where I was finishing up my Ph.D. in medieval English history. I fell head over heels the moment I saw him, little knowing what a relationship with him would entail. After all, one doesn't expect distinguished English historians to have a penchant for biting attractive young men on the neck.

After a rather torrid affair, which lasted the two years he spent in the United States, Tristan and I parted ways. I gained several things from the relationship, including my passport to the world of the undead. I also got the deed to Tristan's house in Snupperton Mumsley, which allowed me to fulfill a longstanding dream of living (you'll pardon the irony, I trust) in England.

After a few months' residence, I had adapted myself happily to village life, which turned out to be more exciting than I had imagined. After that nasty succession of murders a couple of months ago, which I had helped to sort out, things had been rather quiet. I was delighted to have been asked to join the clarinet ensemble a few weeks ago and, until tonight at least, had enjoyed being a member of the group.

Mercifully, Cora had come to the last two bars of her piece, and the oboe wailed mournfully as Cora attempted a blinding succession of arpeggios, ending upon a long note that wavered about three-quarters of a step flat before resolving onto a pitch several steps away from what Dingleton had no doubt intended. I shuddered.

In the ensuing silence, Cora gulped air and watched us all with wary anticipation. Everyone was stunned speechless. Alistair Dingleton leaped into the breach. He came around the side of the piano to clasp Cora's free hand in both of his.

"My dear Cora, what stunning progress you have made! After your performance tonight, one simply could not imagine that you began playing a mere six months ago." He turned to beam at all of us. "I think the time is now appropriate to announce to you all that I have asked Cora to be our guest soloist for our concert in two months' time."

We had all wondered why Dingleton had wanted us to rehearse at this young woman's house. The mystery was partially solved now. Dingleton's hormones must have eroded any residue of musical taste. Cora was in her mid-thirties, and Dingleton had to be at least a couple of decades older. Small, dumpy, fussy, Dingleton looked like an unkempt mouse in evening dress next to the stately and impeccably groomed Cora. He was painfully and obviously infatuated with her. It was the only explanation for his participation in this farce.

"Oh, Alistair," Cora said, "you are such a dear. How you have put up with me all these months I don't know! But thank you all for your generous words of support. I know our concert is going to be wonderful." She laid her oboe reverently aside, taking the reed out and dropping it into a small glass sitting on the piano.

"Now, everyone just relax for a few minutes, and I'll go and see about some tea," Cora promised. She disappeared through the door and closed it behind her.

Lucas Ashworth, a retired banker and the eldest member of the group, broke the appalled silence. "Dingleton, you may be besotted with that young woman, but I am not about to let you make fools of us all with that travesty of a performance!" He heaved up from his chair and stalked over to Dingleton, towering over him. "I cannot believe you are seriously considering letting that woman desecrate our good name!" He paused for a breath—good thing, his face was turning purple. "I founded this group, and I won't stand by and see us made a laughingstock!"

"Lucas is right, Alistair." Zoe Houghton surprised me by actually expressing an opinion. She seemed to have surprised herself as well. "I mean, well, you know, the woman works for my husband. I don't think it's quite the thing to have my husband's secretary featured as a soloist at our concert."

That sounded foolish even to Zoe, who shrank back in her chair. Dingleton sniffed, then focused his attention once more upon his chief adversary.

"Ashworth, I doubt I could *ever* forget that you founded this group. You remind us at every *possible* opportunity." He cleared his throat in his usual annoying way. "But you asked *me* to take over the direction four years ago, and in that time, we have made enormous progress. Lest you forget, *I* am the one with the academic credentials to pass judgment upon someone's musicianship. If *I* say that Cora is ready to perform in public—with this group—then *she will do so.* Surely you have learned to trust my judgment by now."

Vampires are particularly sensitive to strong human emotion, and I was fairly awash in sensation at the moment. The strongest feelings emanated from Alistair Dingleton and Lucas Ashworth, though Zoe and Tony both seemed strongly perturbed as well. Surely they were all overreacting. Since I was the one person in the group who had academic credentials outranking those of our dear leader, who had merely a master's degree (albeit from Oxford), I decided to venture an opinion. Perhaps I could smooth things over a bit, though I was enjoying, I must admit, seeing them break through their normal reserve. "My dear Dingleton, I grant you that Cora has a rather . . . extraordinary presence and a very individual manner of presentation, but do you think that she will be ready in a mere two months' time to face a large audience?"

"My *dear* Dr. Kirby-Jones," Dingleton mocked my friendly tone, "you are still *new* to the group and thus have little idea of how we work. I assure you, I *know* what is best for our ensemble." He glared long enough to be certain that I had been put firmly in my place. I decided that flipping him the bird would be slightly uncouth in the circumstances.

"Now," he continued, "I know Cora might have been a *bit* nervous tonight, since this was her first public performance. But she will be rehearsing with us twice or three times a week in order to prepare for this concert, and she will be *just* as prepared as any of *us* when the time comes."

Tony Clynes, the hitherto silent member of the group, snorted with laughter. Handsome, self-confident, Tony rather fancied himself a ladies' man. A pity, because I could have quite a bit of fun with him, even though he's not my usual type. Cora seems to be *his* type, though, judging from the appreciative leers he sent in her direction—before she started playing the oboe, that is. Apparently Tony has *some* standards after all.

"You won't give one of *us* the chance to perform a solo at the concert, yet you'll stake the good name of our ensemble upon *her*?" Tony nearly shouted at Dingleton in his frustration. In the time I had been in the group, Tony rarely let a rehearsal go by without hinting, and sometimes demanding, a chance to perform a solo at a concert. As the second chair clarinetist, he chafed at Dingleton's overbearing leadership. He was every bit as good a musician as Dingleton, as far as I could tell, but Dingleton kept him firmly in second place. Dingleton reserved all the solos for himself.

Cora came back at that moment with a tea tray, and I sprang forward to assist her. The others were all too busy glaring at Dingleton. Cora bustled around, serving everyone with tea and biscuits. I took a tentative sip of mine (despite what you may have heard, vampires can actually drink other beverages besides blood), and it confirmed my suspicions. Cora made tea no better than she played the oboe. The brew was harsh and left a foul taste in my mouth. I politely set my cup down and munched on a biscuit. Thank goodness, she must have bought these at Tesco's or somewhere, because they were actually edible.

From my vantage point on the sofa, I watched the others. Lucas Ashworth ambled around the room, still very much in a temper, staring at the various pictures Cora had used to decorate the room. One in particular seemed to interest him. He picked it up from the back of the grand piano and stared at it for a couple of minutes before setting it down with a jerk. He stared hard at Cora for a moment before he resumed his wandering around the room. I had seen the photo which piqued his interest. It was a portrait of a young man, slender, almost girlish, cradling an oboe in his arms. I had assumed he was a relative of Cora's.

Zoe Houghton fussed over her tea and biscuits, spilling tea on her mud-brown twin set. Her stolid figure and mousy coloring were a sharp contrast to Cora's blonde voluptuousness. Zoe became clumsier than usual whenever Cora was anywhere near her.

Tony Clynes glowered at the group from his corner by the fireplace. Cora flirted with him briefly as she proffered him tea, but for once, he paid no attention to her. She turned away from him, a slight grimace marring her features. She caught my eye and winked. I smiled back. In the few times I had encountered her before tonight, she had flirted with me outrageously, and I had flirted back. The poor woman was too dim to realize that her efforts were wasted on me.

Now that everyone had been served with tea, Alistair Dingleton once more took center stage. "I have another very important announcement to make."

Glowering, Lucas Ashworth and Tony Clynes resumed their seats, and I wondered what further fireworks we could expect tonight. I didn't think anyone would cause a scene in front of Cora. They were all too English for that, but, then, I might have underestimated them. I settled back to watch.

Dingleton rubbed his hands together gleefully. "I am delighted to announce that Dame Cynthia Howard has accepted my invitation to our next concert. The whole performance will be dedicated to her, as it occurs on the twenty-fifth anniversary of her first performance with the London Philharmonic."

I do believe that Lucas Ashworth actually groaned. I was rather excited myself. Imagine that, Dame Cynthia Howard, the famous flautist, to attend one of our concerts. If we were lucky, Cora might have some nasty virus and be unable to perform.

"How on earth did you manage that?" Lucas demanded.

Cora practically bounced with goodwill. "Oh, that was all my doing. I told Aunt Cynthia about it, and she said she'd like to come."

"Aunt Cynthia?" Tony Clynes said. His voice expressed the incredulity we all felt.

Cora simpered. "Actually, she's not really my aunt, she's my godmother. But I've always called her Aunt Cynthia, because she and my mother were at school together and were *such* good friends."

The little plot had finally revealed itself. Dingleton had designs on more than Cora's ripe charms. He was after the attention of no less a celebrity than one of the world's premier flautists. Perhaps he was tired of being music master at nearby Dylworth Hall, the tony public school to which those with scads of money sent their offspring. Perhaps he had delusions of foisting one of his compositions upon Dame Cynthia, who was known to encourage the work of lesser-known composers. If she performed one of his compositions, his reputation would be made.

"That's quite an accomplishment," I said to fill the lengthening silence. "To have such a celebrity at our concert. I toast you both." I raised my cup to my lips and pretended to sip. The others looked at me reproachfully. Well, they could pretend to sip just as well as I could.

"And you *must* tell me, Cora my dear," I continued, "where you got this extraordinary tea. I don't believe I've ever tasted anything quite like it."

Tony Clynes sputtered into his cup, and even Lucas Ashworth looked like he remembered what a smile was. The irony of my compliment went completely over Cora's head; I should be ashamed of myself, but I seldom am.

"Thank you, Simon," she burbled at me. "It's my own concoction, I must confess. I take Earl Grey and add some special ingredients from my herb garden. I find that drinking several cups a day gives me increased energy and zest for life." She twitched her bosom ever so slightly, and Alistair Dingleton almost swallowed his teacup.

"I have to get back home." Zoe Houghton plunked down her teacup with unaccustomed force and stood up. "My husband is expecting me. He doesn't like to be left alone with the children too long." Having once encountered Zoe and her brood of ill-mannered offspring, I could sympathize with her husband, who by now probably wished that vasectomies were retroactive.

"I might as well be going, too," Tony Clynes muttered. He set his tea aside and went to the corner of the large room where we had been rehearsing and began packing up his instrument and music. Zoe, Lu-

cas, and I followed suit. Alistair busied himself helping Cora pile crockery on her tray.

Cora wished us all good night, then headed to the
kitchen. Alistair accompanied us to the door. "A reminder. We'll meet here again at Cora's for our next
rehearsal, Thursday night. I'll expect to see you all
then, and I expect your full cooperation in preparing
Cora for our concert."

"You're not going to get away with this, Dingleton!
I'll see to that!" Lucas Ashworth stalked out the door
without another word, while Tony Clynes muttered
under his breath and followed him. Zoe Houghton
once again expressed an opinion—twice in one night
was surely a record for her. "I still think you ought
to reconsider, Alistair. I don't think it's right!" So saying, she marched off up the lane toward her expen-
sively restored Victorian villa at the other end of the
village.

"I know I can count on you, Simon," Alistair said,
suddenly chummy with me.

"I'll keep an open mind," I assured him. After all,
there was still time for a reprieve—like a great oboe
heist the night before the concert. "I just hope you've
not assigned yourself too difficult a task."

"Never fear, Simon," Alistair replied as he closed
the door. "I shall prevail, and you'll all thank me in
the end."

Two nights later, we all gathered again at Cora
Dembley's cottage, and the rehearsal was a disaster.
Cora's oboe torturing reached new heights with an
entire clarinet ensemble backing her, rather than a
mere piano. If the perfect pitch fairy (other than
yours truly, of course) had come and sat on her head,
she still would have been godawful.

Alistair Dingleton finally called a halt to the proceedings, and Cora bustled off for tea and biscuits.

Cora looked relieved; I think even she had reservations about Dingleton's plan. The rest of us fiddled with our instruments, cleaning out the accumulated spit of the past hour's suffering. I parked Irmentrude, my trusty Selmer Low C bass clarinet, upon her stand and sat back to watch the others.

Zoe had propped up her contrabass on its stand and was fiddling around in her purse. Dingleton was searching for something in his case. He pulled out what appeared to be a small plastic bottle of oil and set it upon his music stand. Lucas Ashworth had set his clarinet carefully on his chair and had gone over to the piano, staring fixedly again at the same photograph which had engaged his interest two nights ago. Tony Clynes nipped outside for a quick smoke. No one offered to break the silence, and I wasn't feeling sufficiently bitchy to stir things up. One of my off nights.

Tony came back in time to assist Cora with the tea tray, and we all drifted over to the piano to accept our teacups and select biscuits from the tray.

"Cora, my dear, do you have any of those delightful little chocolate biscuits that we had before?" Alistair Dingleton broke the silence.

"Why, I do believe so," Cora said. She set her teacup down on the piano. "Let me just go see!" She bustled off.

The rest of us busied ourselves looking for a convenient potted plant-cum-tea disposal. I spotted it first. I had no idea what it was, but it was about to be enriched by several doses of Cora's herb tea. I was back in my spot, with the others straggling into place when Cora came back into the room with another small plate of biscuits. We all helped ourselves, and Cora set the plate down on the tea tray.

Cora picked up her teacup from the piano. She seemed nervous. "I must apologize for tonight," she said. She paused to take some tea. "I don't know what came over me, but I was a bit nervous while rehearsing." She took another, longer sip of her tea. "I promise you..."

She never finished the sentence. She dropped the teacup from her hands as she doubled over in pain. As we watched, horrified, she fell to her knees and began making ugly retching sounds.

"Oh dear God, Cora, what's wrong?" Alistair Dingleton threw his teacup aside and knelt on the carpet beside Cora, trying vainly to ease her distress.

"Dial 911!" I yelled at Tony Clynes, who was nearest the phone. I had forgotten, in my distress, that 911 wasn't the correct number here, but fortunately Tony realized what I meant. He grabbed the phone and punched in the appropriate number.

Cora had stopped retching for a moment and was now clawing feebly at her chest. I pushed Zoe and Lucas aside and knelt beside Cora and Alistair Dingleton. "Let's try giving her artificial respiration," I suggested desperately, since Cora was now acting like she couldn't breathe.

We worked with her, in vain, until the emergency crew arrived, but by then it was over. Cora died, clasped in Alistair Dingleton's arms, and he had to be pried away from her so the emergency team could remove the remains. Exhausted, I wondered whether he was more distraught over losing Cora herself or his chance to impress Cora's godmother, Dame Cynthia Howard.

The next day, I was working in my office in my cottage, devising the latest adventures of my hard-boiled female sleuth, LuAnn Chippendale (I write them under the name Dorinda Darlington; do look for them on the shelves of your nearest bookstore!). The doorbell rang, and I cursed the interruption. I saved the file, then went to answer the door.

Late afternoon sunshine streaked in when I opened the door. (Contrary to what you've heard, vampires can stand a bit of sunlight, thanks to these wonderful little pills developed by some vampire scientists at the National Institutes of Health in Bethesda—and, no, the Republicans in Congress have no idea that they're vampires.) "Oh, Robin," I said, not all that surprised at the identity of my guest. I knew Cora's strange death would bring out the forces of law and order. "Please, come in." I stood aside to let him enter.

Detective Inspector Robin Chase and I had met over those unfortunate murders I mentioned earlier and had developed a rather interesting relationship. I flirted outrageously with him, and he pretended not to be interested. One of these days, he'll kick open the closet door, and we might have some fun, but until then I'll just tease him unmercifully.

"Well, Robin," I began, leading the way into the sitting room, "have you finally come to clap me in chains and have your way with me?" I turned to face him.

He blushed slightly as I motioned for him to sit down on the sofa across from me. "Now, Simon," he said, "this is purely business. I'm here to talk to you about Cora Dembley." He stroked his moustache, a habit of his when he's nervous. Somehow, I seem to have that effect on him. He does a lot of moustache stroking around me. I guess there's nothing Freudian in that.

But, to business. "So, what did happen to poor Cora?" I asked. "It looked to me like she was poisoned."

Robin nodded. "Most definitely. Now, tell me what happened. What did you see? I have the statement you gave PC Harper, but I'd like to hear it from you."

Settling back in my chair, I gave him a quick and precise description of last evening.

"So none of you actually drank any of the tea?" Robin jotted down something in his notebook.

I shook my head. "That potted plant in the corner got five cups of tea. They could all have been poisoned, for all I know."

"That doesn't seem to worry you," Robin observed. Naturally I couldn't tell him that, if my tea had been poisoned, it wouldn't have bothered me much.

"Somehow, I doubt that any of the rest of us were the intended victims."

"But why would someone want to kill Miss Dembley?"

I shrugged. "If you had heard her play the oboe, you'd understand." Robin is a music lover, but he looked a bit shocked at my cavalier dismissal of Cora's death. To pander to his tender sensibilities, I explained in more detail about Dingleton's plans for the Snupperton Mumsley Clarinet Ensemble's next concert.

"And she was so awful that you think someone killed her to keep her from performing with you?" Robin's tone was frankly incredulous.

"It sounds frivolous to me, too, Robin, but you didn't see how worked up the others seemed to get over this situation. I'm not saying that they would have resorted to murder. There were other, simpler ways to keep Cora from performing with us. But someone killed her, I suppose. There has to be a motive somewhere."

I thought for a moment. "Do you know yet what the poison was?"

Robin looked uncomfortable, battling with his conscience, I thought. He's not supposed to tell me these things, but after those other murders, he learned to trust me. Or else he just couldn't resist my exotic charms.

"I suppose it wouldn't hurt to tell you this much," Robin conceded with barely concealed relief.

"Oh, I won't breathe a word of it!" I assured him.

"Preliminary tests indicate that she was poisoned with foxglove."

"Ah," I said. "Have you checked her little herb garden? She made that vile tea of hers with some of the ingredients she grew herself."

"No, we've not yet checked that," Robin said. "Good point. You don't suppose that she could have inadvertently poisoned the tea herself?"

"Cora was a bit of a dim bulb," I said after a moment's thought, "but I don't think her wattage was that low. I'm sure she would have known enough not to put foxglove in the tea. Still, you should check it out."

Robin left soon after that, promising to call me with any fresh news. I sat for a while longer in my chair, my thoughts turning irresistibly toward Cora Dembley's murder.

I didn't seriously believe that someone had killed Cora to keep her from performing with us. As I had told Robin, there were other, less drastic ways to have her sidelined before the concert. There had to be some other, hidden motive behind it. Of course, it could turn out that Cora was even stupider than I thought, and she had poisoned herself. And, were it not for our ritual dumping of tea into the potted plant, my fellow musicians would all have died along with her. Not I, of course, since I'm immune to poison. That certainly would have been awkward to explain to the police!

I thought back over the events of that night, replaying them in my mind. Something occurred to me, and I went to the phone.

The last vestiges of the sun disappeared from the sky as I let myself out the front door of my cottage. Thanks to those dandy pills I told you about, I don't have to fear the sun as I once might have, but I also don't expose myself to it unnecessarily! I had waited until sundown to complete my errand. When I had phoned him earlier, Lucas Ashworth had reacted with surprise, but he hadn't protested at my inviting myself over for a drink this evening.

Ashworth lived in a neighboring village, between Snupperton Mumsley and Bedford. The drive took me less than ten minutes. I parked the car, got out, and knocked on the door of Ashworth's half of the elegantly modern semidetached.

Ashworth opened the door and invited me in. He took my coat, then ushered me into his sitting room. "What can I offer you?" he asked. "Sherry?"

Suppressing a shudder, I told him that would be fine. I didn't intend to drink much of the nasty stuff anyway.

"It's all rather shocking about Cora Dembley, don't you think?" I asked him as I accepted my sherry. He looked a bit pained as he turned back to serve himself.

"Yes, it is. I'll admit that I was appalled with the poor woman's lack of ability, and I most assuredly did not want her to play with us." He took a sip of his sherry as he seated himself in a wing-back chair. He motioned for me to sit down across from him, but I pretended not to see. I wanted to explore the room instead. That's one of the advantages of being an American; people don't expect you to know quite how to behave all the time.

"But you wouldn't wish for this way out of a particularly uncomfortable situation." I paused in my perambulations to offer him that bit of comfort.

"No, of course not! I can't believe that someone would have murdered her for such a silly reason." He seemed to have forgotten his own vehemence on the subject, just days before.

"She might have been the victim of a rather bizarre accident," I said, and he pressed me for details as I continued to wander around his spacious sitting room. As I related to him the theory that Cora could have poisoned herself, I spotted something of great interest. Something I had hoped, but had not expected, to find. This made what I had in mind much easier.

"The poor young thing was not all that bright," Ashworth said, seeming to take comfort from the idea that Cora had died by her own hand. "It's only by the grace of God that we all got rid of our tea instead of drinking it. She could have killed us all." Shaking, he took another sip of his sherry.

"Who is this?" I asked him, brandishing a photograph I had found stuck in a corner on a small table.

He blanched. "Oh, it's someone I used to know." He became absorbed in examining his fingernails. Then he jumped up. "More sherry?"

I declined, and he served himself. I glanced down at the photograph in my hands. The young man in it was the same as the young man in the photo on Cora Dembley's piano. In this photograph, however, he was playing his oboe, rather than simply holding it.

"I noticed Cora had a photo of this same young man on her piano. Who is he?" I asked him again.

Ashworth gave me a look of pure dislike. This was probably the last time I'd be invited over for sherry. Oh, well, I didn't like sherry that much anyway.

"If you must know, he was a young friend of mine who happened to be quite a talented oboe player."

"*Was?*"

Ashworth nodded. "Yes, he . . . died three years ago."

"What happened to him?"

Ashworth twisted his sherry glass in his hands. "He killed himself" was the quiet response.

"I'm sorry to hear that. He looks like a rather special young man." I set the photograph down and went to stand near Lucas Ashworth.

"Oh, he was," Lucas assured me, forgetting his former reserve. "Jonathan was enormously talented. He had quite a gift. Hearing him play the oboe was like hearing an angel sing." He shuddered. "Which is why hearing that poor woman attempt to play was even more a travesty than it might have been. I don't know how she had the nerve to stand there in front of us, playing like that, after all that she did to poor Jonathan."

"What did she do?" I asked him gently, after he had been silent for a minute or so.

He looked miserably at me. "Jonathan was such a dear boy, but he was confused about a number of things. He was attracted to men, particularly to older men, but he couldn't feel comfortable with that. Cora came along, and she made a dead set at him. He was terribly confused by her. Then she discovered him one day with, um, with someone else, and she made a horrible scene. The names she called him!" He closed his eyes, and tears trickled slowly down his face.

"What happened?"

Ashworth took a deep breath to steady himself.

"Jonathan was very upset also. I tried to comfort him, but he wouldn't listen to me. He went home, and the next morning, his father found him dead in his bed. Drug overdose."

"You cared for him a great deal, didn't you?"

Ashworth nodded.

"And you held Cora Dembley responsible for his death, didn't you?" I had finally found a plausible motive for murder—revenge.

"Yes, I did. She destroyed him!" Then the implication of what he had said hit him, and Lucas Ashworth trembled. "But I didn't kill her! You've got to believe me!"

I held his arm gently. He had no idea how strong I was, of course. "But who else had such a motive?"

"His father, of course!" Ashworth looked at me as if I were being deliberately obtuse.

"Who is his father?" I asked, though I had already guessed the answer.

"Alistair Dingleton" was the reply.

"May I use your telephone?" I startled Ashworth with my request. He pointed me toward the hall.

I couldn't believe my luck. Robin was actually in his office when they put me through.

I explained to Robin all that Lucas Ashworth had told me. After I had finished, the line fell silent.

"What about proof?" Robin finally asked, after what seemed to be an eternity.

I had been thinking about that myself. "If you'll get a warrant to search his house and so on, and you get a hold of his clarinet case, look for his bottle of wood oil. If you have it examined, I'm sure that you'll find it contains enough foxglove extract to poison many cups of tea."

*   *   *

Strong emotion is an almost palpable force to a vampire who is close to the human emitting it. That first night of our meeting with Cora Dembley, after Alistair Dingleton's fateful announcement, I had known that both Dingleton and Lucas Ashworth had particularly virulent feelings about the young woman. Ashworth's feelings had been most obvious when he picked up the photograph of the young man who turned out to be Jonathan Dingleton. Alistair Dingleton had harbored strong feelings for Cora, and I had first misinterpreted his thirst for revenge as mere human lust. Those emotional vibrations can be useful in pointing the way, but they're never reliable. Emotions are so complex that it takes a vampire far older than I to sort out their true cause. At any rate, I had been able to follow what clues I had, add them together with the physical indications I had witnessed, and thus find my way to an answer in the puzzle of Cora Dembley's death.

A careful search of Alistair Dingleton's cottage revealed the fatal bottle of oil. He had thrown it into a trash can, but since the trash hadn't been nosy picked up yet, the police found it easily. The bottle contained only minute traces of wood oil, however, but it did contain enough foxglove extract to bury most of Snupperton Mumsley. You'd think that Dingleton would have made more of an effort to get rid of the evidence, but he was arrogant enough to think that Cora's death would be ruled accidental. He had stage-managed everything else so well that I suppose he figured the police would believe his little scenario. The police did find foxglove growing in Cora's garden, right next to the noxious herb she put into her tea. Thus Dingleton's little plan might have worked.

Had he but known, however, that a nosy vampire had moved into his village, he might have reconsidered.

This romp introduces the first gay vampire sleuth in mystery history. James, manager of Murder by the Book in Houston, is coauthor of the Agatha-winning By a Woman's Hand: A Guide to Mystery Fiction by Women *and* Killer Books: A Popular Culture Guide to Mysteries.

Rock of Ages

Gillian Linscott

To the Editor, The Moorside Gazette
18 June 1997

Sir,

Your readers might like to know that the seat over-looking Toller Crag, to commemorate the sixtieth anniversary of the founding of Tollerclough Hiking Club, is now in place, and we hope that it will be appreciated by all walkers who come to enjoy the peace and quiet of this loveliest of Pennine valleys.

Yours faithfully,
Jack Sinclair
Honorary Secretary,
Tollerclough Hiking Club

To the Editor, The Moorside Chronicle
25 June 1997

Sir,

The fact that this miserable piece of garden furniture is now disfiguring one of the finest valleys in the Pennines does not mean that those of us who have been opposed to it from the start will cease our protests. It is a totally inappropriate way to mark the sixtieth anniversary of a group that was formed to fight for everybody's right to walk the high and open places. Let the moors remain uncluttered by the hand of man and let those who would rather sit than walk remain in their armchairs at home.

Yours faithfully,
Stan Briggs
Former Honorary Treasurer,
Tollerclough Hiking Club

The Moorside Chronicle
2 July 1997

Police are investigating an attack by vandals on a seat overlooking Toller Crag, recently erected to mark the sixtieth anniversary of the founding of the Tollerclough Hiking Club. Several of the bolts anchoring it to the rock appeared to have been tampered with, possibly by the use of a crowbar. The damage has been put right. The honorary secretary and founder member of the club, Mr. Jack Sinclair, 78, said: "Any mean-minded and cowardly criminal who thinks he's going to take that seat away from us can think again. It's staying there and that's that."

On a day in July, with two weeks to go to the longed-for end of the summer term, Alison was called to the staff room to take an urgent phone call. Her mother's voice, tense and tremulous.

"Your grandfather's dead."

"Mum, I'm sorry. How?"

"He was out for a walk early this morning and he had a heart attack."

To Alison, her Sinclair grandfather was not much more than a distant memory of northern childhood holidays. When she thought about him at all it was as a pair of stout leather boots planted among the heather, a level Lancashire voice, and an arm in green weatherproof fabric pointing out this or that rock formation on the horizon to a child breathless from trying to keep up with him.

"Do you want me to drive you up there today?"

Her mind was already running through rehearsals for the end of term concert that would have to be rearranged.

"Your grandmother says no, wait until the funeral, and that may not be until the week after next because of waiting for Stan Briggs."

"Who's Stan Briggs?"

"You know, the one from the hiking club your grandfather was always quarrelling with."

She supposed she'd been told about him, but her mother's gossip from Tollerclough had tended to flow over her mind without leaving much impression.

"If Stan Briggs and grandfather always quarrelled, will it matter very much if he can't get to the funeral?"

"They thought they'd do them both together, because of being founder members of the club."

"Do what to them both together?"

"Bury them."

Her head had been aching before this started. She clutched her forehead with her free hand and told herself to be patient, that her mother had a right to be upset.

"Mum, you don't mean that we've got to wait for Stan Briggs to die before we can bury grandfather?"

"No, he's dead too. Only there's got to be an inquest for him because of it being an accident."

"Accident? What sort of accident?"

"I think Mother said he fell over a rock or something. Anyway, they're trying to hurry up the inquest so that they can have the funerals on the same day. Your grandmother and Mrs. Briggs are sorting it out between them."

As the bearers carried in the second coffin Alison, looking down, saw their boots pacing along the Victorian tiles of the church aisle as if kitted out for the high fells, polished brown leather with yellow laces, green suede and purple fabric, khaki and gray, all on quiet Vibram soles. Like a sturdy caterpillar, wooden-backed and rubber footed. Aware of the hunched and sniffing figure of her mother beside her, and her grandmother, dry-eyed, one place along in the pew, she let her eyes travel upward. The faces were old, heads gray or bald. They were none of them large men, but they carried the coffin without strain, faces grave. Then, as the end of the coffin came level with her, she found with a shock that she was looking at quite a different face. The last coffin bearer was no older than she was, mid-twenties, his hair dark and curling, face tanned. His head turned sideways against the coffin and his eyes met hers from a few inches away. She held the look and her stomach turned over, then he was past her. When they'd got the second coffin settled alongside the first one and the congregation began, *"Father hear the prayer we offer. Not for ease that prayer shall be . . . "* She watched him take his place on the front pew, alongside a thin elderly woman in a black coat and hat that looked as

if they'd been doing funeral duty for half a century.
The other widow.

He introduced himself at the funeral tea in the village hall, while she was standing near the door balancing a cup of tea strong enough to take the enamel
off teeth and half a bridge roll with sardine paste and
a fragment of tomato, wondering if she should be
talking to anybody. As he walked toward her, she
knew with total certainty, although she'd never seen
him in her life before those few seconds with the coffin, that he was going to say something outrageous.
He stopped a few feet away from her. He was only
an inch or so taller than she was, and thin as a whip-
pet, but with a concentrated air about him. He looked
at her before speaking, not hesitant but weighing her
up. She returned the look, neither hindering nor
helping.

"I think," he said, "that your grandfather probably
murdered my grandfather."

Then, as an afterthought, "I'm Daniel Briggs."

His voice had a strong touch of the local accent.
She thought, "But he's had to work to keep the accent. He's been living away from here." She was
thinking irrelevancies, because her mind was trying
to adjust to what he'd said.

"It doesn't surprise you, then?"

She must have controlled her face better than she'd
realised.

"I hardly knew my own grandfather, let alone
yours."

She glanced down the hall toward the two widows,
his grandmother in her ancient black coat and hat,
her own in navy blue jacket and trousers.

"Do they know?"

"I'm not sure. Shall we go outside?"

* * *

They walked out of the corrugated iron porch, into the main street that slanted up steeply from the little river with its packhorse bridge to the beginning of the moors, purple with heather. The cottages, the pink row of council houses and the Woolpack pub clustered near the bridge. At this top end of the street were the village hall, the church and the graveyard. Over the low wall she could see the two new graves, some distance apart, each heaped with hectically colored wreaths that had a foreign look against the grass and daisies. A sheep was already taking an exploratory nibble at a sheaf of carnations. After the churchyard there was an expanse of tough moorland grass, metallic and silvery in the heat, then nothing but heather and crowberry. In the middle distance a black crag towered up a hundred feet or so out of the heather. Toller Crag. The name came to her in her grandfather's voice. As soon as she'd seen it again when she and her mother arrived the night before she'd remembered. Unlike most things that were large in childhood it hadn't grown smaller in reality and still dominated the village like a solidified thunder cloud. As she and Daniel walked up the street side by side without speaking she felt as if she'd stepped out of time and was neither in past or present. In the gap between them anything might happen and surprise wouldn't catch up with her until time started again. The street ended in a tarmac parking space for two or three cars and a footpath sign pointing to a trodden brown streak over the grass, running uphill and disappearing into the heather. He stopped by the sign and looked down at her feet in their black sandals.

"Will you be able to walk in those?"

"Are we going far?"

"Would you mind going up to the seat? It will be easier to explain there. It's no more than a mile."

"The seat where they found grandfather?"

Over the previous evening they'd heard more about it from her grandmother. Jack was in the habit of taking a walk up to the seat early every morning to see no harm had come to it in the night. He'd sit there for some time looking at Toller Crag, then walk down for his breakfast. Only that morning he hadn't come down and a party had gone up hours later and found him sitting there. It was, they'd agreed, the way he'd have wanted to go. Only now, looking out over the miles of heather, smelling the sharp smell of sun-warmed peat, Alison couldn't imagine anybody wanting to go. Daniel had his head on one side, still weighing her up.

"No, I don't mind."

When the path became a narrow peat trough between the heather stems she took off her sandals and walked barefoot. She was aware through her soles of slippery heather roots in the peat, like sinews in dry old flesh.

They came to the bench quite suddenly. It was on a flat piece of rock on a little hump of heather. The ground fell away from it to a steep valley with a dark line running down it that was probably a stream in wetter seasons.

"Toller Clough," he said, and Alison remembered from her grandfather that *clough* was the local word for these pleats in the moor. Across the clough was Toller Crag, grown larger and more threatening than from the village, and at a different angle. It was one great plane of rock, from the triangular summit against the sky to the tumbled boulders at its base, split by a few vertical fissures with stunted rowan trees growing out of them. Alison looked away from it to the bench, an ordinary enough object of dark varnished wood with a brass plate on the backrest.

To mark the sixtieth anniversary of the founding of the Tollerclough Hiking Club June 1937 to 1997.

Daniel said, from behind her, "Most of them were no more than teenagers then, and they'd be working in factories, living in narrow little houses in the mill towns. Walking the moors on their Sundays off was life and freedom to them, but they had to fight for it. No footpaths, only landowners and gamekeepers trying to keep them off, with big sticks if necessary."

"I suppose that's why they wanted the bench here."

She put her hand on the back of it, feeling the wood warm and a little sticky from the varnish under her hand, thinking of her grandfather. She couldn't bring herself to sit down on it.

"Some of them did. That was what their last quarrel was about, your grandfather and mine. Did they tell you that?"

His eyes were on her and his hand was on the bench close to hers. She was aware of an urgency about him, but no hostility. The out-of-time feeling was still on her.

"My grandmother said there'd been vandalism. That was why grandfather came up here so early every morning."

"Yes. He suspected my grandfather of being the vandal—and he was almost certainly right."

"But . . . but somebody had been at it with a crowbar, and your grandfather must have been . . ."

"Seventy-eight, only a few months younger than yours. They probably fought in the play yard on their first day at school and went on fighting all their lives."

"What over?"

"Over everything from the design of haversacks to politics. For instance, when the war came, my grandfather was a conscientious objector and went to prison . . ."

"And mine went into the army and got a medal. I know my grandfather was strong Labour . . ."

"So was mine. You take that for granted round here. But they were opposite wings, and that's even worse than being different parties."

"But they both belonged to the hiking club."

"Both founder members, because the moors and the right to walk on them mattered more than anything. But inside and outside the club they were fighting seventy years cat and dog. This seat was only the last thing in a very long line."

She looked down at it.

"It seems a harmless thing to cause so much trouble. Why shouldn't people sit here and look at the view?"

Deliberately she walked round it and sat down, swinging her sandals in her hand. There was a moment of silence.

He said: "I suppose I take my grandfather's attitude. The moors belong to themselves. The less clutter we leave on them, the better."

She couldn't see his face because he was still standing behind the seat. Then he laughed and came and sat beside her.

"I'm not carrying on the war to the third generation."

"No. You only think my grandfather murdered yours."

She said it lightly because it had come into her mind that he'd invented it as a macabre way of getting into conversation with her. His smile when he came to sit beside her had been placating, self-mocking. It died away.

"I don't think I'd have raised it if I'd thought it would worry you. I thought you might be . . ."

"What?"

"Interested. Like I am."

"Why?"

That made him pause again. Then, slowly: "I think, why I'm interested in all of them is that they didn't have much, but they all knew what they wanted. I keep thinking of them, younger than we are now—your grandfather and grandmother and mine and all their friends—so sure of themselves, so ready to fight for what they wanted, even if it was only the right to walk over miles of moorland. Then the war came and they had to go away into the army or into prison, but they came back still wanting what they'd wanted, and they got it. And somehow, the idea that for two of them, right at the very end of their lives, something mattered enough to . . . to kill and be killed for—well, that doesn't seem so bad to me, it seems in its way *encouraging*."

She looked at him and quoted, "*This strange disease of modern life, With its sick hurry, its divided aims.*"

He sat up straight, electrified.

"Who said that?"

"Matthew Arnold. In a poem about a man who knew what he wanted and kept walking."

"It's exactly what I meant. Their aims weren't divided."

"I wonder. They were probably every bit as divided as we are, only sixty years simplifies things."

He shook his head, slowly. Silence for a while. She was conscious of bees buzzing in the heather.

"Mum said your grandfather fell over a rock."

"He didn't fall over a rock, he fell down a rock. That one."

His eyes went to the hundred-foot slab of rock facing them.

"Toller Crag. He fell all the way down Toller Crag?"

"Yes. The same lot of walkers that found your grandfather dead of a heart attack on this seat spotted my grandfather's body on the rocks down there. Must have ruined their morning."

"How on earth did it happen?"

"When they found my grandfather he had an old hemp rope knotted round his waist. They found the other end of it tied round a rock flake at the top of the crag. It was frayed through just a few feet away from the knot."

"Was he still rock climbing, at his age?"

"Stan had been a very good rock climber in his youth, but according to all of them, he hadn't been on a climbing rope for twenty years. Nobody, including my grandmother, had any idea what he was doing there. He had old binoculars round his neck and there was some suggestion he might have been birdwatching, but he wouldn't have to climb down Toller Crag to do that."

"What did the inquest say?"

"Accidental death. I think the coroner's view was that the poor old man was confused."

"Isn't that possible?"

"He was as sharp as he'd ever been. The day before he died he'd written a report to the Department of the Environment protesting against this wretched seat. It was strong stuff, but as sane as they come."

"And yet he takes a hemp rope to the top of the crag—an old hemp rope, I suppose. Nobody uses them anymore."

"Forty years old, at least."

"So he's at the top of the crag with a forty-year-old hemp rope. He ties it round a rock and starts to climb down. If he wasn't confused, what did he think he was doing?"

"You really want to know what I think?"

He was hesitant now, apologetic even. She nodded.

He began to speak slowly, not looking at her.

"We're almost certain that Stan had already had one go at doing away with this seat. Suppose your grandfather came up very early in the morning and found him at it again. He's annoyed, naturally. He snatches the crowbar from him, not meaning any great harm at first. Stan struggles and somehow or other the crowbar comes down on his head."

He looked at her to see how she was taking it.

"So there's a seventy-eight-year-old man left with a seat, a crowbar and a dead body."

"Yes. Now, I don't suppose he'd fancy the idea of standing in dock on account of Stan Briggs. Too much like a final victory for Stan. As it happened, my grandfather was quite a flyweight. I don't suppose he weighed much more than a hundred and twenty pounds. If Jack was desperate enough, it might have been just possible to have carried or dragged him to those rocks over there, as if he'd fallen down the crag. Then he goes home, hides the crowbar, takes out an old climbing rope and saws through it to make it look as if it's frayed. Up to the moors again he goes, ties the long end round Stan's waist, then follows the path to the top of the crag and knots the short end round the rock flake."

"A tall order for a man of seventy-eight."

"A very tall order. Which is why when he's coming back down the path afterward he feels wobbly, sees his beloved seat, thinks he'll have a sit down on it to recover and . . ."

He shrugged. He'd been looking out toward the crag while he was speaking but then he turned and saw her face.

"I'm sorry."

"It's all right. It's really . . ."

"No it's not. You're crying."

His hand came down on hers, held it tight. The

pressure of his fingers was comforting to a grief she hadn't expected to feel and her own fingers closed on his. For a while they just sat there, then he repeated that he was sorry, let go of her hand, and stood up.

"We must go down. Forget it. All in my mind."

When the path widened on the way down they joined hands again and didn't part them until they were nearly back at the village hall.

Next morning she was up early for the drive south but her grandmother was up earlier, in the sunlit kitchen getting breakfast. She was a small woman with a fluff of soft white hair. When Alison had hugged her awkwardly as they arrived it had been like holding a kitten. But over the day of the funeral she'd come to see that first impressions were wrong, that the old woman was tough. She hadn't shed a tear, even when most people around her were crying, had sat obstinately upright through the prayers and insisted on helping to wash up the cups and plates after the funeral tea. She glanced up, bright-eyed, at her granddaughter and hoped she'd slept well.

"Did you enjoy your walk with the Briggs lad?"

She laughed at Alison's guilty expression.

"No need to look like that, girl. They say there's many a wedding made at a funeral." Then, over her protests. "And if you're thinking I won't like it because of my Jack and his granddad snapping at each other like a pair of old terriers, you needn't bother yourself about that. They were born stubborn and they died stubborn and there was nothing to be done about it."

"Has . . . has Daniel talked to you since they died?"

It was in her mind that he might even have come to her with his theory.

"He came over to say he was sorry, like they all

did. He's a good lad in his way, even if he has got some funny ideas."

"Funny ideas?"

"Like being so interested in us old ones. He went to Cambridge and got his history degree, and we thought that was the last we'd seen of him. But he came back here and got himself a job at the comprehensive. He says he's going to write a book about the hiking club and the old days."

"He was talking about those, yes."

Her grandmother, swishing hot water round the teapot to warm it, gave her another sideways look.

"What was he saying about them?"

"That you all knew the things that mattered."

A laugh. "Oh yes, we knew that all right."

"Like what?"

"Sundays out on the moors and being with your friends."

It wasn't quite the radical program that Daniel had talked about, but she sensed she wasn't going to get any further in that direction.

"And that was when you met grandfather?"

"That was when I met both of them, Stan Briggs and your grandfather. Though I say it as shouldn't, they were both sweet on me. I could have married either of them, and that's a fact."

Alison looked at her, standing with the teapot in her small hands, and saw a tanned girl up to her ankles in heather, breasts rounded beneath a checked cotton blouse open at the neck, and a glint of challenge in her eyes. The glint was still there now and it made her take a liberty that would have seemed impossible a few minutes before.

"Did you ever regret choosing the one you chose?"

From the moment's silence she thought she'd said something unforgivable but her grandmother was only considering the question.

"No, your granddad never gave me cause to regret." Then she turned away and reached up to a shelf of mugs, so that the rest of her reply was muffled.

"In any case, it would have come to much the same thing in the end."

She put two mugs on the table, then two more. One of the mugs was larger than the others, well used and tea-stained inside. She looked at it then caught Alison's eye.

"Jack's. I still can't . . ." Guilty of grief, she made an impatient noise at herself and put the mug away on the shelf. When she turned, she was brisk again.

"You know you're welcome up here any time you like. More holidays than you know what to do with, you teachers."

It was early August when Alison went back. When she met Daniel at the signpost to Toller Crag the silver of the grass had turned to dull pewter and the heather had a dusty look.

She said: "I think your grandfather probably killed my grandfather."

Whatever he'd been expecting, it wasn't that. The smile that had come over his face when he saw her faded.

"Are you saying that to pay me back?"

"No." She felt annoyed, having thought about it and brought it back to him like a gift, a sign of shared interests. "I thought you were trying to understand them, a piece of history. I didn't resent what you said, when we thought it was the other way round."

He turned back, still not smiling.

"You mean that? *My* grandfather killed *yours*?"

"I think he might have. He didn't mean to."

"How?"

"Would you mind going up to the seat? It will be easier to explain there."

He caught the deliberate echo and smiled a twisted smile, but didn't take her hand as they walked over the grass, side by side. When they got to the seat they stood behind it, each with a hand on the back but some way apart.

Alison said: "Imagine it's early morning. My grandfather has come up here as usual to make sure your grandfather hasn't done something to the seat overnight. He sees everything's all right, sits down on his seat to enjoy the view before going down to breakfast."

She walked round the seat, sat down. After a long pause, Daniel came and sat beside her.

"He's looking at the crag. Perhaps he sees a figure there on top of it. At this distance I don't think he'd know who it was, but naturally he'd be interested. He can't make out what the person's doing. He goes on watching, then it happens."

Although Daniel was not touching her, she could feel the tension in him.

"He falls."

"Not yet. What my grandfather sees is some sort of slogan, a notice or a banner lowered down from the top of the crag. Whatever is on it infuriates him so much that he has a heart attack there and then."

"Ye gods. You mean that was what Stan was doing up there?"

"It would fit, wouldn't it? Stan would know that Jack went and sat there every morning and couldn't help seeing it. It would be some slogan protesting about the seat, but especially insulting and meant especially for Jack."

She watched his expression change.

"You're right. It would fit. It would explain what he was doing there, why he was out climbing again for the first time for twenty years. It would be just typical of my grandfather. Then he finds he's gone and insulted poor old Jack to death.''

"He couldn't have known that. From the top of the crag, he couldn't have seen he was dead.''

"Couldn't he just? Those binoculars round his neck. He wasn't birdwatching, he was watching to see the effect on Jack. He'd have known that he'd gone too far—and there was his banner or whatever strung over the crag. He ropes up in a panic to get it down before anybody else sees it . . .'' Daniel was gesturing with his hands, caught up with the excitement of the reconstruction. ''. . . and doesn't notice the rope is fraying on the rock. So . . .''

His hands fell suddenly. He went quiet.

"I'm sorry.''

"No. Don't be. I think you might be right. Your theory explains more than my theory. A fair test.''

"There's another test. Did your grandfather have a toolshed or workshop or anything?''

"A workshop. He liked doing odd jobs. In fact, my grandmother has asked me to clear it out for her.''

"Would you mind if we looked at it together?''

"Far from it.''

His hand moved along the seat, found hers. They sat in silence for a while, looking across the heat-hazed clough to the black crag.

They walked slowly on the way down. Before they were clear of the heather he stopped where a line no wider than a sheep track branched off from the main path. He led the way along it as it went upward and round a rock outcrop, then stepped aside and let her go first. She found herself in a kind of pocket in the moor, closed off by rocks and screened by rowan trees. The heather that blazed on the rest of the moor had stopped at the edges of the pocket and it was

mostly sheep-nibbled turf and patches of white
quartz sand, with a bright emerald patch of moss
where a spring would rise when the rain came. They
sprawled on the grass.

"Did you come back because of our grandfathers?"

"Partly."

"Only partly?"

"Yes."

"I'm glad about that."

Later, when they left, she asked if the place had a
name.

"Not on the maps. The locals have a name for it."

"What?"

He smiled and wouldn't tell her. They went back
down to the village, past her grandmother's house
and the cottage by the stream that Daniel was rent-
ing. His grandmother's house was in a brick terrace
on the road out of the village. She followed him up
the garden path, between rows of beans and an overgrown strawberry bed, to a black creosoted shed.
Daniel lifted the latch.

"I don't suppose anybody's been in here since Stan
died."

It was cool and dusky inside, neatly kept, with garden implements and a wheelbarrow on one side, a
woodworker's bench and a rack of tools on the other.
On the bench was a liter can of red gloss paint and
a paintbrush in a jar of red liquid. Alison touched the
jar.

"Your grandfather was a tidy man by the look of
things. If he'd lived, he'd have rinsed that brush and
put it away."

"I suppose he would."

He seemed fascinated by the way she spoke and
moved, but by the sounds and movements in themselves rather than the meaning of them. The urgency
had passed from him to her.

"So painting with red paint was one of the last things he did."

She picked up something from the bench. It was a piece of stiff card about a foot square with an *O* or a zero cut out of it, the edges of the figure marked with red gloss paint.

"There's a whole pile of them here, different letters."

"You were right then. He was stenciling a sign."

"I wonder what happened to it."

"It would have fallen down with him, on the rocks somewhere. The people who found him wouldn't be looking for anything like that."

"Shall we go and see?"

The sun was down behind Toller Crag and the light in the clough was going by the time they found a white sheet among the rocks. The string attached to one corner had caught round a clump of gorse and the whole thing was twisted and tangled, marked by sheep droppings and peat dust. They stood looking down at it, struck immobile by the flat reality after so much speculating. Then his hand moved into the gorse bush, oblivious of thorns, and together they untangled the sheet and spread it over a flat rock, Daniel up above it, Alison pulling from below. She saw figures first, a 9 and an 8, then a word *CLOUGH*. She took a few steps back, going carefully among the rocks.

"I don't understand."

Daniel climbed down to join her.

She read aloud: *"KISSING CLOUGH JUNE 1938."* Then angrily, "What was he talking about? What's Kissing Clough?"

He said softly: "You know Kissing Clough."

"No. No, I don't."

"Yes you do. It's where we were this afternoon. That's what we locals call it."

A moment of panic came over her, as if dead eyes had seen them, then she thought of the glint in her grandmother's eyes and understood. She spoke in a whisper.

"She couldn't have been more than sixteen or seventeen and she married the other one anyway. But it still mattered to them after all this time."

"What do you mean?"

He moved sideways to look at her face in the dusk. She whispered:

"Your grandfather and my grandmother."

He whistled. "You think so?"

"Sure of it. But to be jealous about it for sixty years. To die of it, both of them."

She shivered, and his arm went round her.

"They were going to die of something. Isn't it better this way—better than nothing mattering?"

They clung together for a while, then picked their way down in the dark, Daniel carrying the folded sheet under his arm.

Next morning, on the pretense of clearing out old stuff from the shed, they burned it on a bonfire in his grandmother's backyard. At lunchtime her grandmother, stirring soup from a tin, said:

"You've got a smut on your nose, child."

Alison rubbed.

"And grass stains on the back of your blouse."

She laughed as Alison twisted her neck backward, trying to see.

"I know where you've been. Only one place where the grass is still green enough to stain on a dry summer like this one. Always was, always will be."

Alison, untwisting her neck in time to catch her

grandmother's look, knew the name didn't need to be said—like other things that mattered.

Linscott departs from her series featuring suffragette Nell Bray to explore generations and passions converging on an imposing crag. The latest Bray novel for former journalist Linscott, who lives in picturesque Herefordshire in England, is Dance on Blood.

Murder at the Soirée

Amy Myers

The greatest philanthropist in England raised the glass of browny-orange liquid to his mouth, drained it and adopted an expression of rapture:

"Delightful. Who would seek to drink wine when—"

He stopped, the expression changed from rapture to staring agony, a strangled cry ended in a terrible gasping for breath, he swayed on his feet and the glass dropped from his hand as he fell to the floor; there the body jerked and shuddered in convulsions. Then it became ominously still.

A moment's hush, then:

"His lordship is not well!" his hostess screamed inadequately.

Auguste Didier found himself rushing toward the platform, where he collided with an eminent Harley Street doctor. The services of neither were required.

Lord Robert Blakeham was dead.

*   *   *

Auguste began to go over the mounting horrors of the evening in his own mind, relieved that Inspector Egbert Rose of Scotland Yard, whom he had met (and helped) in similar circumstances, was on his way. He would need to know exactly what had happened—and why Auguste Didier, master chef, happened to be on the scene once again. Had he heeded the dire warnings of disaster predicted in the tea leaves read for him by that delightful new chorus girl at the Galaxy theater, he would never have come. The sympathy in her lustrous dark eyes when she revealed the imminent death of someone close to him before the end of this month, May 1895, had mitigated the immediate shock, and Maman and Papa in Cannes had since reassured him somewhat crossly that they were in perfect health and well able to stir their own *pot au feu* of life. Now he was torn between relief that the someone close to him was an unfortunate gentleman in the same room and anxiety lest Inspector Rose thought the presence of Auguste Didier was no mere coincidence.

The signs of catastrophe had been there from the time of his arrival, but only an hour and a half ago had the full horror of what lay before him been revealed . . .

Temperance? Had he heard aright? He had been thinking of the perfections of the supper (prepared by himself) awaiting the fortunate guests at this illustrious gathering, honored by the presence of Lord Robert Blakeham, instead of listening to the hostess. Auguste decided he had misheard the dreaded word.

Lady Cecilia Wantage had asked him to provide an exquisite banquet, having once partaken of his *sole au chablis* during his years at Stockbery Towers, and, flattered, he had left the Galaxy restaurant, where he was now employed, in the hands of his assistant, to cater for what he had assumed to be a soirée of the *crème* of society to greet the opening of the London season. Surely he could not have misunderstood?

"We—" Lady Cecilia, from the platform in the ballroom of her palatial home in London's Piccadilly, threw out encompassing arms toward her audience, all thirty-six pearl buttons on her white kid gloves quivering with emotion—"are the Life-Line, the Bells of Temperance."

Temperance? Auguste realized to his dismay he had not misheard. This must be the latest of Lady Cecilia's "causes." A widowed lady of middle years, whose daughter had just become betrothed to Lord Robert, she threw herself into each mission of mercy with gusto until she was enticed by the next new cause. Clearly the excitements of saving the glittering ladies of the night who frequented Jimmy's, Piccadilly's famous café, had palled—perhaps because, so he had been told, on the last occasion an eminent member of the government had mistaken the reason for her presence. So now she had turned to Temperance.

"We still await the arrival from Italy of our artiste," Lady Cecilia trilled, "the great concert diva Madame Isabel Mantini. Her son, it is well known, was lost to the demon liquor, and this little soirée is given in the cause of the killer—*drink*."

Temperance? A terrible suspicion entered Auguste's mind and refused to take its departure. Why, oh why, had he accepted what had seemed the honor of preparing this banquet when he could have been in his usual kitchen at the Galaxy? Why, oh why, had he not been warned? Suppose the "killer drink" were to be banished from the buffet? Surely his exquisite supper should be sacrosanct from such a catastrophe, and if checks for the Bands of Hope were to flow with the ease of a Cahors into a coq au vin, wine would be essential.

"The Muses themselves drank nectar," Lady Cecilia boomed gaily. "We shall follow their example."

Auguste's worst fears threatened to come true. No wonder his proposed menu had deprived the gathering of such delights as his Homard Didier, in which the demon brandy played a starring role. What was a Salade Gabrielle d'Estrées without its delicate truffles, chicken and asparagus being complemented by a mellow white wine, or Rouen duckling without a Châteauneuf du Pape?

"Tonight," Lady Cecilia continued, oblivious to her chef's distress, "we shall sample no less than five delectable nectars created by the truly inspirational hand of my butler Mr. Alfred Maple, who has himself seen the light and is to be one of our speakers this evening. Our honored guest Lord Robert Blakeham and our speakers shall have the privilege of tasting them first." She beamed beneficently at her audience.

Why did they not rise up in instant protest? Auguste fumed. And since Lady Cecilia had insisted on all her servants' presence in the audience (discreetly hidden at the back), he had to put up with listening to Alfred Maple—that lumbering black presence who had made his day a misery, by remaining locked in his butler's pantry, to which Auguste had been forced to demand entrance when necessary to request essential ingredients. With some pleasure, Auguste recalled the liberal quantity of Madeira he had added to the pheasant casserole as an innocent and inspired afterthought.

There had been no instant rapport between himself and Mr. Maple, and now Auguste realized why. A butler should have a proper respect for the products of the grape. Moreover he had a distinct impression he had met the gentleman before, though he could not quite place him. The hunched shoulders, the bowed head, and the black coat had reminded Auguste of a vulture, and there was no such thing as a reformed vulture.

"As we are still without Madame Mantini," Lady Cecilia beamed, "my dear daughter, Lord Robert, and I," pause for modesty, "will now read a scene from the celebrated Temperance drama: *Ten Nights in a Bar-room*. My daughter will play Little Mary, Lord Robert the evil landlord Simon Slade, and myself the drunkard Joe Morgan. 'Farewell, *friend* Slade!' " With this foretaste of delights to come, Lady Cecilia tripped gaily to her guest in the front row in order to conduct him to the platform and glory.

She was unable to do so, for he was forestalled by the late arrival of the famous artiste. Little Mary's fervent prayers were postponed (rather to Auguste's regret) as the main doors were flung open. A striking and amply proportioned Madame Isabel Mantini, clad in bright red velvet, swept up to the platform with her accompanist, where she bowed to the gathering before her. "Pray do forgive me, Lady Cecilia, Lord Robert, ladies and gentlemen. The high seas delayed our passage."

Lady Cecilia gushed her welcome, clinging firmly to Lord Robert's arm (lest he attempt escape, Auguste thought uncharitably), having sat down once more at his side. "And which songs of the path to light are we to have the pleasure of hearing you sing for us tonight, Madame Mantini?" she cried.

"Let the choice be yours, dear Lady Cecilia." Madame Mantini's hand was thrown across a bosom well able to support it.

"What could delight us more than to begin our evening with that melancholy warning to all who squander life, 'Come Home, Father'?"

A great deal, in Auguste's opinion, as the full mellow voice of Madame Mantini soared out plaintively:

"Father, dear Father, come home with me now..."
Auguste had heard Little Mary's song many times
and his interest in brother Benny's departure from
this world with the angels of light was extremely limited. At the Galaxy he could have been preparing the
hollandaise for the asparagus, waiting for that delightful and glittering moment when the chorus girls
in their bright dinner gowns and jewels would arrive
with their masher escorts.

Mr. Alfred Maple, the first speaker, did not invite
comparison with the lovely ladies whom he had so
foolishly abandoned for the evening. Nor did any of
the three other speakers sitting to one side on the
platform. One at least looked interesting, a woman
in middle years, gaudily dressed in bright yellow silk
which did nothing to flatter the layers of paint on her
haggard face, which looked pale with shock as
though in surprise at finding herself in such a position of prominence. The other two were more con-
ventional, a tall lean man with a hawklike gaze and
a shorter rounder gentleman with an amiable somewhat lost expression as though he'd wandered in
here in mistake for the temple of the magic arts of
Messrs. Maskelyne and Devant.

Fulfilling Auguste's worst suspicions, Maple had
brought to the stage a silver salver bearing five labeled glasses, which he had placed lovingly on an
isolated table at the back so that their full rainbow-
colored magnificence might be contemplated by the
audience.

Their creator now cast his eyes to heaven, and began the moving story of his life:

"A sinner was I..."

Now Auguste remembered where he had seen that
face before. Inspector Rose of the Yard had kindly
shown him round Scotland Yard's Convict Supervi-
sion Office, with its huge collection of photographs

of habitual criminals. One of those faces, though less
well shaven than the virtuous Uriah Heep who stood
before them now, was undoubtedly Alfred Maple.
Only then he had rejoiced in the name of Slasher Joe.

After relating how he had been saved from a Lime-
house den of unspeakable vice, Slasher turned toward the fruits of his endeavors. Something that
might have been a blush came to the proud man's
face: "I call 'em Dazzle, Jollity, Fun, Froth, and
Smile."

His reputation was in ruins! Auguste was aghast.
He might even be thought to be lending his name to
such an outrage to the civilized diner. Never would
he disbelieve tea leaves again. How could he serve a
banquet of exquisite gourmet food accompanied by
a drink called Smile? He fidgeted, longing to ask the
footman next to him whether he had seen any signs
of decanters respectably filled with red wine being
transported into the supper room behind them. Even
Lady Cecilia must have some compassionate feelings
for her guests.

"Now perhaps 'Rocked in the Cradle of the Deep,'
dear Madame Mantini," Lady Cecilia cooed, as at her
side Lord Robert led the applause for Slasher's stirring words, and the singer dutifully echoed her
words as the first line of the noble song rang out.

The voice was magnificent, and yet how could he
enjoy it with the threat of disaster ahead? Auguste's
attention fled back to the plight of his turbot, denied
its due homage of a delicate white wine accompani-
ment, until his interest was caught by the next
speaker, who was introduced by Lady Cecilia as
"poor dear Jenny." To his surprise the voice was low
and educated, although her attire left poor dear
Jenny's present occupation in little doubt.

"The demon drink drove me to my present state,"
she faltered. She kept her gaze fixed firmly on the

back wall, Auguste noticed, as though she could not bear to look at the audience. "In the unhappiness of my marriage I met a man who forced vile liquor upon me, until I brought disgrace on the noble name I bore. Cast out, I took work at an illegal gaming establishment for baccarat but a short distance from this very house."

For the last few words, she suddenly raised her voice, almost in accusation. Or was he imagining it? Auguste wondered. Certainly there seemed something melodramatic about this parade, he decided, almost regretting they had been deprived of *Ten Nights in a Bar-room*—especially when Lady Cecilia announced that as the next speaker was American it was applicable to ask Madame Mantini to sing perhaps the most tender of all Temperance ballads.

"On a dark and stormy night a little girl clad only in rags," she informed her rapt audience, "shivered outside the home of the President. Asked why she did not go home, this poor child replied: 'I have no home, Father's a Drunkard and Mother is Dead.' Tonight we are privileged to have Madame Mantini sing Bessie's song for us."

She sank down beside Lord Robert, overwhelmed with the sadness of her story. *"Out in the gloomy night . . . "* From Madame Mantini's opening words to the very last *"God pity Bessie, a Drunkard's lone child,"* her hostess punctuated the words with sighs of audible and deep emotion.

Auguste thoroughly enjoyed this impromptu duet, despite his grievance, and began to look forward to the next speaker, the short, rounded gentleman with the amiable expression

"My name's Horace Pennyfather," he beamed at his audience, "and I'm a plain-speaking man. I'm not Temperance. I like my glass of whiskey. So why am I here? Trade!" Auguste warmed to him even more, as a hiss of shock ran round the room at the unmentionable word in polite society. Not whiskey, but trade. Horace Pennyfather seemed unaware of his solecism. Indeed he spoke with pride. "Now I manufacture Pilgrim's Cherry Shrub, a Temperance drink if ever there was one. Tastes like alcohol but not a drop in it. Based on cherries, as good as grew on George Washington's tree. It's made me a million in America but you won't have heard of it here because someone," he paused, looking straight at his audience, his voice heavy with meaning, "has been determined to stop its distribution. I'm a persistent fellow though; I believe in Pilgrim's Cherry Shrub, and want you to have the chance of tasting it too. I'm providing five thousand bottles of it, free, here tonight, and you're welcome to take as many as you like home with you."

"You're too kind, Mr. Pennyfather," Lady Cecilia gushed, as Auguste's bonhomie toward this speaker promptly vanished. Pennyfather bowed and returned to his seat. "And now, Madame Mantini, pray give us that stirring exhortation to those who are drowning in a sea of evil liquor, 'Throw out the Life-Line.' "

To Auguste's grim delight, Maple lumbered to his feet, stood behind the singer, clapped a sou'wester on his head, drew himself up, and displayed a small model of a lifeboat which he held out on one hand. "*Throw out the life-line . . .* " Madame Mantini began, as Maple obediently threw a miniature lifebuoy on a string from his model in case anyone missed the point. Unfortunately it hit Jenny by mistake, bringing an unscheduled few notes. Madame Mantini then exhorted the audience to join in the choruses, with all the dedication of one not long rescued from the terrors of a cross-Channel steamer.

The last speaker, he of the hawklike stare, proved to be Ernest Higman, the successful brewer. Unlike

Pennyfather he believed in glaring, not beaming. "I daresay you think it strange to see me at a Temperance meeting. The reason's simple. If you can convince me that Dazzle and Smile are as commercial as beer, I'll begin producing them, *and* I'll do my best to distribute your Pilgrim's Cherry Shrub for you, Mr. Pennyfather. With the government set on making life difficult for the publican, I need to think of the future." There was belligerence in his voice—reasonable enough, Auguste supposed, since he was on presumably hostile ground.

Auguste regretted that Lord Robert was not to speak, for he had listened to one of his crusades against drink, and though naturally he could not agree with his views, he knew he was an impressive and passionate speaker. Indeed, in Auguste's opinion, Lord Robert was almost too impassioned, for his own reaction had been to rush away and admire the wonders of a Château Margaux at the earliest opportunity.

Disaster, he realized, was growing perilously close as he heard Lady Cecilia say: "For your last song, pray give us 'Temperance Bells.' What better to conclude this part of our entertainment?"

Perhaps with the thought of her coming supper, Madame Mantini threw herself into her task with renewed gusto: *"Hark the Temperance Bells are ringing."* For Auguste, facing the probable prospect of supper with Fun and Froth, they seemed to be tolling a death knell.

When the Bells ceased, Lady Cecilia, after coos of thanks to Madame Mantini, turned to her neighbor: "If I might ask you, dear Lord Robert," she boomed for the edification of her audience, "to join our speakers on the platform, Madame will hand round our delicious drinks, one to each of you. And of course

all our lucky guests here this evening will have the
opportunity of tasting them at supper."

Auguste's last hope that his buffet might be spared
vanished. With hate in his heart, he watched Slasher
Joe walk to the back of the platform, pick up the silver salver with the five glasses, each bearing a label
with its name, and bring it to Madame Mantini's side.

Her hand hovered. "Now which of these appealing
drinks shall I give you, Lord Robert? I think—" The
hand grasped the stem of the glass containing a
browny-orange concoction—"Froth!"

Madame Mantini handed it to Lord Robert, who
regarded it with polite enthusiasm, as Lady Cecilia
consulted her list from the front row. "Ah yes, a most
delightful mixture of toast and boiled water, very
suitable for our poorer Band of Hope members, fla-
vored with cinnamon, sugar, and I believe—yes, a
hint of fresh orange."

Lord Robert stared into his glass without enthusiasm, as the next libation was offered to the small circle.

"Dazzle," intoned Madame Mantini, clutching the
stem of a glass looking to Auguste uncommonly like
a glass of milk with brown and yellow spots, and
handing it to Horace Pennyfather.

"Egg, milk, rosewater, and nutmeg," Lady Cecilia
cried, as though she would dearly love to storm the
platform, snatch the glass from his hand, and drink
it to the very dregs herself. She didn't, Auguste noticed.

"Fun for you, Mr. Higman." Madame Mantini
handed an evil-looking yellow mixture to the eminent brewer.

"And who would not have fun with this cocktail
of lemonade, sugar, and a hint of curry powder?"
Lady Cecilia trilled.

He for one, Auguste shuddered. *Curry* powder?

"And for poor little Jenny, Jollity!" Then no doubt remembering how Jenny's was achieved, Madame Mantini hastily held up the remaining glass, without waiting for Lady Cecilia's intervention. "And for myself, Smile." Smile was pink, *very* pink.

"Scalded strawberries, with a soupçon of cucumber purée." A soupçon of red wine might make it more palatable in Auguste's unsought opinion.

Balked of one of her great moments, Lady Cecilia's voice dropped to suitably grave and dramatic tones: "And now pray toast our great cause, the conquest of evil."

Lord Robert raised the glass of browny-orange liquid to his mouth, drained it, and adopted an expression of rapture . . .

"Cyanide most probably, according to the doctor." Inspector Egbert Rose joined the group at the back of the ballroom who were surreptitiously glancing toward the police constables in the process of moving Lord Robert's body. "And probably only in the glass, since the decanter from which it was poured in the pantry doesn't smell of it. So, Mr. Didier," he looked toward Auguste, "what I'd like you to tell me is who at this party could have poisoned that drink."

"Soirée, Inspector Rose, not party," Lady Cecilia moaned faintly, determined to maintain the last vestiges of civilized life.

Most of the audience had now been allowed to leave, some bewailing the lack of supper, others only too glad to retreat to their clubs where they could get a decent glass of claret and spread the news.

"No one on the platform could have added anything to Lord Robert's or anyone else's drink, Inspector," Auguste replied, "for we would all have observed it. Just as we would have noticed if Madame Mantini had added anything, as she handed the glass to Lord Robert."

The evident truth yawned before them. Inspector Rose voiced it. "Where did you pour out those drinks, Mr. Maple?" Auguste longed to whisper, "Slasher Joe" to the inspector.

The butler was indignant. "I poured 'em out in my pantry and it was locked." There was a pause, while Slasher contemplated the effect of this statement, then burst out even more indignantly: "Why should I want to murder the bloke? He's against the demon drink just like me. Anyway," his eye gleamed as he realized how little he liked Frenchie chefs, "*you* came into the pantry. Popping in and out you were, like a cork in an old lady's gin flask."

"I am a stranger here," Auguste protested.

"Yes," said Slasher Joe lovingly. "Who knows what you got against Lord Robert?"

"I went into the pantry too," said Lady Cecilia, to Auguste's relief, since it deflected both Slasher's and Inspector Rose's attention from him. "I had to compose my list of drinks and ingredients. Such exciting ingredients," she added mournfully, "but I would hardly wish to kill my future son-in-law. And the disgrace, oh, the disgrace."

"Neither Lady Cecilia nor Maple nor I," Auguste stated firmly, "could possibly tell which glass would be handed to Lord Robert. And the same applies to Mr. Higman, Mr. Pennyfather, and—er—Jenny. Madame Mantini alone chose the glass to hand to Lord Robert."

Madame Mantini grew very pale, steadying herself on the arm of her accompanist. The bosom swelled. "Is this man suggesting I deliberately chose to give Lord Robert a poisoned drink?" She ignored Auguste and addressed herself indignantly to Inspector Rose.

"How could I have known which glass was poisoned?"

"Madame Mantini is right," Auguste agreed hastily. "She came straight from the boat train to the platform, and the glasses were brought onto the stage by Slash—Mr. Maple after her first song. She did not go near them. Nor did the others on the stage."

"Too right," agreed Horace Pennyfather, giving Auguste a nod of approval.

"I certainly didn't." Jenny's face was white.

"Nor I," barked Ernest Higman. "I'm not in the habit of carrying cyanide around with me. Nor, in case you're interested, do I make a habit of creeping into my hostess's butler's pantry."

"Not beyond a bribe are you, Slasher?" Rose asked him cheerily, to Auguste's amusement. "Someone ask you to drop something in a glass, did they?"

Mr. Alfred Maple was hurt. "Inspector, throw a lifeline to a repentant sinner. I wouldn't take a bribe even if the Archbishop of Canterbury were to plead with me. And murder, I ask you. *Me*?"

Rose raised his eyebrows, but only said:

"So what it boils down to is this: no one on the platform or in the pantry would have poisoned the drink because they didn't know which glass Madame Mantini would offer to Lord Robert, and Madame Mantini can't have poisoned it or Lord Robert himself because they would have been seen. In short, no one did it."

"So it appears," Auguste murmured unhappily.

Rose sighed. "A pretty pickle, Mr. Auguste, like that tasty pickle of pork I recall you serving one day at the Galaxy."

"*Petit salé*, Inspector. Perhaps, however, the ingredients of your problem can be rearranged."

"You're the cook."

"Suppose you investigate *why* Lord Robert was murdered?"

"How can there have been cause to murder a man so good?" Lady Cecilia wailed.

"The only apparent motive," Auguste continued doggedly, "is that of Mr. Higman, who is heavily reliant upon public house trade. For all your brave words, Mr. Higman, if Lord Robert had his way, your profits would have plummeted."

Ernest Higman glared, then changed his mind and laughed. "I'm afraid, Mr. Whoever You Are, you're wrong. I'd every reason to want him alive. So far from wanting to banish drink, it's my belief Lord Robert was actually in my camp. I began to notice that every time he took his crusade to factories in one town or another, my profits went up. At first I thought it coincidence, but I concluded his crusade was cleverly designed to encourage men to drink more, not less."

"Inspector, I believe Mr. Higman may be right," Auguste exclaimed, remembering his own reaction when he heard Lord Robert speak.

"This is slander!" cried Lady Cecilia.

"I'm not so sure it is." Horace Pennyfather had been thinking. "I've had a suspicion for some time it could have been Blakeham behind the blocking of my Pilgrim's Cherry Shrub."

"Nonsense, Mr. Pennyfather," Lady Cecilia said in dogged defense. "You dishonor the name of one of the great statesmen of England."

"Yes," Jenny chimed in quietly. "The name of Robert Blakeham, perhaps. But I knew him under another name. I recognized him immediately this evening. Have you never heard of Arthur Noir, the puppetmaster of half of the vice of London, from opium and back-street drinking dens to the apparently highly respectable houses that mask illegal gambling—including the one for which I worked? He was the man who ruined me."

"Nonsense, Jenny dear," Lady Cecilia repeated feebly. "I cannot believe that."

"I can," growled Slasher. "I knew Mr. Noir— once," he added vaguely. "Thought his lordship looked familiar first time I saw him here. The lady's right. I did hear," he said carefully, "as there was two organizations, one run by Noir, the other by White."

"And you worked for White?" Auguste asked innocently.

Slasher Joe cast him a look that made him glad he was standing next to Inspector Rose.

"This gets us no further." Horace Pennyfather voiced Auguste's own thoughts. "Even if all of us had a motive, none of us could have done it."

"Inspector," Auguste suggested, aware that his brain needed space to think, like a jelly to set, "in the adjacent room a most excellent supper lies fully prepared. Could I not serve it to these ladies and gentlemen? Your Sergeant Stitch could remain with us there, while you continue your work uninterrupted here."

Rose regarded him reflectively for a moment, then grunted: "I've a better idea. Stitch can stay here. I'll come with you."

"If I might suggest, Lady Cecilia, a few bottles of claret from your cellar and perhaps some Sancerre might have excellent *restorative* powers. Unfortunately the police would not allow us to drink Mr. Maple's most interesting creations." Auguste used his best endeavors to sound as though the matter were of little concern to him.

It was noticeable, however, that the faces of all the guests immediately acquired a look of great interest. Lady Cecilia looked doubtful.

"For medicinal purposes after shock, of course," Auguste added.

"Of course." She brightened up immediately, and a constable was dispatched with Slasher Joe to the cellar.

"You don't think it might appear a little too *jovial*?" she wavered anxiously as they disappeared through the door.

"The proper appreciation of food is a serious matter," Auguste reassured her, as he happily glided into his accustomed place behind the serving tables.

Half an hour later, Auguste looked round the tables with weary satisfaction. They were splendidly ravished. Eager diners had trilled the perfections of the *cailles en Belle-vue*, and quacked appreciation of the *mousse de canard*; they had sung the wonders of his *paté d'alouettes*, the *Homard à la Chevrenne* had vanished, the salmon *à la Norvégienne* had swum, and the *ballotines de pigeons* flown, swiftly followed by *salades composées*, *éclairs*, *compôtes de fruits*, and *bavarois*. Not to mention countless bottles of the *true* nectar of the gods.

Disaster had been mitigated. The ending of a life by such a means was terrible, however unpleasant the victim, yet only one of those now present had not deserved the best he, Auguste Didier, could offer in the way of consolation for their shock. The only problem now remaining was: which one?

"This claret is as good as Pilgrim's Cherry Shrub," Horace Pennyfather declared, refilling his glass approvingly. "The food isn't bad either. Despite what's happened, I shall be rocking in the cradle of the deep darned well tonight." He slapped Auguste on the back. "What's this?" He stuck a fork into an unrecognized object on his plate.

Auguste shuddered at such lack of appreciation. "That is a slice of truffle of Périgord."

Even as he was saying it, he had a sudden memory of Madame Mantini's spirited rendering of the song to which Mr. Pennyfather had referred—and the jelly in his head at last began to set.

"Inspector," he said, trying not to be overheard, but in vain since the guests showed a mysterious reluctance to be separated from the claret and food. "About Madame Mantini's second song—"

Rose sighed. "Stitch checked. She was on that boat train all right."

"Yes, but 'Rocked in the Cradle of the Deep' is not a Temperance song."

Rose shrugged, and Auguste subsided. The point could hardly be of importance. "Foie gras. Very rich," he muttered in vengeance as Rose helped himself to a large portion.

"Quite like a party, isn't it?" Rose looked round at the gathering. "Only needs a magician and Punch and Judy."

A crazy idea occurred to Auguste. Ingredients of the puzzle swirling around in his mind began to come together. "Do you have a pencil and paper, Inspector?" he asked eagerly.

Rose regarded him sourly. "I'm not on the beat now. Ask Stitch if you want to play Consequences."

"No." Excitement seized him. "That's not it." Auguste could not wait for a pencil. He looked round wildly for something in which to express himself. There was only one possibility—and it was worth the terrible sacrifice. He seized a knife and spoon and began to write letters on the spotless damask tablecloth in black clumps of his beloved Provençal olive paté.

"Well?" Rose looked blankly at his efforts: *CRFTT*.

"I was wrong." Auguste felt all the more foolish for having been so sure he had the answer. Then a further idea struck him, and more hesitantly now he asked humbly: "Inspector, could you please ask Sergeant Stitch for the accompanist's music?"

Stitch, complaining loudly when the constable told him it was for the Frenchie, marched in from the ballroom and ostentatiously placed the music in front of Rose. Auguste rushed to leaf through the pages. "Ha!" he cried in delight—and relief. "*Now* I can tell you how this crime was committed."

"In food?" Rose was not easily impressed. "Why not try mayonnaise-this time?"

Auguste ignored the sally; indeed, intent on his theory, he did not notice it. "It is obvious who committed the crime once the importance of the impossible is given due weight. Why *had* the crime to be impossible? Because blame must not be attached to any one person."

"You going to tell me they were all in it together?" Rose asked, unimpressed.

"No, but consider a duet."

"Go on." Reluctantly Rose showed some interest.

"Madame Mantini could not have added poison, but it is not impossible that someone else added it, or bribed Maple to do so, and then intimated to Madame Mantini which glass it was in."

"This is an outrage," the singer cried faintly.

"That could only be Maple, you, Mr. Didier, or Lady Cecilia," Rose pointed out. "And you and Lady Cecilia weren't in a position to tell Madame Mantini anything. You were both in the audience." He looked round the group. "By golly, the others could have whispered it somehow: Maple, Pennyfather, Higman, or Jenny. And my money's on Slasher Joe. You worked not for Mr. White but for this Arthur Noir, didn't you, Slasher? This sweet duet was between you and Madame Mantini."

"I'm an honest man now," Slasher howled virtuously, alarmed. "I'm glad the macer's dead, but you can't prove I had anything to do with it."

"And you, Madame," Rose addressed the singer, "you had good reason to want Noir dead too, isn't that so?"

"I did," she replied unhesitatingly. "My son was his victim, but I fail to see how I could have been implicated. Had the name of the poisoned drink been whispered to me, others in the circle would have heard."

"Inspector," Auguste was unable to suppress it any longer, when Rose paused nonplussed, "do you know the party game of Magic Writing where taps on the floor from a walking stick spell out the letters of the answer?"

"There's no magic wand around here," Rose said impatiently.

"No, but in this duet of death, Madame Mantini sang five songs in which the initial letters of the first lines spell—" Auguste waved his hand to the table-cloth where he had now rearranged the olive paté into *FROTH*.

"Hell and Tommy." Rose stared at it in disbelief. Then conviction grew. "I'll never say another word about French food. Who was it then?"

"Only the lady who chose the songs and whose daughter was about to marry that most ignoble peer, could have shared in this duet. After all, Lady Cecilia's soirée, as she herself told us earlier, was given in the cause of the killer drink."

Amy Myers, a resident of Kent in England, writes delectable mysteries with Victorian chef Auguste Didier, who

appears most recently in Murder Makes an Entree *and* Murder With Majesty. *In this story, more deviltry exists outside of "Demon Rum" when a lord drops dead in front of Didier at a Temperance meeting.*

Mystery Man

Jennifer Rowe

In April Street, Annandale, people generally kept to themselves. Violent death, however, brings with it a release from social pressures. On the day the police came to see about the murder in number 18, the neighbors gathered. And Ena McGillicuddy, seventy-nine, plumber's widow, the street's oldest inhabitant, was in her element. Because it was she who had discovered the man lying four days dead in the kitchen.

Verity Birdwood, who also lived in April Street, was with Mrs. McGillicuddy when the crisis occurred. So she, too, could have basked in the limelight if she wished. But Birdie, as her friends called her, wasn't keen on limelight. In the limelight, one became dazzled. Birdie preferred to see clearly. Especially on this occasion, when the shadows surrounding the death in number 18 seemed to her to hold such mystery.

April Street was a narrow by-way in Sydney's inner city. It was closely lined on both sides by small

175

single-storied terrace houses, yet it had little sense of community. This quite suited Birdie. Her office was at home, and in her line of work—private investigation and research—an atmosphere of discretion was an asset. But the paradox had interested her. Until she realized it wasn't a paradox at all.

Over the last thirty years, the street had been gentrified. One by one, the old residents died, or moved away. Young, childless professionals wanting to live near the city moved in. And as a result April Street was transformed, in more ways than one.

Inner-city life brought with it enormous satisfactions—not least that an inner-city address was now so fashionable. But modern plumbing, a state-of-the-art kitchen, an attic conversion to create a third bedroom with harbor glimpses (if you stood on your toes) notwithstanding, a terrace house was, and always would be, a terrace house. And if real personal space could not be increased, a sense of it had to be created for those raised in now-despised, leafier suburbs.

Living cheek by jowl, their cute and carefully renovated workers' cottages strung together like paper dolls, the present inhabitants of April Street instinctively kept their eyes averted from their neighbors.

There were few backyard chats over side fences now that the chattering classes had moved in. Pleasant greetings, as well-groomed people emerged together from their front doors to go to work, civilized words as they set their car alarms in the street at night, were of course expected. But out the back, they were not. If, watering pot plants outside one's own back door at seven A.M., one saw one's neighbor wandering, slippers flapping, to her clothesline, one instantly assumed a protective cloak of invisibility, and an air of blindness and deafness. It was an unconscious community safety measure, born out of an educated awareness that rats in uncomfortably crowded quarters tend to start eating one another.

"The street's got no heart, these days, love," Mrs. McGillicuddy was wont to say to Birdie, when they met at the corner store. Mrs. McGillicuddy lived in number 22, across the road from Birdie in 21, and had an advertising project manager on one side of her, and a pair of computer programmers on the other. She was prepared to be tolerant of her neighbors' youth, money, music, clothes, and sexual preferences, but the fact that they politely rebuffed her every attempt at conversation and offer of help irked her.

Birdie had no need to snub Mrs. McGillicuddy for fear of being hailed over the side fence on a constant basis. And, actually, she liked the feisty old woman, and enjoyed their chats walking home from the corner store. They only met on weekdays, anyway, because punctually at six-thirty every Friday night, Mrs. McGillicuddy was collected and borne away for the weekend by one of her five married children.

Like a man who says he reads *Playboy* for the articles, Birdie told herself that it was Mrs. McGillicuddy's April Street reminiscences she found fascinating.

"In my day none of us had two pennies to rub together," Mrs. McGillicuddy would say, as they reached her house, and Birdie prepared to cross the road to her own. "But everyone was in the same boat. Everyone knew everyone else's troubles, and there wasn't one who wouldn't give you a hand, or the shirt off his back if you needed it. Well . . ." (She'd always stop and correct herself here.) ". . . a few wouldn't. But you knew who *they* were."

She'd open number 22's iron gate, painted blue to match the window frames and door of the otherwise white house, and her mouth would droop as she

eyed the tastefully barred windows of number 20
(cream-and-heritage-green), and the ball-on-a-stick
kumquat in a pot chained to the front porch of number 24 (cream-and-heritage-burgundy).

"Those days are gone," she'd sigh.

A good thing, too, Birdie would think. She didn't
want to live in her neighbors' pockets. Or for that
matter to do without a phone, a washing machine, a
refrigerator, or an inside lavatory. But she was sorry
for Mrs. McGillicuddy, whose "day" had passed,
who had lost to time not only her husband and
friends, but a feeling of familiarity with, and command of, the world in which she lived.

The reminiscences *were* interesting. But when
Birdie was feeling particularly honest, she admitted
to herself, with a little guilt, that she also enjoyed
Mrs. McGillicuddy's other conversational gambit—
gossip.

Mrs. McGillicuddy's intense interest in her fellow
creatures was undimmed by age. She no longer knew
everyone in her street by name. But this didn't stop
her from talking about them. She simply used nick-
names of her own invention. She discussed the do-
ings of "Bambi," the young woman with big eyes
and long slim legs who graced number 17. She was
riveted by "Bandy" and "Coot," the so-cool couple
in number 20. She jeered at "Poll," the woman in 24
with the bleached-white crest of hair. Sighing, she
hoped "Whiskers," number 18's single middle-aged
man, the newest April Street resident, was looking
after himself properly. Men, she assured Birdie, normally didn't. They lived on baked beans, sardines,
bread, and beer if you let them.

Mrs. McGillicuddy had been keeping a close eye
on "Whiskers" ever since his arrival two months before.

"He must be that lonely," she said. "He never gets

a visitor. He's only got that black kitten for company—and it's just a stray from the back lane."

The fact was, "Whiskers" was a real thorn in Mrs.
McGillicuddy's side. He went out at night, but was
home all day. Mrs. McGillicuddy knew (because she
unashamedly peeped through his gappy back fence
from the lane that ran behind their houses) that he
spent most of his time out in his backyard, dozing in
an old cane chair, reading the newspaper, smoking
roll-your-own cigarettes, drinking tea and beer, and
fixing up old furniture.

But despite his availability, she hadn't managed to
exchange a word with him. Her resultant pique had
made her curiosity even more intense.

Birdie's interest was aroused as well. Like Mrs.
McGillicuddy, Whiskers was an anomaly in present-
day April Street. With his tartan shirt, his cigarettes
and droopy moustache, he looked like a ghost from
the street as it had been long ago.

But he wasn't. He'd only taken the lease of number
18 a couple of months back. Birdie couldn't quite understand why he had.

The house was unrenovated, and had been rented
to a succession of tenants for years. ("Since poor Ivy
Sneedway passed on," Mrs. McGillicuddy said, ex-
plaining. "The family's still fighting about who gets
what.") It had no kumquat in a pot. Just a frangipani
tree that hung over the rusty fence, carpeting the
footpath with fragrant white flowers every summer.
It had no heritage colors, its cracked cement render
bearing only the faintest memory of its last coat of
apricot-pink. But Birdie knew that despite its shabbiness, the house would carry a high rent. And
Whiskers didn't look well off.

"Poor thing's a migrant, you know," said Mrs.
McGillicuddy. "Can't speak a word of English. If you
try to say hello he just nods and backs off."

"He might just be deaf," protested Birdie. "Or shy."

"Pigs!" snorted Mrs. McGillicuddy rudely, blue eyes snapping. "He's Italian, or Greek or something. You can tell by the moustache."

Late each weekday afternoon, Whiskers slouched off down April Street in the same tartan shirt and baggy trousers in which he spent his days, an old canvas knapsack slung over his shoulder, his old checked cap on his head. The sun glinted on his gold wire-framed glasses, and behind the glasses his gray eyes dreamed. A skinny cigarette hung between his lips, its glowing tip wagging perilously close to his drooping pepper-and-salt moustache. The next morning he'd come slouching back, his footsteps quickening as he reached his gate, as though he was glad to be home.

Mrs. McGillicuddy thought he was a night watchman somewhere, though Birdie thought this unlikely. Whiskers didn't look like security guard material to her.

"You'd be surprised," Mrs. McGillicuddy retorted, when Birdie voiced this opinion. "Some companies'll hire anyone, as long as they're cheap."

Birdie had no answer for that. Instead, she murmured, "He looks quite happy, Mrs. McGillicuddy. It's probably best to leave him alone."

"Don't you worry, I'm not one to impose myself on anybody," the old woman snapped back with sublime disregard for the truth. "I'm finished bothering with him. He can stew in his own juice! Serve him right if he ends up starving to death, or the Mafia gets him."

Birdie knew it was useless to argue further about Whiskers's origins, or his possible fate. She therefore simply congratulated Mrs. McGillicuddy on her resolve.

She didn't think it would last, but soon it seemed she'd been wrong. The next walk back from the corner store was devoted to that morning's attempt by Bambi's German shepherd, Barney, either to consume or to mate with the chihuahua from number 9. Barney's intentions were unclear, but the results of his aggression were spectacular.

Whiskers wasn't mentioned at all.

Work was scant for Birdie around this time. She'd advertised in the local paper, but the results had been disappointing. A snooty-sounding woman called Mrs. Cecily Aronsten called, wanting Birdie to follow her retired husband. She suspected him of philandering while she was at work because he'd started using breath mints and looking happy. Birdie politely advised the lady to do the job herself. A soft-voiced man called Joe rang, inviting Birdie to meet him by the canal, any night that suited her. She declined. Then Philomena Briggs, a sweetly blonde teenage girl Birdie was hired to trace, arrived home with a shaved head, three nose rings, and a tattoo.

At a loose end, Birdie became perversely fixated on the mystery of Whiskers. Like a silly song it kept chanting unwanted in her head, till late one Friday afternoon she found herself following him at a discreet distance as he plodded gently away from his house, down April Street, and past the corner store.

Having crossed Gallantry Parade, into which April Street ran, he turned left and began slouching up the hill. Birdie had seen him do this before. She'd always assumed he was heading for the main road, about ten minutes' walk away. But she'd never confirmed this theory.

Almost against her will, she began climbing the Gallantry Parade hill herself, keeping an eye on Whiskers toiling up the other side of the road and not too far ahead.

"I'm going to HomeWork to get a door mat," she told herself, referring to the three-story hardware store complex ("Everything for the home-lover") that took up the corner of Gallantry Parade and the main road.

She held on to the thought firmly, but it made her feel only slightly less foolish. And it didn't help her at all when she saw Whiskers himself slow down at HomeWork, then disappear inside.

Gritting her teeth, she followed him.

The store was quite crowded. On entry, Birdie skirted a large stack of door mats covered with pictures of cozy houses and hearts, and looked around for Whiskers's tartan shirt.

There it was, beginning to glide in company up the escalator toward the first floor. Birdie lunged forward in pursuit, and collided with someone darting from concealment behind a case of wicked-looking drills.

Birdie's glasses were knocked askew. Hands scrabbled at her for support. Half-blind, locked in a lurching embrace with a furious partner, she stumbled against a nearby table. A pyramid of car-washing kits ("Bonus sponges! Crazy price!"), crashed to the floor.

Birdie disentangled herself and pushed her glasses back onto her nose. As the world came back into focus she saw to her astonishment that the person who had been clutching her so feverishly was Mrs. McGillicuddy.

"Look what you've done! We've lost him!" the old woman screeched, stamping with rage. Beneath her feet, tubes of car wash exploded with tiny pops, and bright green liquid oozed gently out, transforming the pink bonus sponges into hideous lumps of solid slime.

"Stand still, Mrs. McGillicuddy," said Birdie evenly. Her ears were ringing, but she knew someone had to stay in control of this situation.

Besides, a man in bright red overalls marked HomeWork was bearing down on them.

Things were strained between Birdie and Mrs. McGillicuddy on the way home. Mrs. McGillicuddy didn't believe that Birdie had gone to HomeWork to buy a door mat, and she was irritated because she'd given herself away before she could think of a similar story.

"So I followed him. Not a crime, is it?"

Birdie said nothing.

"You did the same thing," Mrs. McGillicuddy muttered.

"You didn't follow him," Birdie accused, changing the subject. "I would have seen you. You were waiting for him in there."

Mrs. McGillicuddy took refuge in defiance. "That's because I saw him go in there yesterday! And the day before, if you want to know. He goes in there every blinking afternoon, and he doesn't come out. He works there. Doing what, I don't know. Today I would've found out. Except for you."

"Oh." Birdie found this vaguely disappointing. If Whiskers was employed at HomeWork, there was no mystery as to why he lived in April Street. The extra he spent on rent would be offset by the savings in fares.

She glanced at Mrs. McGillicuddy, and saw with a pang that the old woman was limping.

"Are you all right, Mrs. Mac?" she murmured.

"As right as I'll ever be till I'm dead," Mrs. McGillicuddy retorted smartly. "Don't you worry. I'm going to my Jan's tonight. She'll look after me."

Birdie felt rebuffed. As, of course, Mrs. McGillicuddy fully intended she should.

*　　*　　*

That night, Birdie slept badly, beset by weird dreams. She woke with a headache and the prospect of a dreary weekend ahead. As well, a niggling need to know the absolute truth about Whiskers, however banal, was tickling at her brain.

Her father rang at midday, asking her if she wanted to come over to his place, go out on his boat the following morning. She thanked him but declined. An old school friend rang at two to ask her to dinner. She declined that, too. She was in the grip of a general feeling of apathy from which she didn't seem able to rouse herself.

The afternoon crawled by. She considered going up to HomeWork to make inquiries about Whiskers. But after yesterday she didn't really feel she'd be welcome in the store. Finally she decided to give up on life, and went back to bed.

When she woke, it was dark. Her headache was worse. She took a couple of aspirins, realized she should eat something, looked in the refrigerator and discovered that she had no food worth eating, and the milk was sour.

She grabbed her wallet and bolted from the house.

The evening air was soft. The smell of dinner-party food cooking wafted through April Street, and from Bandy and Coot's house, there was already laughter. But the lights in the corner store were still on.

Birdie stayed on her own side of the road. She'd cross later on—when she was past number 18. The little house was as dark as always. But Whiskers was no doubt sitting in his chair out the back, looking at the night.

Silently, she slipped down the footpath. As she reached Bambi's house, there was sudden gleam of light from across the road. She looked, and to her astonishment saw that the front door of number 18 had swung open, and that Whiskers was standing talking to someone.

He had a visitor! Whoever it was must have been knocking at the door as Birdie left her own gate.

The frangipani tree obscured vision, and the porch light was dim, illuminating only Whiskers. He didn't look happy. Or maybe that was just the effect of the shadows. It was hard to see much of the other tall figure, except that he or she was wearing something dark.

At the bottom of the street the corner store awning was being rolled up. The shop was closing. But Birdie didn't move. She lurked in the feathery shadows of Bambi's acacia, and spied.

After a few more seconds' conversation, Whiskers stood back (reluctantly, it seemed to Birdie) and let the stranger in. The front door closed, and the light was extinguished.

Birdie ran across the road, her mind racing. They're going to the back. I'll go round to the lane, she told herself. See if I can get a look at them through the fence. It'd be quickest to cut through Mrs. McGillicuddy's. I'll . . .

And at that point, she stopped.

I'm going mad, she thought.

She turned on her heel, and pelted back to her house as if pursued by demons. In two minutes she was talking to her father on the phone. Saying she'd love to go out on the boat tomorrow. Love to come over and spend the night . . . Could he give her dinner as well?

Birdie returned home on Monday morning, loaded with provisions from her father's local supermarket, and feeling herself again. Calm, intelligent company, Sunday's sun and water, had banished the demons as though they'd never been.

She spent the morning tidying her study, and, as if to reward her for her diligence, the phone rang twice with offers of work, and a check arrived from the Briggses, with a grateful note saying that Philomena had agreed to remain at home if *they* agreed to her giving up the flute, and training to be an apiarist.

She interviewed her two new clients in her freshly admirable study in the afternoon. She gave them good coffee and shortbread, and impressed them mightily. She didn't think about Whiskers all day, and she didn't see Mrs. McGillicuddy.

On Tuesday she went out early, made satisfactory progress on both cases, had dinner with a friend, and came home late. As she locked her car she saw the lace curtains in Mrs. McGillicuddy's front window twitch. She turned her back, and hurried inside.

On Wednesday, in the late afternoon, there was a knock on her door. It was Mrs. McGillicuddy.

"Sorry to disturb you," the old woman said, in a strained, rather formal way. "Just—I've been a bit worried—about him—" She jerked her head in the direction of number 18.

Birdie, back in her right mind, could afford to be benevolent. "What's the problem?" she asked, carefully casual.

"The kitten's been yowling for food at my back door three mornings in a row. And Whiskers hasn't been going to work. Hasn't left the house since—you know—Friday."

"I saw him on Saturday," Birdie said. "Not since. But I've been busy. Look, Mrs. McGillicuddy, if you're worried, why don't you just go and knock at his door?"

"I've done that." The old woman's veined hands were fumbling together anxiously. "No answer. That was yesterday. He wasn't out the back, either, but the back door was open. Screen and all, standing open, and the flies getting in. And it was still like that just now." Her faded eyes were filled with a kind of dread.

Birdie felt an uneasy stirring. She had a sudden memory of Whiskers's face, as she'd seen it on Saturday night. And the dark figure standing on his doorstep, screened by the frangipani tree.

"All right," she said. "We'll have a look."

They went through Mrs. McGillicuddy's house and out into the lane, the kitten wailing at their heels. Birdie called and knocked at the wooden gate of number 18. It swung open under her knuckles.

A tangle of shrubs. Spiderwebs and butterflies, lizards basking on a cracked concrete path. Under a rusted awning, an old cane chair, a tobacco pouch, a half-empty can of baked beans with a spoon sticking out of the top. Some bacon rind on a plate, swarming with ants. Screen door swinging on its hinges, the house beyond dim and full of secrets.

"Hello? Anyone there?"

No answer.

They walked gingerly to the house. Birdie called again, knocking at the back door. As she did, she looked behind her. The black kitten was sitting on the path, watching with huge golden eyes.

She turned back to the house. She took a step inside, Mrs. McGillicuddy close behind, and flicked on the light. The old-fashioned kitchen was very clean and tidy. Like an exhibition in a folk museum. Except for the body of the stranger lying dead on the floor, with a bloodied hammer beside him.

"The deceased is not the man who lives in this house. You came to see the man who lives here, but you don't know his name. He doesn't speak English, and he works at a hardware shop as a night watchman. Right?"

Detective-Sergeant Dan Toby was doing his best with Mrs. McGillicuddy, but he was finding it tough going. The old woman was in the grip of a shocked excitement that had by now rendered her almost incoherent. Nothing this exciting had happened in April Street since Doris Murchison's mother-in-law went mad and set number 10's outside loo on fire. With Doris Murchison in it.

She nodded hazily, her eyes drifting across the scene-of-crime tape to the front door of number 18.

"Dan, we don't actually know he doesn't speak English. Or that he's a night watchman," murmured Birdie hurriedly. "That's just what Mrs. McGillicuddy thinks."

Toby gave her a hard look. He and Birdie had met over dead bodies before, and never by his choice. But he couldn't tell her to go away and stop bothering him this time. She was a witness.

Birdie returned the look with a composure she didn't feel.

He turned his glare of disapproval toward the other April Street residents, standing bunched together on the road. "What is this, a street party?" he growled.

Bandy and Coot were there, looking cool. Bambi had her dog with her, either for protection, or to pretend that she had simply dropped by while walking. Poll was munching soya chips. Mrs. McGillicuddy had regaled them all with her story, and answered all their questions, before Toby arrived. The uniformed constable had been unable to contain her. This pleased Toby not at all.

He turned his back on them. "Have either of you seen the dead man before?" he asked.

"I think I might have," Birdie said. "On Saturday night. About five to seven. Whiskers was letting him in."

"You didn't tell me that!" accused Mrs. Mc-Gillicuddy.

"What?" demanded Toby. "The *kitten* let him in?"

"No," said Birdie tightly. "The man who lives here. We call him Whiskers. Because of his moustache," she added lamely, as Toby made a note, staring steadily at her.

"And did you see—Whiskers—after that?" he asked.

Birdie shook her head.

"I did," volunteered Bambi, surprisingly.

Toby whirled to face her. She stood on one leg and blinked at him. "I saw him come out of his house on Sunday morning," she said. "At about six A.M. Oh, wow! He was making his getaway, I guess."

"Never!" exclaimed Mrs. McGillicuddy, incredulous that Bambi had noticed anyone or anything. Let alone being up and about at six.

Toby went to talk to a man in overalls who had emerged from number 18 carrying a wallet in a plastic bag.

"Why're you trying to pin the murder on Whiskers?" hissed Mrs. McGillicuddy to Bambi.

"I can't help what I saw," Bambi protested. "And she"—pointing at Birdie—"sorry, I don't know your name. But you're the PI from number 21, aren't you? Well, anyway, you saw Tartan Shirt let the dead guy in last night. Well, he wasn't dead then, but—"

"Exactly! And Whiskers didn't kill him," insisted Mrs. McGillicuddy. She nudged Birdie vigorously. "You'd better tell your copper mate about—you know—the Mafia thing."

"Mrs. McGillicuddy, that's ridiculous!"

The old woman firmed her lips. "That's what you said before," she remarked coldly. "And see what it led to."

"That's really unfair—" Birdie was beginning. But just then Toby returned.

"There are no fingerprints in the house," he spat, as if somehow this was her fault. "It's been cleaned. You could eat your bloody dinner off every surface in the place. Plus there's no paperwork. No bills, nothing. This merchant cleared out properly. Hasn't left us a clue on who he is, or where he came from."

"Have you asked the agent who handles the property?" Birdie asked, determinedly ignoring Mrs. McGillicuddy's elbow in her ribs, and the word *Mafia* hissed in her ear.

Toby sneered. "The agent's useless. He's got nothing for us but the name Owen C. Plofmay on a lease—"

"Plofmay? That's not Italian!" exclaimed Mrs. McGillicuddy.

"It's not anything," snapped Toby. "It's a fake. The bloke's been hiding out. That's clear as a bell. His references are fake as well. He paid cash fortnightly, according to Call-me-Gavin at the agency, and was a nice quiet tenant. He would be. Wouldn't want to attract attention to himself, would he?"

"Have you tried HomeWork yet?"

"Yeah. They've never heard of Owen Plofmay, and haven't got anyone on staff who looks like your description. So what do you make of that?"

Birdie didn't know what to make of it. She plowed on. "You found the dead man's wallet. Who was he?"

"Adrian Aronsten, fifty-two years old, 32 Nester Street, Annandale, according to the driver's license. Took early retirement after a lottery win four months back. Got a million, but shared it with some old deadbeat he'd bumped into outside the lottery office. The ticket was in his name, but he paid up like a gentleman. Said a deal was a deal."

"How do you know all that?"

Toby grimaced. "Wife reported him missing Monday morning. She'd been away for the weekend. We thought he'd just nicked off. But it seems not. Name mean anything to you?"

Strangely, it did. But Birdie, for the life of her, couldn't think why.

Poll said an interior decorating company called Aronsten Interiors had "done" her front room. Aronsten's wife was an interior decorator, Toby said. No one could see how Poll's front room could have anything to do with the murder, but Toby took down her details anyway, then told them all to go home. Their statements, he said, could be signed in the morning.

No one wanted to leave. Everyone wanted to theorize about why Adrian Aronsten had visited Whiskers, aka Owen C. Plofmay, and ended up dead. Bandy was going for blackmail, Plofmay being an illegal immigrant, and Aronsten having known about it. Coot said no one who'd be moral enough to share a million dollars with a stranger would stoop to blackmail, and they had quite a little squabble about it.

Mrs. McGillicuddy had abandoned the Mafia, and her conviction that Whiskers was innocent. Obviously, she said, Whiskers was the deadbeat with whom Aronsten had shared the lottery ticket. That's how he could afford to rent number 18. The two men had argued about money, and this had led to Aronsten's murder, and Whiskers's flight. Money, she said darkly, was the root of all evil.

Everyone agreed solemnly. Then they all adjourned to Bambi's place. Bandy said it seemed awfully callous to have a party when someone had just died. Coot said wakes were quite okay, and after all it wasn't as if they'd known the dead guy. Which Bandy said was illogical.

Bambi only had cottage cheese and a bunch of radishes in her refrigerator, and nothing but herbal tea, soy sauce, and dog food in her pantry, but she did have a vast dispenser labeled "Pure Spring Water," the man from number 13 contributed a large tin of Scandinavian butter cookies he'd been given for Christmas, and in the end the gathering didn't break up till midnight.

Birdie was wide awake when she got home. Her mind was spinning with solutions to the mystery, none of which made sense. At two A.M. she decided to be firm with herself. Warm milk, perhaps, would help her to sleep.

She was pouring out the milk when she suddenly remembered why the name Aronsten had rung a bell with her. She couldn't imagine why she hadn't recollected it before—except that she'd so thoroughly repressed the recent past that even small details had slipped her mind.

By then it was two A.M. and too late to do anything—except think. So Birdie thought. And slowly all sorts of little details started coming together. She forgot about the milk, and made tea instead. She thought some more. She found a pen and paper and scribbled thoughtfully for a while. When she was finished, she felt rather sad. But by the time she rang Dan Toby, dragging him from his bed at six A.M., she'd worked the whole thing out.

Toby didn't believe her at first. But when he'd had a chat to the pathologist, done a bit of background checking, and talked to some of the Aronsten family friends, he decided to get a search warrant.

He rang Birdie later in the day.

"We found the clothes," he said, sounding tired.

"Beat the St. Vincent de Paul pick-up by about half an hour."

"Good," said Birdie. "And?"

So then he told her that yes, he'd arrested Cecily Aronsten for the murder of her husband Adrian Aronsten, aka Owen C. Plofmay, aka Whiskers. Mrs Aronsten had admitted visiting number 18 and killing her husband, but claimed in her defense that she'd lost her temper because he was deceiving her and living a double life.

"It wasn't that!" exclaimed Birdie. "She just saw a chance to get rid of him without being the obvious suspect!"

"Don't worry. She won't get away with it," Toby said grimly. "Not after pretending she was going away, to trap him into staying in number 18 for the weekend so she could get at him there. Not considering she hit him from behind. Not when she spent all night cleaning the place of fingerprints, so no one would realize that her husband and Whiskers were one and the same. Not after changing the poor bloke back into his Adrian suit after he was dead, and going off in the morning wearing the Whiskers disguise herself. And not considering her so-called friends' testimony that she's money-mad. The jury won't like her. They'll put her away somewhere where she won't like the decor, no risk."

Birdie was glad to hear it, because she hadn't liked Mrs. Cecily Aronsten from the moment she'd first heard her snooty voice on the phone. But she was sad for Whiskers, for "Owen C. Plofmay," whose name was an anagram for "place of my own," and who had enjoyed his place only in the daytime, and for two short months, before death overtook him.

"He was happy for a while, love, anyhow, with his house, and his kitten and his smokes and his wood-

work," said Mrs. McGillicuddy in her kitchen, later.
"That's what counts. A bit of happiness is all any of
us can ask for in this life. He couldn't have kept it
up forever. She was onto him, according to you,
pretty well straightaway. Only she thought it was a
woman."

Birdie thought how tough the old become. She was
still depressed.

"Cunning, wasn't he, old Whiskers?' Mrs. Mc-
Gillicuddy said, spooning out cake mixture from a
blue-striped bowl. She was making patty cakes. Some
plain, for Bandy. Some with sultanas, for Coot. "Telling his missus he had to share the money with an
old bloke from the lottery queue and all the time the
old bloke was him."

"He must have seen it as his one chance to escape.
Dan Toby says their house looks like an operating
theater with zebra-striped curtains. Baked beans, beer
and bacon, kittens and smokes, unfashionable
clothes, strictly forbidden."

"She was a better detective than us," said Mrs.
McGillicuddy. She clattered pans into the oven. "I
never thought that moustache was false. Did you?"

"No," said Birdie truthfully. "It looked just right
on him. Like the clothes, and the glasses, and everything else. But she had an advantage. She lived with
him. It wouldn't have taken her long to realize he
was using the HomeWork men's room as a changing
area, and to find out where he was spending his
days. All she had to do was hang around and follow
him for a while, instead of going to work." She
sighed. "I told her to try that. I wish I hadn't."

"You weren't to know." Mrs. McGillicuddy patted
her shoulder, then turned to the sink and started
washing the mixing bowl.

The black kitten miaowed at the screen door.

"There's a bit of fish in the fridge, love," said Mrs.

McGillicuddy. "Give it to him, will you?"

Birdie did. The kitten had his own saucer now, she noted.

"You've adopted him."

"Oh, well." Mrs. McGillicuddy shrugged. "Thought I'd call him Whiskers," she said casually. "In memory, you know?"

Birdie's eyes suddenly stung, behind her glasses. I'm overtired, she told herself. But she went on looking out at the little cat cleaning his plate. It made her feel better to know that he, at least, had found another place of his own.

Verity Birdwood, the sleuth of Australian Jennifer Rowe (Lamb to the Slaughter, Death in Store, The Makeover Murders, Grim Pickings), is a PI and researcher investigating her new reclusive neighbor who is killed by a mysterious male stranger. Or is he?

Writer's Revenge

Barbara Burnett Smith

Deborah Adams, Eileen Dreyer, Jan Grape, and Joan Hadley were eating at a nearby table as I waited for the hostess to seat me. I recognized them from book jackets and magazine articles, and I'd read almost every word any of them had ever published.

I tried not to stare, but this was my first mystery conference, and to say I was in awe is to understate the situation. It felt like the first day of school and I was the transfer student.

"Right this way," the young hostess said, leading me on a winding path between tables in the Atrium restaurant.

Before I'd gone more than five feet, Jan Grape said, in her thick west Texas accent, "I know that lady."

I paused, looked around, and realized she was really talking to me. "Hi," I said.

"You're Jolie Wyatt; I saw you checking into the conference when I was downstairs. Are you going to eat?"

"Uh, no, I was just going to get something to drink."

"Well, shoot," Jan said. "If you don't mind sitting with a bunch of lethal ladies, come join us."

"Oh, no, really—"

"Eileen, move over a little and make room for Jolie Wyatt, who drove all the way in from Purple Sage. Jolie just sold her first mystery."

As chairs were moved to make a place for me, they said:

"Congratulations."

"Good job."

"Nice going."

It was like completing a home movie and being congratulated by Spielberg.

"Oh, thank you," I gushed. "It's very nice to meet everyone."

Deborah Adams, delicate and lovely, leaned forward and said, "Call me Deb. And that's Joan, and Eileen."

"Hi." I pulled a chair up to the table, sat down, and stowed my things on the floor. When I looked up, everyone was watching me, but no one was talking. "I interrupted your conversation."

They exchanged glances and finally it was Deb who said, "We were just discussing our dear sister in crime, Heather James."

"Heather James will be here?"

Eileen Dreyer nodded, her eyes glinting wickedly as she said, "And how lucky we are. This woman is special, and she's going to be at this conference."

I thought I caught a note of sweet sarcasm, but wasn't sure.

"My conference," Jan added. Besides writing short stories, Jan was one of the organizers of the event we were attending. "Heather James, can you imagine? We're in tall cotton, now!"

I knew the woman they were talking about; not personally, of course, but Heather James was the hot new star in the mystery field. So far she had published three books. The first had been selected as a *New York Times* "Notable Book," and had gone into eleven printings. The second had been sold to Hollywood for a reported seven figures. Up to this point, no film had been made, but it was rumored that Demi Moore and Whitney Houston had both vied for the lead role.

Meanwhile, Heather's third book had won two national literary awards; not mystery awards, mind you, but literary awards, which had moved her into a whole new realm, with a new agent and a new publisher. I'd read that she'd nabbed a huge advance for her next book, as well as a monstrous promotional budget for everything from radio commercials to her own dumps—bins—at the bookstores. Those were to feature not only her first books, but a life-sized picture of Heather, raven-haired and gorgeous, holding her now-trademark knitting.

Book number four was coming out next month.

"What's Heather James like?" I asked.

Eileen said, "Like Hannibal Lecter."

"Well, I'd describe her as the prom queen," Deb said. "And Miss Congeniality and president of the student council all rolled up into one, only—"

"On the side she's boinking all the teachers," Joan added.

"Naughty, naughty." Deb paused to consider it. "She's definitely a social climber, only she's confined herself to the publishing field. So far."

"She's all of those things, and worse," Jan agreed.

"And poor Joan," Deb said, eyeing her, then raising an eyebrow. "You're stuck with the same publisher. Glad it's not me."

Joan flipped her permed, white-blonde hair back

from her face and smiled sweetly. "I am not someone to be trifled with, although . . ."

"Speaking of trifle, is anyone having dessert?" Deb asked. The waitress was standing at her elbow, so Deborah ordered a fudge brownie and I ordered my diet cola.

As the waitress moved away, Jan said, "Joan, spill the beans; I want to hear your story."

Joan exaggerated her slight Southern drawl. "Well, I'd just love to tell it." After settling her black-clad body more comfortably in her chair, she began. "When Heather's second book came out a tour was arranged by her publishing house. And it was being paid for by her publishing house, I might add." Joan looked at me. "Don't expect that unless your book goes platinum."

"How about number fifteen with a bullet?" I asked.

"Don't upstage me. Where was I? Oh, yes, so they have this tour set up, and on the first stop, she is supposed to be signing with another author. Only, dear Heather calls her publicist on the day of the signing—the very day, mind you—and tells her publicist that she just doesn't feel it's fair to be expected to draw a crowd for other authors. It puts such a burden on her, you know, signing with these authors of *little* books."

"Oops," I said.

"Oops, my ass," Joan responded. "And would anyone like to guess who this author of *little* books happened to be?"

"You," Deb guessed.

Joan touched her finger to the tip of her nose. "Correct in one. And at that time I had twenty-three *little* books out, and she was on number two."

Obviously the others knew the story; they looked

at me expectantly as if that was my cue. "So, what did you do?" I asked.

"Fifteen minutes before the signing I marched myself into the bookstore and moved all her stuff to the other end of the table. Then I plopped myself down in the only chair, just like I belonged. When the lady from the bookstore came up—and it was a pretty lousy thing to do to her—I just told her that my books seemed to be missing." Joan waited for the polite applause that followed, then went on. "And as it turned out, I had more fans there than Heather did, and I signed twice as many books. Heather couldn't have been nicer to me. Calls me her best friend."

Deborah sighed. "I love that story. I tell it to myself at bedtime when I can't sleep."

The waitress delivered my drink, and placed a huge brownie with ice cream, nuts, and fudge in front of Deborah. "That's incredible," I said, feeling deprived because I had put myself on a diet to lose the extra five pounds that were creeping toward ten extra pounds.

"I never eat at home. Only when I'm on the road, really," Deb claimed, picking up a spoon and taking a quick bite. "It's tofu and lettuce most of my life. Honest." She licked whipped cream off her lip.

"I'm not that disciplined," I said. After a sip of my drink, I found myself frowning.

Eileen noticed. "Bad drink? Or bad thoughts?" she asked.

"I was just wondering how Heather James became so famous."

"You don't know about the claw?"

"The claw?"

All eyes shifted to her. "You see, it's our theory of fame and fortune; I heard it on a panel once, and claimed it for my own."

"Eileen normally only tells stories about animals,"

Joan said. "Ducks and snakes and such . . . read *Bad Medicine*, you'll see—"

Eileen said, "But in this case, I'll make an exception. It's very simple. When you sell a book you become one of those little stuffed animals, the kind that you see in the glass toy machines. You know, all the toys are jammed together, and every once in a while someone comes along and puts a quarter in the machine and the claw goes to work—"

"Keep in mind," Joan added, "the claw is blind. It can't see the toys, doesn't read—"

"It just swings out, drops down, and grabs someone." Eileen made a claw with her hand, dropped it down to fetch a napkin, then whisked it up in the air. "If the claw gets you all the way to the chute and sends you out, then voila! You are John Grisham. But, if the claw drops you on the way"—she shook her head sadly—"you're a one-book wonder and next year people won't remember your name."

She placed the napkin carefully back on the table.

I could feel myself stuttering before I'd said a word. "But, but, wait a minute. This just happens? This Fame Claw just does its thing?"

"That's right. Once a year or so."

"And it grabs someone, not because they're a wonderful writer, or told a great story, but just because of clueless luck?"

Eileen was too polite to snort, but Joan did it for her. She also leaned closer as she said, "Do you have any idea how many wonderful writers there are in this country? Know how many great stories are published every year?"

"Well, no. Several thousand, I guess."

"More like sixty thousand."

That was a lot, but for reasons of my own I wasn't ready to give up and accept the claw theory. "What about the publisher? Can't they make a best-seller?"

"They put the quarter in," Eileen said. "But they get no guarantees."

"And the claw just picked up Heather James?"

Joan gave me the evil eye. "Have you ever read the middle of one of her books?"

"Actually," I admitted, "I've never made it past chapter four of any of them."

"I rest my case."

"But, wait a minute," I said. "So what happens if the claw doesn't pick you?" My first mystery was due out in exactly seven months. I dreamed about it the way an astronaut must dream about his first space launch, but I didn't feel the presence of any claw hovering above me.

Eileen said. "Then you have to succeed on your own. Claw your own way to the top of the heap and struggle off to the chute by yourself. Make sure you have good medical insurance before you start."

Not exactly what I wanted to ponder at my first mystery conference. Standing in line waiting to get books autographed would have done more for my morale.

"So, when is your first book coming out?" Joan asked, sweetly.

"Seven months."

"Then," Eileen said, "you have a year or two when the claw could get you."

"And if it does," Deb chimed in, "be nice. Not like Heather James."

"Who is a bitch on wheels," Jan added. She looked around quickly. "Who said that? I didn't say that. Did y'all hear that? I must be possessed or something, because I wouldn't say that."

Eileen patted her arm. "We know you wouldn't."

"Hey," Jan said with a shrug, "if she wants to miss her own signing, that's her business."

"A formal signing?" Eileen asked.

"Well, nobody was in black tie and tux, but it was confirmed by her publicist in writing. And three times by phone, and twice by fax. And I had complied with all their demands—I mean requests. Anyhow, makes me no nevermind if she decides that we're too little to bother with after I sent out umpteen jillion postcards, and press releases, and bought ads in the *Statesman* and the *Chronicle*. So what if all those people lined up around the store and then got mad at me because Heather never showed up?" Jan took a breath. "Her publicist called to apologize three days later; that makes it all okay, doesn't it?"

"I think you should tell people about it," Deb said. "Write an article."

"I can't afford to say anything about it."

"Why? Do you think her whole publishing house would refuse your orders?" Deb asked. "The authors would stay away in droves? Is that what you think?"

"What I think, is that if Heather James told them to, they'd all fly down to my store and moon me, that's what I think."

Nobody laughed, which was scary in itself.

"Certainly she doesn't have that much power," I said.

Four pairs of eyes turned to stare at me. With pity. Deb shook her head. "Saddam Hussein has less power than Heather James. Did you hear what she got on her last contract?" She named a figure that rivaled John Travolta's film salary. "And when the house said they couldn't front that much, Heather simply told them to cut all their other authors' advances."

"Which they did," Eileen snapped. "By a bunch."

"It's hateful," Deb said. "So, do y'all want to hear my story?"

"I do, I do," Joan said.

Deb nodded. "Heather was going to give me a

quote, a blurb, you know, saying how wonderful I am," she added for my benefit, "for the jacket of my book. She offered to do it; I swear to you I did not ask. Anyway, two weeks after she gets the manuscript, Heather sent a letter to my editor that said, 'Thank you for sending me Deborah Adams's latest manuscript. I enjoyed the Fall Creek book.' Can you imagine? Not only does she damn me with faint praise, she has the audacity to call it the Fall Creek book! Fall Creek is a vineyard! I write the *Jesus* Creek series."

A woman who had been skirting our table stopped abruptly and stared at Deb. "Oh my God! You do write the Jesus Creek series! You're Deborah Adams! I love your books—I've read them all." She dug through a large handbag and pulled out a paperback. "See, I read it on the plane. Oh, would you sign it for me?"

"Of course, I'd love to," Deborah said, beaming out a smile Miss America would envy. "Would you like it personalized? What is your name?" The woman told her; Deborah whipped out a pen and began to write. When she was finished, she looked up at the woman. "You said you flew in. Where were you coming from?"

They went on for a good five minutes and by the time the woman left, I think they were planning to vacation together.

I was open-mouthed. Joan noticed. "Can you do that?" she asked.

"I don't think so. Is there a class?"

"It's called The South."

"Y'all are making too much of it," Deb said, resettling herself at the table. "When someone approaches you and they've read all your books, or even one, and love your writing, you know important things about them already. You know they are a person of incredible breeding and impeccable taste. Of course you want to get to know them. There are far too few people in the world like that."

"Actually, Deb's a special case," Joan continued. "She may carry the whole thing a teensy bit too far, but we try not to hold it against her."

"It's simply part of my character," Deb said. "And character is the key to everything, don't you think? Even Heather."

"Does she really knit?" I asked. "And carry her knitting everywhere?"

Eileen smiled wickedly. "Rumor has it it's just a sex toy."

The waitress was handing out checks, and Jan pointed to the lobby below us where a crowd had gathered. By peering over the railing I could see the Atrium bar as well as the front desk, both mobbed with people. A uniformed chauffeur, several bellmen, and at least sixty others were jammed together.

"What is it?" I asked, trying to determine the cause of the commotion.

Jan threw money and her check on the table. "I'd better do something official," she said, dashing toward the escalators.

The others were also up and moving.

"What?" I asked again. "What's going on?"

It was Joan who said, "You're going to have to be quicker than that if you intend to keep up." She headed after Jan, but said to me, "Come on. This should be fun." When I hung back, she turned and said, "Don't you get it?" She struck a pose and enunciated distinctly, "Heather . . . has . . . arrived."

We weaved our way through the crowd, and by sticking close to the others I ended up near the front of the crowd.

"This is too much; I'm going to my room," Eileen

said, trying to veer off, but Heather spotted her before she could move.

"Eileen!" She almost impaled her with a knitting needle from the tapestry bag she carried. "Sweetie!" Heather air-kissed her twice.

Eileen lurched sideways to avoid another run-in with the needles before gasping, "How are you, Heather?"

"I'm practically insane! I have been touring so long I hardly remember my own name anymore, and everywhere I go there are people. Not just on tour, either; I mean everywhere. I can't even play racquetball without a crowd watching. God, now I know how Princess Di felt."

Deb made a delicate gagging noise which was lost in the general confusion.

Up close Heather James wasn't as magnificent as her press photos, but she was very attractive. Her hair was a brilliant black with a shine that said it was natural. Her skin was smooth, but missed the creamy description by at least an inch or two. The glow was missing, and in its place was a dull grayness which could have come from too many nights on the road.

Her eyes were the focal point of her face, dark, wide, and ringed with thick eyelashes. I guessed her age at a few years younger than I, about thirty-five.

A young man whose name tag read "Manager" appeared beside her. "Miss James, on behalf of the hotel, I'd like to welcome you to Austin." He was glowing with exuberance. "If there is anything I can personally do to make your stay more pleasant, please don't hesitate to ask."

He'd approached with hand extended cordially, and now Heather shoved her knitting bag into it. "You can get this to my room immediately; and those things, too," she said with a gesture toward a luggage cart that held an elegant matching set of tapestry luggage.

"I'll get a bellman right on it—"

"No," Heather snapped the word. "You said 'personally.' I don't like just anyone handling this knitting bag." She poked him lightly in the chest with a needle. "I've already had one needle disappear on this tour, and another is unacceptable." Then she touched the lapel of his suit jacket with her index finger. "Thank you so much." She dipped those magnificent lashes down, coyly.

"Yes, Miss James—"

Before he could finish the sentence, she turned away from him, spotted Joan, and smiled. "Jynx, my dearest friend! How are you? It's been ages."

"I'm fine, Heather," Joan said. "We were just going up to my room—"

"No, no, I know about your little parties! I insist you be my guest in the bar." The lobby bar was completely open with a small stream running through it. "But if it's going to be another mob scene—" She glanced with distaste at those standing close to her, primarily me.

Jan stepped forward. "Miss James, I'm Jan Grape, one of the organizers, and I'd like to welcome you. I'm sure you know Deborah Adams, and this is Jolie Wyatt, a new mystery writer."

Heather's look made me feel as if I was the dweebie freshman who had accidentally gotten gym class with the cheerleaders.

She gave us a duty smile. "Yes, of course."

Jan pushed on, somehow keeping her tone warm and caring. "I'm so glad you could take the time to come." She stepped back. "I've got to go do the opening welcome, but I'll send your packet straight over to you."

"Thank you."

As Jan hurried away, Heather spoke directly to the three people standing closest to her, whom I later learned were her publicist, a secretary, and the chauffeur who doubled as a bodyguard. "Maureen, Allen, Jennifer, you come with us to the bar, as well." She linked arms with Eileen and Joan. "Oh, my good buddies! Isn't this fun?" She towed them away.

I looked at my watch. The conference was about to start, and I didn't want to miss a single thing, especially not a warm, Jan Grape-style welcome.

"I'm heading for the opening," I said to Deb. "It was nice meeting you."

"You, too, Jolie," Deb said. "I know we'll see you later."

One welcome and three panels later I needed to come up for air, real air that hadn't been air-conditioned, reconditioned, or breathed by anyone else first. I was in overload from the wealth of information about writing and publishing that was being funnelled into my brain; I stumbled outside into the baking heat and blinding sun. Even at six o'clock it was staggering, which is my excuse for walking directly into a woman not far from the entrance.

"Jolie!" Deb Adams was the woman. "Are you okay?"

"I'm not sure," I said, blinking.

"Your first conference?" When I nodded she shook her head sympathetically. "It takes most of us like that the first time. It's a lot to absorb."

"So I'm discovering."

"You need a break. Have you eaten?"

"Food?" It was the first I'd noticed that my stomach was on empty. "No, I hadn't even though about it."

"Then you must come with us!" Without waiting

for my response, she led me to a bright blue mini-
van parked a few feet away.

Jan Grape was already there. "Jolie, hi," she said.
"Having a good time?"

"Wonderful, thanks. You did a great job."

"We aim to please."

Deb smiled. "Jolie is going to come with us."

"What?" That from Jan.

"It will be a lot of fun," Deb went on, "And so
what if Heather invited herself? She'll just have to
get over it, won't she? Besides, I'll bet Jolie hasn't
seen the bats, either. Have you, Jolie? We're going to
see those first."

I blinked again. "Bats?"

"Millions of them; they come out at sunset from
under the bridge over there. If you're squeamish . . ."

"She kills people for fun and profit—she is not
squeamish." Jan opened the front door. "You can
ride shotgun."

I climbed in, and while Deb went around the front
of the vehicle to get in the driver's seat, Jan moved
a box of donuts off the dash. Embossed in the plastic
were the words, "Do not place items on airbag."

It was then that Eileen, Joan, and Heather came out
of the building. After a pause to put on their sunglasses, they headed toward us.

"You see," Eileen was saying, "the rental place had
a plethora of mini-vans, and when in the urban jun-
gle . . ."

Heather was carrying her knitting bag, and she
gestured toward the van with it. "I'll ride in the
front."

This wasn't said to me, nor did she bother to ask
me to move; she merely stood there as if I would
evaporate. I didn't. Instead I forced myself to smile
and dutifully stepped out of the van. Heather

climbed in, Joan helped her by putting the knitting bag on the dashboard.

"I'll take the middle," Eileen said

Joan pulled me to the backseat. "You can ride with me."

"What about Jan?" I asked as doors all around the vehicle began to close.

"She can't go," Joan said. "She has to run to the store. Mysteries and More, she owns it with her husband, Elmer."

Jan waved us off and Deb pulled smoothly away from the curb, while Eileen leaned forward and pushed Heather's knitting bag farther up on the dash. The two needles were pointed straight toward Heather.

"Who was that woman?" Heather asked.

Deborah rolled her eyes, while Joan said, "One of the conference organizers. You met her this afternoon, remember?"

"But I've met so many people this afternoon. I've been mobbed repeatedly," Heather said. "You just don't have any idea what it's like. Which is why you have to get me away from the hotel so I can relax."

"Our pleasure," Deb said. She headed the van across the parking lot toward the Congress Street exit, testing the brakes, then the steering. "Sorry, y'all, but I've never driven one of these before." She popped the brakes and we all rocked forward. "Oops."

"No damage done," Joan said.

I started to say something about the knitting needles. Something motherly, but while I am the mother of a sixteen-year-old son, I didn't think Heather would take the warning well. If she even deigned to hear it.

Deb was pulling out into the street, threading into fast-moving homeward-bound traffic when Joan smacked her forehead. "Oh, no, I forgot my other glasses. All I have are my sunglasses; I can't see bats at twilight with those."

"We can go back," Eileen said. "It will only take a second."

The literary superstar clacked her tongue and ran her hand through her black hair. "What else can go wrong? I can't be out all night; I have to give the luncheon keynote address tomorrow, and I need my sleep. Be quick!"

"We'll eat fast," Deb assured her.

"And watch fast," Eileen added.

Deb turned the vehicle around, and while she did, I tried coming up with an excuse to leave as soon as we reached the hotel. Not that I didn't like most of the women in the van. They were my idols, icons in the mystery writing field, and most of me was thrilled to be this close to them. The adult part of me, though, was realizing that Heather James was a royal pain in the rump, a bitch without a cause, and not someone I wanted to spend even another forty seconds with. Everything was about her, as if even the gods on Olympus knew her name personally, and targeted her.

Joan began climbing over me. "I'll hurry. Just screech to a halt, Deb, and I'll jump out."

I couldn't see what happened next, but the sensations are riveted in my mind. The van picked up speed, no doubt to placate Heather. Then Joan yelled, "Look out, that's Jan!" The vehicle swung to the right, someone screamed, and I heard the tires squeal as we began to skid. There was a crunch of metal and we slammed to a stop, throwing me against the middle seat. Almost simultaneously there were explosions, two of them, like gunshots inside the van. Joan bounced forward, then pitched back onto me. I let out a grunt.

She moved enough for me to see out. Luckily we hadn't hit any person, just a stone barrier in front of the hotel.

"Is everyone okay?" Deb asked, her voice shaky. "This thing scared the hell out of me." She slapped at something on her lap, then leaned back and closed her eyes.

"I'm fine," Joan said.

Eileen was next. "I'm not hurt."

"Are you okay, Jolie?" Deb asked.

"I'm fine," I said. "What exploded? Was that a tire? Two tires?"

"The airbags," Deb said.

Jan pulled open the front passenger door. "I didn't see y'all, because of the sun—"

"We're all okay," Joan said.

Jan's words became stiff as she stared first at Heather, then back at us. "Not all okay. Not Heather." She must have touched Heather's wrist, or felt for a pulse, because she turned white before she said, "She's dead. The knitting needles got her."

Deb turned to stare first at Jan, next at Eileen, and finally at Joan. Her eyes widened as big as UFOs. "I don't frigging believe it."

Jan's face was even grayer now. "Who could have believed?"

Eileen's head moved around until she could look Joan in the eye. They exchanged one long look, before she said, "I don't even believe it."

Deb started at Heather, then leaped out of the van. "I believe it. Why are y'all just sitting there with a dead body?" We were out of the van in seconds. "It's disgusting," she went on. "I'm going to be sick . . ."

Jan clutched a fender, her body bowed. "I have a medical background—I know what to do." She sat on the curb, placing her head between her knees, leaving Deb to fend for herself.

"I'm an ER nurse," Eileen said. She had stepped to the front of the van and now inspected Heather quickly. After a brief check she said, "I'll go call the police."

Joan reached inside her purse and pulled out a cigarette, a lighter, and a silver flask. After a swallow from the flask, she dropped it back into her bag, and in quick successive moves put the cigarette in her mouth, lit it, and took two huge hits, blowing the smoke out her nose like a dragon. Then she shoved the cigarette at Deb, who inhaled like it was oxygen itself. When she saw me watching her, she said, "I never smoke at home. Only when I'm on the road. Honest."

The police came, and after seeing Heather's body, escorted us to an office on the second floor. There were mauve couches and drapes, and eight magazines on a side table that I counted repeatedly until it was my turn to leave with the female officer and answer questions.

I could only tell the woman what I saw, or heard, and that was very little. We had been in the van because we were going to see bats, and eat dinner. And no, I didn't know whose idea it was. I had been invited at the last minute, just before Heather arrived with Eileen and Joan.

As for the knitting needles, Heather carried them everywhere because they were her trademark. We were hurrying because Heather had asked us to. She had asked Deb to speed up. I hadn't seen Jan step in front of the vehicle, but Deb had swerved hard.

"An accident?" the officer asked.

"It was no one's fault."

I said that. I think maybe the officer even said it. And I know that's what went on the official accident report.

Later, as I walked through the Atrium bar I noticed Joan, Eileen, Deb, and Jan, their heads bent together, the four of them whispering.

At the other tables, people were saying what a tragedy it was. But it was no one's fault. These things just happen.

Joan spotted me. "Hey, Jolie. Are you okay?"

I nodded slowly. "Oh, fine."

"Join us for a drink?" Deb asked.

"Me?" I stared at them, four of my idols. "Uh, no. No, thank you. I think I need to go to my room and lie down."

"You look pale," Eileen said. "Elevate your feet."

I nodded and continued walking, straight across the marble lobby, straight to the elevators.

I kept wondering if it was true. Was it no one's fault?

I wasn't sure. But one thing *was* very clear to me: if the claw grabbed me, and if it got me all the way out the chute to fame and fortune, I was going to be very nice to all the other people in the business.

Four of them in particular.

Real-life mystery writers star in this tale of an obnoxious colleague reaping her just reward. Jolie Wyatt, Smith's protagonist, is featured in this story, the Agatha-nominated Writers of the Purple Sage, *and most recently in* Mistletoe from Purple Sage.

A Deliberate Form of Frenzy

Daniel Stashower

I found Mabberley in the smaller of the two interior rooms, his back to the fireplace. A half-empty pint of Speckled Hen sat on the low table in front of him. There was a dead soldier next to it, but I couldn't be sure it was his.

"You know something about theater, don't you?" he asked, by way of greeting.

"A bit," I said.

"That fellowship of yours, the, uh . . ."

"The H. Darmstadter Contemporary Playwrights Fellowship," I said, pulling out a low stool. "What about it?"

"Do you know anything about Joe Orton?"

"A little. I've read him. Seen *Loot* a couple of times."

"He stole my wife."

"Joe Orton stole your wife?"

"Uh huh."

"He's dead, isn't he? Orton?"

"Yes."

"Wasn't he queer, too?"

He looked at me strangely. "Is that a problem for you, Brian?"

"No, no. Just marshalling my facts. So: Joe Orton, the dead, homosexual playwright, stole your wife. Is that it?"

"You begin to understand. Let me buy you a drink."

He stood up and walked three steps to the bar, fumbling in his pocket for a handful of change.

I barely knew David Mabberley. Once, when I was fresh off the boat, he'd pointed me toward the office of the Domestic Bursar. Another time I sat next to him at lunch, but he didn't look up from his newspaper. Every so often I saw him brewing his tea in the Senior Common Room, which is what they call the faculty lounges at British universities, and if he saw me coming he would leave the kettle boiling. This was the extent of our intimacy. We both drank tea. So it caught me by surprise when he called me out of the blue that night, in tears, to say that his wife had left him and would I please meet him for a drink, now, please.

He had told me to join him at the Rose and Crown, where he wouldn't be likely to run into any of his students. Apparently the plant biology crowd favored the livelier atmosphere of the King's Arms. The Rose and Crown, a smallish pub on a quiet, terraced street, catered to a more exclusive set—itinerant Washingtonians, Brits with marital troubles, that sort of thing. I'd always liked the place. The tiny rooms and low ceilings gave an impression of intimacy, even where none existed. The back room, where Mabberley had settled himself, featured a large rowing trophy and a battered player piano.

Mysteriously, the walls were covered with hockey memorabilia.

Mabberley ordered two pints and then leaned heavily on the bar, bracing his foot against the railing. He looked as if he'd been through it. His brown hair had formed itself into loose spikes at the front of his head. His eyes were pink and watery. Dull flecks covered his suit and some sort of yellow crust clung to his sleeve, like military braiding. It looked like an omelette gone wrong, and I guessed that Mabberley was unused to cooking for himself.

Oxford is not exactly a center of fashion, at least not among the college faculties. One finds a great many plaid-on-plaid ensembles, and the neckwear tends toward the wide and shiny. Chances are good that Monday's soup stain will still be on view the following week, and a cuff button, once lost, is never seen again in this world. Mabberley was the exception. He had several suits of recent vintage, all of them woven from known fibers. His ties were at peace with his shirts, and his socks invariably matched. He was thought to be a bit of a dandy.

He glanced up and his eyes met mine in the mirror behind the bar. He turned to give an overly broad wave, as if to a departing ship. I wondered how many drinks he'd had.

"Pistachio nuts," he called.

"What?"

"You can get them by the pint. That's why I come here. Pistachio nuts."

"I see."

He paid for the drinks and carried them back to the table. "Look," he said, "did I get you from something? Because if I did—"

"No. It's fine. But you'll have to start at the beginning. You can't just—"

"Sure." He set down the drinks and settled himself in the corner. "Ever met my wife?"

"No."

"I think perhaps you have. An attractive girl. But you wouldn't say 'girl' in America, would you? You'd say she was an attractive *wo-man*. Mustn't call anyone a girl. Heaven forfend." He sipped his pint. "A-ttrac-tive. Would that be considered demeaning? I'd hate to—"

"I think we can let it pass."

He considered it, then gave a curt nod. "A bit younger than I am, my wife. Twelve years. Former student of mine, I'm afraid. The usual thing."

"And now she's left you."

"Erm."

"For Joe Orton."

"Orton, yes. Subject of her dissertation, you see. I think she found him alluring, somehow. She may have identified with his rough upbringing. She's a Leicester girl. A bit coarse around the edges, but I soon smoothed her out. Perhaps that's how she fastened on Orton. It wouldn't matter, except that now she spends more time with him than she does with me. Used to kid her about it. I'd say, 'My dear, you spend more time with Joe Orton than you do with your own husband.' I often say clever things like that to my young wife. To demonstrate what a keen and lively mind I have." He lifted his glass. "I'm being ironic, you realize. You lot have no sense of irony, I'm told. None at all. So I thought I'd best let you know."

"It's good of you."

"Perhaps that's what drove her away. The irony."

I watched as he took another long swallow. "David," I said, "isn't there someone else who might help you with this? I don't mean to be unkind, but we barely know each other. Surely one of the others—"

"You're an American. From the U.S.A. I can talk to you. The distance has a liberating effect. We don't talk to each other here. Not really. We have all that plucked out at an early age and stored away and we must obtain special permission to use it. The paperwork is quite extraordinary. So we learn to do without. A man could have a psychotic episode without ever spilling a drop of his Earl Grey."

I reached for a pistachio nut.

"But of course I'm dramatizing. You're not the only one who ever read theater. That's how I captured my wife's affections, by the way. Originally. At first, I dazzled her with my knowledge of Restoration drama. What I don't know about William Congreve isn't worth knowing, I can tell you. Bunyan? I'm your man. Locke? Look no further. I've got it sussed. I'll fight any man who says different."

"I doubt if it will come to that."

"Am I talking too loudly?"

"A bit."

"Alcohol will do that, you know. It never fails. There is undoubtedly a direct proportion between units of alcohol and decibels. I may commission a study." He ran a finger around the rim of his glass. "So," he said, dropping his voice to a conspiratorial whisper, "when Janice began her affair with Orton, I did what any self-respecting academic would do. I went to the Bodleian."

"You brushed up on Orton."

"More than that, my boy. I devoured the man. Read all the plays, all the criticism. Took in a biography or two. But Janice only resented it. Said I was trying to usurp her field. She was right, I suppose. Not that there was much danger of that. She's become quite the rising star in the academic heavens.

You've heard about her Wolfson award? No? Puts me quite in the shade. But do you know something? I couldn't stop. It was fascinating. I developed a genuine passion for Orton. The plays are marvellously clever. Crafted, you might say. And Orton's life: Extremely compelling. The working class background, the failed acting career, the blaze of talent extinguished in its prime. I genuinely—I honestly thought Janice and I might collaborate on a project, perhaps we might edit of collection of essays or some such. Was that so unreasonable?"

"Sounds a little out of your field, David."

"That's what Janice thought, as well. She insisted that I give him up. And I did. I took up woodworking instead. But she continued to stay away at night, with her trips to London and her Firehouse production of *What the Butler Saw*. Based on Trevor Nunn's original script notations, you'll want to know. And while all this was going on, I stayed at home, building things. Night after night. Improving our happy home. You should have seen me—drilling and gluing, gluing and drilling. I've become quite a dab hand with a spokeshave, I can tell you that. I started with a set of bookcases, naturally, but soon I was eager to stretch myself. Ever built a Welsh dresser?"

I shook my head.

"Not for the faint of heart. Extraordinary amount of precision cutting. But I prevailed. Then, emboldened by my success, I took a notion to put a nice little work island in the kitchen. I'll finish it yet."

He stood up abruptly and stepped over to the bar. Protocol dictated that I should have bought the next round, but I'd only worked through half my pint and apparently he'd grown tired of waiting. I'll never understand how they do it. I have friends who can put away anywhere from ten to twelve pints in an evening without so much as a discreet belch. I might be able to stomach the alcohol, but where do they put all that volume?

Mabberley set two more pints on the table. "Halliwell," he said. "That's the key."

"Excuse me?"

"Halliwell. Orton's partner. I suggested that Janice concentrate on him. He's the truly interesting player in the drama, if you want my view."

"Halliwell was the artist, right?"

"Of a sort. Frustrated actor, really. He and Orton met at RADA. Must have cut quite a figure. Twenty-five years old and totally bald. And who could blame him? When he was eleven years old, his mother got a wasp sting on her tongue. She choked to death right in front of young Ken's eyes."

"God."

"It gets better. A few years later, he came down to breakfast one morning to find that his father had stuck his head in the oven. Halliwell always claimed he stepped over the body, turned off the gas, fixed himself some tea, and called the police—in that order." Mabberley leaned back. "An intense young man, you might say. Very intense."

I leaned back. My eyes drifted along a string of NHL pennants dating all the way back to the Cleveland Barons. Near the bar, a framed photo of Gordie Howe enjoyed pride of place. There seemed to be a signature, but I couldn't be sure in the dim light.

"David," I said. "I'm not sure I—"

"Context, dear boy. I'm establishing the context." He cracked a pistachio. "You'll have to bear with me. This sort of thing is difficult to say. It helps to approach it from familiar ground."

"But why exactly are you—"

He held up the palm of his hand, and resumed as if I had not spoken. "Halliwell took Orton under his wing. Gave him food and shelter. Initiated him into the ways of the homosexual lifestyle. And most importantly, gave him an education. Halliwell was quite intelligent. Fancied himself a novelist. He'd inherited a bit of money from his father, and he used it to buy a cramped little bed-sit in Islington. A horrible place, by all accounts. Dark, suffocating. But once they'd failed as actors, they resolved to become writers, and this was to be the crucible of their genius. At first, Orton did the typing, transcribing Halliwell's ramblings onto the page. But over the years—"

"The pupil became the master. I remember."

"After the prison stretch, yes."

"Prison?"

"The two of them used to deface library books. A form of cultural terrorism, I suppose. A means of revenging themselves on a society that refused to recognize their brilliance. They would slip books off the shelves and alter them to reflect erotic themes. Quite witty, actually. On the cover of one book, I recall, the title character was seen to be gazing fondly at a set of male genitalia. Another, a historical romance called *The Queen's Favorite*, was embellished with a pair of nude wrestlers. They also typed false blurbs onto the jacket flaps. Lovely stuff."

"Sounds harmless enough."

"Some would disagree. In the end they'd defaced a staggering number of art books. They pulled out the plates and carried them home for cut-and-paste artwork. The walls of their little room were covered with dark, brooding collages. And one day there was a knock on the door. They each got a six-month prison term."

"Six months? For cutting up books?"

"Erm. That's where Orton's career truly began. He flourished in prison. Wrote a play, sold it to the BBC. When he got out, he wrote two more. By the time he was thirty, he was the toast of the West End. 'The Oscar Wilde of Welfare State gentility,' they called him."

"And that's when your wife left you?"

"Patience, dear boy. We're nearly there. You owe me this much."

I fastened my eyes on Gordie Howe.

"And another drink. I believe you owe me another drink, as well."

"I think—"

"This is no time to come over all puritanical, Brian. It doesn't suit. Off you go."

The room felt hot as I made my way to the front. I pressed a hand to the back of my neck. The bar man, waiting for the first pint to draw, pushed a Lucite clipboard toward me. "Sponsor the dongola race, sir?"

"Excuse me?"

"Never mind."

David was picking at his sleeve as I returned to the table. "I know what you're thinking," he said. "You're thinking, 'What was Halliwell doing all this time? What was Halliwell doing while Orton was drinking in the critical plaudits, opening on Broadway, cruising the cottages?' "

"Actually, David, I—"

"Halliwell, I'm afraid, was spiralling downward at a precipitous rate. It pains me to tell you this. He attempted suicide once or twice. Orton's success reduced him to the role of personal assistant and housekeeper. 'A middle-aged non-entity,' someone called him. Can you imagine? Can you imagine what that might do to a person's ego? He tried to make a go as an artist. He tried to sell his collages, had an exhibit, I think, but it didn't go anywhere. And Orton, he just heaped coals on the fire. Excluded Halliwell from his work, banned him from the rehearsals of his plays, flaunted his sexual conquests. Orton won a drama award, refused to take Halliwell along to the ceremony. Out of pure spite. Pure spite." Mabberley punctuated the two words by jabbing a finger into the foam of his bitter. "And meanwhile he was writing those famous diaries, and leaving them out on his desk for Halliwell to read. 'What's to be done about Kenneth?' That sort of thing. Orton was making money now, real money, but they still lived in that same little flat in Islington, with the collages covering every surface. It must have been a hideous place. Oppressive. I remember somebody saying the place made her want to put her elbows out and stretch the walls. Not her arms, mind you, her elbows. They talked about moving to a better place, but they always found a reason to stay. I suppose that's why it happened." He pressed his palms flat on the table.

He paused. I knew I was supposed to ask what had happened, but I decided to wait him out. It didn't last long.

He curled his fingers around the base of his glass. "You still haven't twigged, have you?"

"Twigged."

"An expression my wife uses. Thought you might have heard it."

"No."

He lifted his glass, but did not drink. "One morning, a limousine pulled up in front of the flat. Orton had a meeting with some sort of film producer. The driver went inside and knocked on the door of their room. No answer. He went outside and called his boss, just to make sure he had the right address. After a few minutes he went back inside and knocked again. Then he bent down and looked through the mail slot. He spotted a bald man lying on the floor. Eyes closed."

"Halliwell."

"He knew it wasn't Orton. He'd seen Orton before. So he went back outside and called the police, who got there a few minutes later and broke down the door. Halliwell lay naked on his back in the center of the room, near the writing desk. His hands, chest and head were spattered with blood. On the floor nearby sat an empty glass, a large can of grapefruit juice, and an empty bottle of barbiturates. His pajama top, caked with dried blood and gore, was draped neatly over the back of a desk chair.

"Orton's body lay on top of his bed a few feet away. His head was open. Halliwell broke it open like a coconut. No—not a coconut, really. Like a squeezed grape. The insides had spurted out like a squeezed grape. Contents under pressure. They say the sight of it made one of the officers sick. Skull fragments all over the place. Pieces of Orton's brain clinging to the ceiling. Blood dripping from those dreadful collages. There was a hammer on the bed near the body. A Warrington hammer, the sort of thing one might use to drive finishing pins into a bookcase. The imprint of the hammer could be seen in the exposed tissue. He kept banging away long after it had ceased to matter. Up and down. Up and down. The police report called it 'a deliberate form of frenzy.' Lovely phrase, that. A deliberate form of frenzy."

Mabberley ran his fingers through his hair. "The part that used to baffle me, the bit I just couldn't get a handle on, was what set it off. Orton's diary breaks off in mid-sentence, a full week earlier. So I was always left to wonder what had happened, what triggered the explosion. Was it a slow, gathering storm of rage, or a sudden outburst, dropping in out of the sky like a mortar shell? Perhaps Halliwell had been sitting alone that night—brooding, wondering. Another lover? Was that what set it off? He was always ready to forgive in the past. Perhaps a cruel remark from Orton? It bothered me. But now I believe I've come to an understanding. I think Halliwell simply got tired of waiting. He just picked up the hammer and did what he had to do. And when it was over he calmly folded his pajamas and took his life. A brilliant scene, really. Crafted, you might say."

He had pressed his hand to the top of his pint glass, as though he might push it through the table. "Sometimes I tried to picture it in my mind. The gurgle of rage. The upswing of the hammer. The rising spume of dark blood. I used to wonder what it had been like. Often."

He sat back and spread his fingers on the table. I said nothing. A log cracked and settled in the fireplace. From the doorway, a pair of young women scanned the room for familiar faces. The barman struggled with a fresh keg. Mabberley picked at the yellow crust on his sleeve.

I cleared my throat. When I spoke, my voice sounded faint and reedy. "David. It's late. You've had a lot to drink. You can't be trying to tell me—"

He reached across the table and gripped my forearm. "No one is blaming you," he said.

"But—"

"Context, dear boy. Context is so important, don't you think?" He drained his glass. "Last orders, I think. And then, I believe, you may wish to use the telephone."

This story has its roots in Stashower's Raymond Chandler Fulbright fellowship at Oxford and centers on the intriguing premise of well-known (and gay) playwright Joe Orton

breaking up a marriage. Stashower is the author of the Edgar-nominated The Adventure of the Ectoplasmic Man, Elephants in the Distance, *and* Conan Doyle: Teller of Tales, *and has started a new mystery series featuring Harry Houdini.*

The Error of His Ways

Margaret Yorke

Shooting began at eight o'clock that morning.

It was a fine, sunny day, though cool, as was to be expected in October, but the evenings were still light, and in the hours before darkness fell, the routine of those who lived in Lower Foxbourne was to be severely jolted.

Martin, the schoolboy who delivered newspapers in the High Street, had witnessed the early controlled commotion as he trudged along, pushing his bicycle with the bright yellow bag balanced across the handlebars down the wide main street, where thatched, timbered cottages, modernized within, nestled beside relatively modern houses which had been built more recently. Objections from preservationists had made further development in this part of the village very difficult, though occasionally consent was given. The vicarage was new, neatly fitting into a section of the former vicarage's large garden. Martin had posted the vicar's *Independent* through his letter box, and the *Financial Times* through that of the former vicarage, Mr. Mole's *Telegraph*, Mrs. Hopgood's *Times*, and various copies of the *Express* and the *Daily Mail* were safely delivered, but there were hazards on his round. At Honeysuckle Cottage a snappy Airedale leaped up and grabbed the paper before the boy released it through the flap in the door; when he first began the round, Martin's fingers had only just missed the dog's snarling teeth, but he was wary now and poked only the rolled-up corner of the paper into the slot. The house he dreaded most was Hawthorn Lodge, a Victorian villa fenced off with railings and a hedge behind which Nero, a Border collie cross, was always free to roam. Both Martin and the postman approached the house with trepidation, but Martin had solved his problem; having had his ankles nipped several times, and his school trousers torn, now he left the paper at the gate where, in rainy weather, it got wet, and Mr. Norton had to come grumbling down the path with an umbrella to retrieve it, cursing the sloth of modern youth as he laid the sodden newsprint on the hot rail in the bathroom to dry it out so that he could read it. He had complained to Mr. Scorer at the Snacky Shop, which, besides newspapers, sold groceries, sweets, and tobacco, but Mr. Scorer had had experience of the dog, for he did deliveries when boys overslept or were off sick. He wanted no schoolchild employed by him to be savaged; down that path lay lawsuits and damages. He told Mr. Norton that the answer would be a large lidded box fitted by the gate, or for Mr. Norton to fetch his own paper; he was, after all, retired; the day was his own. Mr. Norton, formerly a civil servant and more recently a churchwarden and a loquacious member of the parish council, had protested, but Mr. Scorer had said that the choice was his. It was Mr. Norton who favored a scheme to prevent parking in the village square outside Mr. Scorer's shop; he and some newcomers wanted to plant trees and install cobblestones, ignoring the fact that such embellishments would hinder trade. Besides the Snacky Shop, Lower Foxbourne had a post office, an antique shop, and a butcher.

Neither solution to the problem had seemed acceptable to Mr. Norton until today, when Martin saw that a box had been attached to the gate. It was sturdy enough, stained brown, with a hinged lid and a large interior. The words POST AND PAPERS were neatly painted in black on its surface.

Martin, who had been thinking partly about his math homework and partly about the stereo system he was saving up for, and only marginally about his deliveries, was distracted by the sight of a large pantechnicon from which were being unloaded props—street lamps from an earlier era, a red telephone box, and vegetation, in the form of rose trees in full bloom and assorted shrubs, which men were placing against the walls of some nearby houses, denoting that it was high summer. Martin dropped the *Express* in the new box and stood watching as a large, brightly painted sign was hoisted into place outside The Crown Inn, renaming it The Pig and Whistle. Various people in drab, out-of-date clothes stood about, talking and smoking, and farther up the road the camera crews were setting up their equipment. Cool, thought Martin. A girl with a radio handset was standing near them, and she waved on several cars who were coming down the street, their drivers on their way to work; Martin saw the same ones every morning, and most hoped not to leave before he had deposited their papers, though some stopped at the Snacky Shop to collect their own. He had no time to wait and see what else would happen; mounting his bike, he pedaled back to leave his satchel at the Snacky

Shop, and then set off toward home, a small stucco house beyond the recreation ground, where he would snatch a quick breakfast before catching the school bus outside the cricket pavilion.

"That Mr. Norton's got a box now, by the gate," he told his mother as she poured him a cup of tea. His bowl of Coco-pops stood ready and his younger brother and sister were finishing their own breakfasts. His father, a hospital porter, was on nights this week and was not yet home. His mother had a cleaning job, including among her clients the family at the former vicarage. "Oh, and there's a lot of trucks and things in the High Street. Some telly stuff. The Crown's been called The Pig and Whistle."

"That's today, is it?" said his mother. "They had a note about it at The Old Vicarage. I'd forgotten when it was." She didn't go there today, which was a pity; she wouldn't have minded seeing some of the filming.

Mr. Norton, however, had not forgotten; he, too, had had an informative notice, stating that the film company would keep the disruption to the minimum. As a member of the parish council, he knew that a donation for village funds had been promised; indeed, he had hoped to channel the money into the improvement scheme for the square, while others considered renovations to the cricket pavilion were more important. He was ready to find the film company a nuisance even before the first van had driven up the road. Now, discovering that Martin had made a mistake and delivered, instead of his *Daily Mail*, the *Express*, he was irate.

Before he could go up to the Snacky Shop to complain, he did his morning chores: washing up his breakfast things and putting them tidily away; vacuuming and dusting round the sitting room, because it was Friday and his day for that, ready for the weekend, though guests were rare at Hawthorn Lodge. He cleaned round the whole house on Mondays. Standards must not slip, even though he lived alone. At last he was free to go marching up the village, his dog on a lead at his heels, the offending newspaper tucked beneath his arm.

By now cameras were set up on the footpath outside Hawthorn Lodge, about to film a scene in front of the thatched cottages opposite, and the girl with the radio, whom Martin had seen earlier, asked him to stop for a few minutes while it was shot. Immediately, Nero started barking and a fierce crackle came down the line to her.

"Yes," she said, and turned to Mr. Norton. "Please, we're shooting," she said. "Could you keep the dog quiet for a few minutes? It won't take long."

"I'm going to the shop. I'm a busy man and I have business to conduct," said Mr. Norton crossly. Nero, catching his mood from his master, was now growling angrily.

The girl, whose name was Claudia, turned slightly away from him and spoke into her radio. A further crackle came down the line and she waved Mr. Norton through. Some you couldn't win, she thought, an opinion fortunately shared by the director.

The actors engaged in this fragment of the film were dressed in clothes typical of the forties. One of the men was in army battle dress. They stood on the pavement in front of Primrose Cottage, whose walls had been dirtied so that it looked unkempt and dilapidated. They watched silently while Mr. Norton stalked past, head high, Nero at his heels still growling softly. A group of people—extras, dressed as civilians—stared at him, and the male star, the man in battle dress, well known but not to Mr. Norton, tried a friendly smile which went unnoticed.

"Gauleiter," said someone, and there was a snigger.

Mr. Norton looked round sharply but could not tell who had spoken. Apart from the cast, a number of residents of Lower Foxbourne who had time to spare were grouped out of camera range, obediently silent and enjoying both the autumn sunshine and the novel intrusion of the film crew; the words could have come from anyone. Not sure if he had heard correctly, he strode on, intent on making trouble for Martin in the shop. Behind him, he heard the director issue instructions, and the activity he had interrupted resumed.

Righteous in his indignation, Mr. Norton went into the Snacky Shop, banging the door behind him and stepping to the counter, where, at some length, he made his complaint. Mr. Scorer listened patiently, apologized for the boy's mistake, mentioned Martin's reliability, supplied a copy of Mr. Norton's chosen paper in exchange for the one rejected, and said that he would point out the boy's error.

"The village is not what it was," said Mr. Norton, far from mollified. "There's a crowd of film folk down the road. They're holding the traffic up. What if the fire brigade or an ambulance wanted to pass? They're blocking the road. Blocking the traffic. And defacing property. Primrose Cottage is covered in dirt."

"They'll make it good," said Mr. Scorer mildly. He'd seen the grimy cottage. "They'll paint up Primrose Cottage like new. They didn't ask to use your house, then, Mr. Norton?"

"I'd have told them where to go if they did," was the answer.

"They always make it worth your while," said Mr. Scorer, who had done a deal with the company for inside shots after hours the following night, Saturday, and on Sunday. They needed to rearrange the interior to resemble a village shop from decades ago, before the introduction of self-service; afterward, they would replace shelves and fitments in a more convenient layout than at present. He was extremely satisfied with their agreement. "They need people for the crowd scenes," he added. "Thirty pounds a day it is, for extras, so I've heard. They've bused them in. Pity they didn't use locals."

"Local people should have more sense than to go guying themselves up," said Mr. Norton. "What's the point of it?" He spoke rhetorically. He did not want to know. Dissatisfied with his interview, for Mr. Scorer had not been sufficiently abject in his apologies, he was about to leave when he heard a howl, followed by sharp barking from Nero, left outside tethered by his lead to a ring in the wall placed there for the purpose; dogs were not allowed inside the Snacky Shop. If Nero went on howling, it would certainly annoy Mr. Scorer and might continue to upset the film people, assuming their microphones were within range. He turned back. "I might as well get a few items while I'm here," he said, and began to scrutinize the shelves. Biscuits were always useful, and he could buy a tin of Nero's favorite food. He took his time choosing, picking up first digestive biscuits and then exchanging the packet for one of custard creams, a weakness of his at teatime, though more expensive. Eventually he settled for rich tea, which were cheaper, mused over the dog food, knowing all the time what he would select, and listened complacently to Nero's prolonged wails. At last he went to the counter and took out his purse to pay, taking his time, picking out the correct money.

As he left the shop, bidding Mr. Scorer a stern good day, two elderly men and a gray-haired woman entered the shop. All were chattering together. Mr.

Norton knew none of them by sight. He brushed abruptly past them, collected Nero, and set off homeward.

Nero was quiet as they walked back toward the High Street. Ahead, the filming seemed to have made no progress since they left; the same group of characters were outside Primrose Cottage, whose owner, a widowed potter who had a studio in her garden, stood outside among the spectators, and now he was stopped again, this time by a young man who was armed with a hand-held radio.

"May I ask you to wait for just a few minutes," said the young man, holding out his arms as if to prevent Mr. Norton passing. He was quite tall; to get by, Mr. Norton would have to be aggressive, and employ Nero's attacking qualities. The dog had begun to growl softly; he started quivering at his master's side and then, as Mr. Norton bent to speak to him, he barked. Meanwhile, the young man's handset made a sound and he listened to it, then asked Mr. Norton if he was going to Hawthorn Lodge.

"Yes," said Mr. Norton. "I live there. You have no right to deny me access."

"Please continue on your way," said the young man, and he made a sweeping gesture with a bow as Mr. Norton, oblivious to the mockery, walked on.

Nearing his house, Mr. Norton saw the group of actors more clearly than when he had gone past earlier. Among them, now, was an actress whom even he recognized. She stood in the open doorway of Primrose Cottage talking to two men, the one in battle dress, and another wearing a shabby sweater and corduroy trousers tied at the knee. They stopped their conversation as Mr. Norton drew level and, taking his time, opened his gate and went up to his door.

Once inside, he was curious enough to watch the

resumed action, concealing himself behind the net curtain in his window, peering through the lace. The actress retreated into the cottage, the man dressed as a farm laborer moved away, and the man in battle dress knocked on the door. Out came the actress.

"Goodness, George! Is it really you?" she cried, though Mr. Norton, shut inside his house, could not hear her words. She was clasped to the ample khaki chest of the actor on the threshold, the farm laborer approached, and angry words were exchanged. Then the scene was cut, to be repeated several times until Mr. Norton lost interest and moved away.

The other residents of Lower Foxbourne who were watching were enchanted with the proceedings, content to stand in the sunshine being entertained; the hired extras, not required yet, were gathered outside the newly rechristened inn, where the three who had entered the shop while Mr. Norton was leaving joined their fellow thespians.

Mr. Norton remembered what Mr. Scorer had said: thirty pounds a day for standing about doing nothing. He would never have considered it; of course not, though funds were tight on his pension. Six years before, and after thirty years of marriage, Isabel, his wife, had suddenly left home, saying that she could stand his company no more and now that their only son was married, she was off to live in Spain. He had been obliged to pay her half the value of their house and a lump sum instead of maintenance. She had not run off with a lover—which would have saved Mr. Norton money—but had chosen to live alone, accusing him of unreasonable behavior. When detailed, this seemed to amount to no more than preferring Nero's company to hers. Now he, who during his working life had commanded obedience and respect, had to pinch and save, or else sell his house and move to something small and poky, which Nero would dislike.

His limited interest in the filming lost, Mr. Norton went to put his shopping away, and discovered, when he reached into his pocket for his purse, which must be put away in a drawer of his bureau, that it was missing. It contained nearly twenty pounds, his bank card, and the driving license which he still kept up, though he no longer had a car.

Mr. Norton felt quite faint and had to sit down with a cup of tea before he could think clearly about what could have happened to it.

One of those extras must have stolen it, pushing past him in the doorway of the Snacky Shop. Their shoving was a ruse, to mask their evil pickpocketing designs upon a law-abiding citizen. They'd come from some other area; Mr. Scorer had told him so. No doubt their backgrounds had not been checked. The shopkeeper was quite right; local people, who would have been accountable, should have been employed.

He'd call the police and have every one of them searched. His purse must be found. He'd telephone just as soon as he felt well enough. As it was, he felt quite shaky.

Meanwhile, the filming was continuing. The shots outside Primrose Cottage were concluded, and a further scene was rehearsed outside the pub. When a police car came into view, although it was too modern for the period in which the film was set, some of the spectators thought it was part of the action.

A makeup team was sitting on the pavement in the sun opposite what was now The Pig and Whistle. Actors' faces needed touching up between takes, especially when it was hoped that at last the scene would be a wrap. The two women watched as a young police officer got out of the car and came to ask them if they could tell him which house was Hawthorn Lodge. He was new to the area and unfamiliar with the local layout; in these villages few houses were numbered, which meant they were difficult to locate and made emergency calls a nightmare. The girls did not know the answer, but the location manager, who was nearby, was able to direct him. The police officer had been patrolling not far away when he was directed to Lower Foxbourne, where a man had reported the theft of his purse and insisted that a member of the film's cast was responsible. Mr. Norton had demanded swift response before the actors could all leave the village with the stolen property.

Nero greeted the police officer with frenzied barking when he rang the doorbell, but no one came to answer it. After a while, the constable walked round the house to try the back door, with no more success. Strange. The call had been so urgent. Then he peered in at the window. He saw the old man sitting in his chair, a teacup on the floor beside him, vacant eyes staring into space. Indubitably, he was dead.

Reinforcement came: further officers and an ambulance.

They had to break the door down, and the dog immediately went for the entering police officers, barking furiously and snapping at them with his sharp teeth; two were bitten before they accepted that Nero, now crouched, growling, in front of the body of his master, would let no one pass. Eventually, captured in a net, he was removed. Luckily the bitten officers were up to date with tetanus injections.

The first police constable had come to take details of the theft of a purse, to be confronted with a sudden death. When Mr. Norton had telephoned to report his loss, only his insistence that he knew who the thieves were and that they were still in the vicinity, filming in the road outside, had lent urgency to the investigation. Now, in the face of his sudden death, the theft was of secondary importance. The doctor, pronouncing life extinct, could see no reason to suspect foul play; there were no signs of a break-in, or a struggle, or any visible injuries on the body. The man had most probably died of natural causes, a sudden heart attack, for instance, but a postmortem would confirm this view. The investigation was conducted in a calm, controlled way, while filming in the village street continued, the crew and actors ignorant of what had happened to cause the police presence. The director was anxious to complete his day's schedule, and as the police cars were not in shot since the action had moved on, paid no heed to them.

An officer went up to the Snacky Shop and Mr. Scorer confirmed what Mr. Norton had already reported: that he had been in earlier and had bought biscuits and dog food, which the police had already seen on the kitchen table at Hawthorn Lodge. He was quite upset, Mr. Scorer reported, annoyed because the film people were obstructing the road and they had objected to his dog. There was no need to mention Martin's delivery error, which was the real cause of the old man's fit of temper. Mr. Scorer had seen no theft, and as yet, the Snacky Shop had not needed to install a security camera. As for the customers who had come into the shop as Mr. Norton left, it was true that there had been some jostling at the door, and they had been quite noisy, laughing among themselves, and why not? They were extras hired for the film, Mr. Scorer had discovered, pensioners from a luncheon club. Why should they steal? Someone else must be the culprit, and the haul was unlikely to be large, for Mr. Norton was a man of modest means, even if he liked to give a different impression. It was Mr. Scorer, in the end, who officially identified the dead man, since no one knew where to find a relative, though papers revealing addresses were found in his desk, but that was later.

The film crews and the actors, extras included, would be returning the following day. Further inquiries into the theft could be pursued then, it was decided.

Martin had not heard of Mr. Norton's sudden death. Next morning, he set off on his paper round as usual, and in the rush Mr. Scorer forgot to mention it, putting up the papers but omitting Mr. Norton's *Mail*. Martin, however, had not realized that, and, reaching Hawthorn Lodge, put one in the new box. At the bottom of it lay a purse.

Funny, thought the boy, but did not touch it, laying the paper over it. He'd mention it to Mr. Scorer, which he did, reporting that he'd been one *Mail* short on his round.

"No, really?" Mr. Scorer was extremely interested. "A purse in the box, you say? Did you touch it?"

"No."

"Hm," said Mr. Scorer, thinking that fingerprints might be found on it which would trace the thief, who must have dumped it after emptying it. "I'll deal with it," he said. "You get off now, Martin." Then he added, "Mr. Norton's dead. He had a heart attack yesterday afternoon. Or it might have been a stroke. Died suddenly, in his chair."

"Oh," said Martin, rather shocked. "I didn't hear the dog today. He always barks, even though I don't go up the path. I suppose he's gone, then."

"I expect he's been put in kennels somewhere," Mr. Scorer said.

"Poor old guy," said Martin. "He'll not been wanting any papers, then."

"No," agreed Mr. Scorer. He'd have to drop a *Mail*
down to the house Martin had, perforce, missed.

The film's director, vexed because the police had
said, the night before, that they would want to interview all those involved in the shoot, solved the mystery. In the rushes he viewed in the evening, Mr.
Norton was clearly shown returning from his shopping trip, intruding on the scene as he pushed his
way down the street, bending to speak to his dog,
goading it, the director suspected, to bark. It jumped
up beside him, and as it did so, something fell from
the man's rear pocket: a small object, barely noticeable, and the shot ended. Mr. Norton's incursion was
the reason for the instant cut. A later shot revealed a
woman stooping down to pick up something, which
she scrutinized. She was not one of the extras employed as villagers but the owner of Primrose Cottage who had spent much of the day watching the
activity involving her house. She had discovered Mr.
Norton's ownership from his bank card, and, aware
of the fierce nature of his dog, she had put the purse
in the box by his gate. She telephoned to tell him
where it was, but first his line was busy, and then
she could get no answer. By the time the police arrived, the film crew had moved away from Primrose
Cottage, and she had locked up and left, going to
spend the evening with friends. The contents of the
purse, retrieved by the police, seemed to be intact,
some twenty pounds, a bank card and a driving license. Mr. Norton, dead of a stroke brought on by
rage, had become the victim of his own mistake.

In this story, Margaret Yorke plumbs the mysterious death of an unpopular village resident. Yorke's latest mysteries include Act of Violence *and* False Pretenses. *Yorke lives in Buckinghamshire in England.*

DEN OF ANTIQUITY MYSTERIES

by
TAMAR MYERS

LARCENY AND OLD LACE
78239-1/$5.99 US/$7.99 Can

As owner of the Den of Antiquity, Abigail Timberlake
is accustomed to navigating the cutthroat world of rival
dealers at flea markets and auctions. But she never thought
she'd be putting her expertise in mayhem and detection to
other use — until her aunt was found murdered . . .

GILT BY ASSOCIATION
78237-5/$5.99 US/$7.99 Can

A superb gilt-edged, 18th-century French armoire Abigail
purchased for a song at estate auction has just arrived
along with something she didn't pay for: a dead body.

THE MING AND I
79255-9/$5.50 US/$7.50 Can

Digging up old family dirt can uncover long buried
secrets . . . and a new reason for murder.

SO FAUX, SO GOOD
79254-0/$5.99 US/$7.99 Can